A DISCONCERTING DISCOVERY

Despite her well-known self-control, Felicia felt a shiver run through her as she was waltzed out onto the terrace by Edward Crawley. Was it apprehension about being alone with this lascivious lord—or something else? His hand was still at her waist, its warmth passing easily through the muslin to her skin. It was a large hand, twice the size of her own, and it felt comfortable there.

"Miss Adlam," he said, "I'd like you to tell me why you must always pretend to be so damned composed."

"I don't pretend!" she protested.

"Oh, yes, you do, and it accomplishes little other than to make me want to discover what will disconcert you."

"You talk nonsense, sir."

"Do I?" he said. And before she had time to discern his intent, he pulled her close and kissed her . . . and though she struggled, it was more against the surge of her own unexpected desire than his. . . .

SIGNET REGENCY ROMANCE
COMING IN OCTOBER 1993

Sandra Heath
Cruel Lord Granham

Anna Barbour
Lady Liza's Luck

Emily Hendrickson
Julia's Spirit

THE FICKLE FORTUNE HUNTER

by

Amanda Scott

A SIGNET BOOK

SIGNET
Published by the Penguin Group
Penguin Books USA Inc., 375 Hudson Street,
New York, New York 10014, U.S.A.
Penguin Books Ltd, 27 Wrights Lane,
London W8 5TZ, England
Penguin Books Australia Ltd, Ringwood,
Victoria, Australia
Penguin Books Canada Ltd, 10 Alcorn Avenue,
Toronto, Ontario, Canada M4V 3B2
Penguin Books (N.Z.) Ltd, 182–190 Wairau Road,
Auckland 10, New Zealand

Penguin Books Ltd, Registered Offices:
Harmondsworth, Middlesex, England

First published by Signet, an imprint of New American Library,
a division of Penguin Books USA Inc.

First Printing, September, 1993
10 9 8 7 6 5 4 3 2 1

Gordie's book

1

UNTIL the first two gunshots cracked in the distance, the silence of the sunny mid-March morning had been broken by nothing more alarming than the chirping of birds in the tall beech trees lining the country lane and the muffled but steady clip-clop of the horses' hooves as they ambled companionably along it. The three riders had remained silent since leaving the Longworth Park stable, two of them out of compassion or simple courtesy, the third because even the sound of his own voice was enough to set fiendish devils pounding against the inside of his skull. He had come out riding against his will, finding it easier to submit than to argue when his companions—both of whom he had known since childhood—insisted that a ride in the crisp morning air would clear the effects of the previous night's carousing from his befuddled brain.

The first shots were followed by two more before one of his companions, plump, fair-haired Peregrine, Lord Dawlish, collected his wits and exclaimed, "Gunshots! Poachers, I'll wager."

"You're daft," said Sir Richard Vyne, a taller, leaner man whose generally glum expression frequently led others to think him ill-tempered even when he was in excellent humor. "A pony says it ain't poachers at all, Mongrel, but merely farmers shooting at rabbits."

"Done," said Dawlish, taking not the least exception to the odd nickname for the simple reason that he had been saddled with it since his school days. His most famous relative being a duke, his chums had first called him Pedigree Dawlish, then Pedigree Dogless, but the name had soon afterward been shortened to its present form, and he had long since stopped protesting. He held out his right hand now to clinch the wager with a handshake, then grinned at the silent gentleman. "You want a piece of this action, Ned? Poachers or farmers?"

Edward, ninth Baron Crawley, taller and broader of shoulder than either of the other two, but of sterner countenance and a leaner, lankier build than even Sir Richard, had paid little heed to the first shots, and none to his companions' conversation, but the second set of shots captured his attention. He drew rein, frowning as he struggled to concentrate through the merciless pounding in his head. Just then another shot rang out, followed by the unmistakable sound of a horse's scream.

"Good God!" Crawley looked at his companions, his head feeling instantly clearer, his dark brown eyes becoming more sharply focused. "The York Mail passes through here about this time each morning. Do you suppose it might—"

"Come on," Sir Richard shouted, giving spur to his mount.

Crawley followed with Dawlish, who called out anxiously, "I've not so much as a pistol by me, Ned, and the Royal Mail is always well-guarded. If they *have* been attacked—" With a grim look, Crawley drew a horse pistol from his saddle holster, whereupon Dawlish, a smile lighting his cherubic face, cried, "We shall do now. At them, lads!"

The lane ended at the highroad, and the scene that greeted them when they emerged from the woods might have daunted three lesser men. A heavily laden mail coach, its identity printed in gold lettering around the royal crest on its door panels, was drawn up at the side of the road. Two armed villains held the guards and driver, as well as the several passengers, at gunpoint while two others were busily emptying the contents of several mail pouches onto the road.

The sudden eruption of three horsemen from the woods at the side of the road startled the robbers, who turned as one to deal with them, giving one of the guards who thought more quickly than his compatriot the opportunity to snatch up his blunderbuss. When one of the mounted villains fired his pistol, Crawley fired back, and saw his man tumble from his saddle. When the second armed man fell almost in the same moment to a blast from the guard's weapon, the remaining villains threw down their weapons and raised their hands.

Ignoring cries of gratitude mingled with exclamations of outrage from the passengers and guards, Crawley guided his mount toward the man he had shot. "Damn," he muttered, looking down at the lifeless figure.

"What is it, Crawler?" Sir Richard demanded, reining his horse nearer. "Someone you know?"

"No, of course not, but I didn't mean to kill the fellow, only to wing him. My aim was all over the shop, Dickon. Really, I must stop drinking so much. Throws my aim right out."

The guard who had fired the blunderbuss said, "Don't you never mind about him, my lord. That villain meant to kill you right enough. And us, too, I reckon. He ain't no loss."

Vyne looked down at the corpse, his gray eyes narrowing. "Are you sure he's dead?"

Swinging his right leg over the saddle bow, Crawley slid to the ground and moved to have a closer look.

"Have a care," Vyne growled. "Knew a fellow once who got himself killed through thinking a wild boar he'd shot was dead when it wasn't. Turned on him and ripped his gullet out when he bent down like that to see if it was finished."

Crawley saw blood oozing through the fallen man's jacket. There was no sign of life. A breeze stirred, sending a bit of paper skittering along the road, followed by another. Without thinking, Crawley put his foot on one just as a female passenger shrieked, "The mail! The wind is blowing the letters away!"

The mailbags the robbers had ripped open had spilled most of their contents onto the road and a capricious wind was scattering letters hither and yon. One of the guards ran after two letters that blew into the woods, and several of the passengers chased others along the road and plucked still others from the nearby hedgerows.

The second guard ignored the commotion, keeping his blunderbuss firmly trained upon the other two robbers, while one of the passengers bound their hands behind their backs with cords from the remaining pouches.

Crawley, glancing at the driver to make certain he was attending to his nervous horses, saw yet another letter come to rest between the left wheeler's rear hooves. The animal moved just then, putting one large hoof down on the letter. Grimacing, Crawley moved to rescue it. Smacking the horse's flank, he reached down and picked up the letter when the animal shifted its weight again.

He could not make out the direction, although it had been written in an elegant copperplate hand. The frank was illegible, too, but that was no fault of the horse.

"What's that, Ned?" Dawlish demanded.

"Just another letter," Crawley said, turning it over, "but this one won't be delivered, I fear. Impossible to read the direction, thanks to old Dobbin, there, and of course the frank can't be deciphered either."

"Franked, is it," Dawlish said, peering down at the missive and paying no heed to Crawley's last comment. "Nobility then. One would think that when a chap's had a decent education, he'd learn to write his name clearly on the corner of an envelope so others might decipher it. Hope the letter ain't too important."

The seal, a plain gold wafer, had been broken. Glancing at Dawlish, Crawley unfolded the single sheet and looked at the salutation and signature. "To Aunt Augusta from someone named Felicity," he said. "No help there."

"You might as well chuck it into the woods then," Dawlish said. "Some bird will appreciate having an extra bit of paper for its nest. Here, what are you doing? You mustn't read that! It ain't at all the thing to be reading a lady's private letter."

Crawley paid him no heed. He was reading what little he could make out in hopes of learning more about the sender or the intended recipient. He was curious, incorrigibly so, as Dawlish roundly informed him.

After a moment's reading, Crawley laughed and said, "Dickon, by all that's holy, here's a commission for you! And she's a beauty, by the sound of it. Oh, but wait—beautiful and well-dowered! Damned if I won't cut you out of this one, my friend. Now, whom can I cajole into presenting me to this tempting bird as the greatest amongst the new portrait artists? No, you don't," he added, jerking the letter away when Vyne, riding nearer, reached down to snatch it from him.

Dawlish, watching them, chuckled. "Shame on you both.

Ned, you have come to a pretty pass indeed when you must take advantage of reading a gentlewoman's letter to try to recoup your losses. What does she write?"

Crawley grinned at him. "You don't expect me to read it to you right here in the highroad! That *would* be bad manners. Moreover, we must see to tidying up this mess first."

Little of their help was required, however, for the two guards assured them that they would deliver the live highwaymen to the constable in Stamford, and one of the male passengers volunteered to remain with the dead ones until a wagon could be sent back to fetch them.

"Not meaning to travel beyond Stamford, m'self," he said when one of the other passengers protested that the coach could not be expected to wait for him. He added placidly, "Just see that my trunk is let down at the inn."

Matters were soon thus arranged and after another round of thanks from driver and guards for the timely intervention, the three friends were left to continue their morning ride.

Crawley's head was clearer, and feeling more cheerful, he thought a little more about the letter in his pocket.

Vyne said nothing, but Dawlish, who had been watching him narrowly, barely waited until they had returned to the quiet lane before demanding to know more about the letter.

"You oughtn't to have taken it away, Ned," he said. "I am persuaded that that must be some sort of desperate offense—tampering with his majesty's mail."

"Nonsense," Vyne interjected. "He said no one could make out the direction, so what harm can there be? He is keeping it only from those scavenging birds you mentioned, and they can find some other scrap for their damned nests."

"But there were some interesting bits of information, were there not?" Dawlish declared.

Crawley smiled lazily at him.

"Come now, tell us!"

"Perhaps there were, Mongrel, but as you so rightly pointed out before, a gentleman does not read a lady's letter—at least, not aloud to all and sundry."

"Well, I like that! Listen to him, Dickon, pretending all at once that he's got scruples. Have you ever abducted anyone,

Dickon? Have I? No, we have not. Has Ned? Aha! There you are. Scruples indeed!"

Vyne was smiling now, too, the expression doing nothing more for his gloomy features than to make him look rather sleepy. "I did hear about an abduction, Mongrel, but as I recall the matter, it was thwarted before Welwyn. That hardly counts, though it might serve to warn the next heiress Crawler makes up to. Did I hear you mention a dowry, old friend, and a commission?"

Crawley was remembering the so-called abduction, the willing victim of which was now safely married to one of his best friends and living on family estates in Ireland. But Vyne's comment reminded him of his present woes, the same woes he had tried unsuccessfully to drown in several bottles of good port the night before. He glanced at Sir Richard. "The words 'and so well-dowered as she is' fairly leapt off the page at me," he said with a wry twist of his mouth.

"But you did say my name was mentioned, did you not?" Vyne murmured gently.

Amused, Crawley said, "Did I? My wretched memory. I fear I cannot at all recall having—"

Dawlish exclaimed, "Now, dash it all, Ned, you said you would tell us the whole when everything was tidied up, so cut line, I say. If you know who wrote that letter, courtesy demands that you return it to her, and that is all there is about it."

"Just what I thought myself," Crawley replied. "But there is no legible direction, you will remember. You'd think the fool woman might have written 'We remove to Blank House, Grosvenor Square, on the eighteenth instant.' But she writes only 'We remove to London' on that date. Utterly unhelpful."

Vyne said, "You might consider my feelings, dear friend. If you annoy me now, I shan't tell you about my new commissions."

"That likelihood also occurred to me," Crawley admitted, "but before sharing this letter, I propose another wager. Did I not win the last one, by the bye? It was not poachers or farmers, after all—"

"Or anything you suggested," Dawlish pointed out.

"Rubbish, I said it was the York Mail, and so it was."

"He did," Vyne agreed.

Dawlish glared at the artist. "That is a mere quibble, Dickon, and you know it."

"It is plain fact," Vyne said. "Truth is truth."

Crawley chuckled. "Don't look so glum, Mongrel. Think how good you will feel, knowing I can pay a few of my debts."

"I thought you had matters well in hand again," Dawlish said. "Didn't Thorne pay everyone off for you before he went to Ireland?"

"He did," Crawley agreed, "but I must repay him one of these fine days, you know, and in the meantime, Quarter Day has a way of coming round before one has recovered from the last one. And then that bleater Dacres seems reluctant to come up to scratch. I have explained to Belinda the necessity for acquiring a husband with forty thousand or so per annum, but she just sits and stares out the window, or sighs when I mention his name. Damned foolishness! Be a good deal easier, I expect, to find myself an heiress. That is much the simplest way to save my groats." He patted the pocket into which he had put the letter. "I believe I shall soon be off to London to seek my fortune."

Vyne grimaced. "To masquerade as a portrait painter?"

Crawley grinned at him. "Can't be too difficult. One has only to be surly of manner and gruff of voice, spatter paint liberally about one's person, and tell everyone who wishes to gaze upon one's work that it is not yet fit to be seen. By the time she realizes I am no genius, I shall have flushed her from her covert and cajoled her neatly into the parson's mousetrap. In point of fact, Dickon, my friend, I sketch quite well enough to compete with you, and have done since our school days."

Vyne shrugged. "Perhaps."

Dawlish laughed. "The only time you don't tell the truth, Dickon, is when you speak of your work. I suppose next you will say that the king and queen would see no difference between one of Ned's spatters and that delightful painting you did of the Princess Amelia last year. Or that Lady Sefton would be as pleased by the result if he, not you, had painted her children. You are the rage, man, and well do you know it.

No schoolboy sketches of Ned's would ever be mistaken for a true Vyne."

Amused, Crawley said, "I wouldn't expect to fool their majesties or Lady Sefton, just one young heiress long enough to make her fall in love with me. Do you think I cannot do it?"

"Not," Dawlish retorted, "if you mean to behave like Dickon does, all surly and rude. And he's got such a reputation for it that if you mean to impersonate him, you cannot then decide all at once to be charming and . . . and whatever else you mean to be to seduce this unknown beauty."

Crawley had been watching Vyne and, seeing his lips tighten ominously, knew their bantering had gone far enough. The artist's temper was none too predictable at the best of times, but when there were definite storm warnings, it behooved one to heed them. Sighing, he said, "I don't suppose for a moment that Dickon would allow me to impersonate him, so I shall just have to set up as his competitor. That cannot be too difficult, after all. I shall simply tell some duchess that I wouldn't sully my brush with the colors necessary to do justice to her complexion, and every wealthy woman in London will come begging me to paint *her* picture instead."

He was glad to see Vyne's eyes, which had resembled two bits of flint, begin to twinkle. The artist said, "It is odd how that came about, all because I refused to cater to a woman's vanity."

Crawley shook his head. "It wasn't that. It was because, when she said you had made her figure much rounder than it was, you replied that, had that been the case, anyone viewing the portrait would mistake the subject for a whale instead of merely for a sow about to give birth. She might well have murdered you on the spot, and you know it, had her husband not chanced to come in just then and exclaim over the way you had given life to her image in a way no other artist ever had succeeded in doing. He was delighted with the result, and told everyone he had found a painter who was less concerned with his subjects' vanity than with making them spring to life on the canvas. It was that observation—and, admittedly, a bit of talent—that made you what you are today. I need not impersonate you at all. Just tell people that you know of another painter as rude as you are yourself. Then when I choose to be charming to the heiress, she will think that she alone has tamed me. What do you say?"

"I say that you had better go soak your head, Crawler."

There was more good-natured bantering, but they soon reached the well-tended stables and turned their horses over to the grooms. Despite Crawley's reputation for carelessness, he took excellent care of his horses.

The house, built of golden brick on a sloping hillside, was not so well cared for, but the air of general shabbiness did nothing to detract from its comfort. Crawley's father had engaged Robert Adam, the great architect of his day, to refurbish an older house; however, as often occurred with great houses, though the plans had been magnificent, they were never completely carried out. Still, in the end, much was improved, but the best of Longworth was that visitors always felt instantly at home there. One knew that one could put up one's feet or lounge in one's chair and that Amelia, Lady Crawley, would say not one word unless it was to offer one another cushion. Crawley's dogs roamed freely in the house, their desires catered to by everyone except his sister Belinda's three cats, who expressed sibilant disapproval whenever one of them ventured too near.

When they returned to the house, Crawley left his two friends to their own devices, for each had interests to occupy him. Vyne had taken over a small parlor where the light, he said, was excellent for his daubing, and had set up an easel there. What he was painting no one knew, for not even Belinda had the temerity to defy his orders and sneak a look when he left the room, but whatever it was, it drew him now to his work.

Dawlish repaired to the library to read the morning papers, delivered to Longworth only a day later than they might be read in London, and Crawley went to his dressing room, where he took the letter from his pocket and read it again.

The handwriting was the same elegant copperplate as in the direction, but the writing was so small that anyone with vision less acute than Crawley's would need a magnifying glass to read it. The correspondent did not cross and recross her lines as did so many others, in order to save the expense of a second sheet, but had clearly planned her letter carefully, for the last line was as neatly written as the first and as evenly spaced as all the others, not scrunched in as if the writer had suddenly realized she was about to come to the end of her paper.

Not a young woman, he decided. Most likely a middle-aged or even an elderly one. He had purposely not discussed the letter any further with his friends. There was something about it that had struck him, something aside from the intriguing description of the young lady with the dowry.

He found himself pondering its contents while he changed his clothes. He had thought he discerned quiet desperation in its tone, and despite the careful writing, one sentence stood out from the rest. She wrote that she was often at her wits' end but assured her aunt that solutions to each of her problems generally presented themselves before she was tempted to seek solace in a bottle or a watery grave. Since such bits of the letter as he could make out seemed to enumerate trials and tribulations of a large and demanding family as well as the writer's acceptance of responsibility for coping with all of them (the very thought of which appalled his lordship), the mention of a watery grave sent chills up his spine. He hoped she was being melodramatic or making a poor attempt at humor, but decided that, whatever her mood, the remark was a lapse by one unaccustomed to expressing her deeper feelings in her correspondence.

Despite his interest in the well-dowered beauty, he found himself exerting more energy to try to imagine the correspondent than to imagine "dearest Theo" who was to have her portrait drawn once the family was settled in London. Theo was a ridiculous name for a young woman, Crawley thought. But then nowadays no one was called Felicity, for the modern— and in his opinion, much more appealing—form of the name was Felicia. Felicity sounded like something dreamed up by Roundheads for Oliver Cromwell's Puritan daughter. But Theo was infinitely worse—mannish. He sighed, telling himself he ought not to be nitpicking when the fact—lowering though it was—was that he coveted that dowry.

Crawley was not a deceptive man by nature and did not

think he would be able to maintain any charade for long. Nor did he want to do so. But he did want to meet the heiress before she became the primary target of every fortune hunter in Town.

He stared out the window at the vast land that was his. His friend Thorne had told him flatly that with a little proper management, his estates would pay for themselves and give him a tidy profit. Easy for Thorne to say. He was a marquess, the eldest son of the wealthy Duke of Langshire. Moreover, both Thorne and his new bride were tiresomely interested in modern planting methods such as those advocated by Mr. Coke of Norfolk. But what answered in Norfolk or in Ireland did not necessarily answer in Nottinghamshire, and Crawley did not aspire to be a farmer. His last two stewards had been rogues, too. Really, he thought, being a landowner meant a lot of work, which did not suit him. He much preferred spending time at his club in London, in the company of his friends. He liked to hunt in the 'Shires, to spend summer in Brighton with the rest of the *beau monde*, and to enjoy the round of winter house parties without concerning himself over difficulties at Longworth. Time enough for that later, when he was older and more settled in his ways.

He supposed he was a pretty frippery fellow, but a man was what a man was. Moaning about it did no good. That he had not expected to inherit Longworth for many a year was beside the point, too. His friend Thorne had always wanted to have a finger in the Langshire pies, and the irascible duke had forbidden him to dabble in the running of their estates until shortly before Thorne's marriage. But Crawley had always enjoyed spending the income from his father's estates without being burdened with the bother of looking after them. The discovery, after his father's untimely death, that the estates did not simply run themselves had come as an unwelcome shock. In the three years since that dreadful day, Longworth had declined from a profitable, well-run place to a landlord's nightmare, but Crawley had neither the training nor the inclination to prevent it. Were it not for his mother's money, carefully saved from her marriage settlements, his sister Belinda would be spending her second Season at home. It annoyed him to know that he could not afford to frank her himself, that, in fact, he frequently had to borrow from his friends merely to support himself in the style he liked; however, until he could devise a way to recover his losses without isolating himself in Nottinghamshire, that was how it would be.

As if merely thinking her name had somehow conjured up her presence, his sister's familiar knock sounded just then upon his door. "Come in, Bella."

She entered at once, a pretty young woman dressed in a simple white muslin frock, her elfin face wreathed in smiles, her turquoise eyes twinkling with mischief. "Art sober, Ned? I want to ask a favor, so if you still have a sore head I shall take myself off again, for I do not want mine bitten off."

"I would never bite off such a pretty head," Crawley said. "I like the new way you are doing your hair, Bella."

Her glossy chestnut tresses had been cropped into a tumble of curls around her face, with the longer strands behind twisted into a knot atop her head. The style made her eyes look enormous, particularly now when she widened them in such a way as to warn him that she meant to ask a favor he would not like.

"Ned, Mama said I cannot go to Mary Westfall's birthday party if you do not lend me your escort. Mama has vowed not to set foot in Lady Westfall's house, or to speak to her until she takes back what she said last week about having been prettier and more popular than Mama was when they were girls. Really, it is so silly. But will you take me? Rosa will be as angry with me as Mama is with Lady Westfall if I do not go."

Crawley grimaced. "Lady Westfall gives me a pain, Bella. And Rosa simpers so that I want to drown her in their fish pond."

"I know," Belinda said, grinning at him, "but that is only because she has decided to adore you from afar."

"What?" Crawley felt a little sick.

His sister's grin widened. "Unrequited love, dear brother. The very most romantic kind. Rosa is a trifle unbalanced that way, no doubt from reading entirely too many silly romance novels. I am glad to say," she added with a superior air, "that I am not addicted to such stuff. But will you take me, dearest Ned, kindest of brothers?"

"I do have guests of my own, you know," he said, throwing out the reminder without much hope of its doing him any good.

Nor did it. "Bring them. Extra gentlemen are always welcome, and Lady Westfall will be thrilled to tell her friends she has entertained a duke's nephew, not to mention the great Sir Richard Vyne. He will be rude to her, I expect, but no one ever minds his impudence, do they?"

"No."

"It is very odd." She tilted her head, regarding him quizzically. "Will you do it, Neddie? Please?"

He reached out and tweaked a chestnut curl. "I will, but I do not mean to make a habit of indulging the likes of Lady Westfall, let alone the idiotic Rosa. When did I say we would depart for London, brat?"

Her eyes widened again. "You did not say. Mama hoped she might persuade you to remove there before Easter, but she said she feared you might be difficult because of the added expense of living in Town."

"Can you be ready to depart within a fortnight?" he asked.

Her eyes sparkled. "Oh, Ned, do you mean it? Of course I can. It will mean purchasing gowns in London rather than in Nottingham, but Mama will not mind that, I daresay. She says every penny she spends on me now is merely an investment in the future. I only hope I do not disappoint her."

"Well, just don't go whistling another fortune down the wind as you seem to have done with Dacres," Crawley said sternly. "Forty thousand a year and practically living in your pocket all last Season. I cannot think why you couldn't manage to bring him up to scratch."

The smile faded from her face. "I know you are displeased, Ned. I am dreadfully sorry to have failed you."

"Don't be foolish, brat. I am not displeased with you. In

point of fact, I ought never to have brought Dacres up again, for he is now past history." Shooting an oblique look at the letter on his dressing table, he added, "Perhaps, with any luck at all, we can both make our fortunes this Season."

2

AUNT FELICIA, have you seen my small satchel?"
"Felicia, which bedchamber is to be mine? I cannot abide street noises, and this wretched footman says I am to be in the front blue chamber. *Tell* him!"

"Pardon me, Miss Felicia, but where did his lordship say he wanted this large trunk?"

"Miss Felicia, I must know how many mean to sit down to dinner. And what time shall I order it served, if you please?"

"Aunt Felicia, Aunt Felicia! Freddy put a toad down my back. Oh, get it out! Get it out!

"Here, Felicity, where the devil has Foster got to? I want my coin collection, and I can't find the dratted fellow."

"Felicity, what on earth is all this pandemonium in aid of, and why did you not write to warn me of your arrival?" demanded the slender, well-dressed lady of middle years and needle-sharp features who appeared just then in the open doorway of the tall narrow house at number twenty Park Lane, Mayfair. "Had I not chanced to pass by on my way to Devonshire House, I should not have known you were in Town at all."

The soberly attired young woman standing in the midst of the huge pile of baggage littering the hall paused long enough to remove a wriggling green frog from the bodice of the stillshrieking little girl before she turned and smiled at the newcomer. "Hello, Aunt Augusta," she said calmly. "I did write to you. Hush, Sara Ann. A lady does not shriek. Go and tell Miss Ames to tidy your hair and to give you a fresh sash before you have your dinner. Come in out of the chill, Aunt. Here, Peters, take this poor frog out into the garden and set him free. Be careful now. Do not harm him." Turning from the open-mouthed footman, she said, "Papa, your coin collection is in the library, and Foster has gone to see if your wine was delivered by Oakley and Campion this morning, as they assured you it would be. Mrs. Heath, we will dine at eight. The two younger children will have their supper in the schoolroom with Miss Ames at six. Tom may dine with us tonight, but I do not yet know how many we shall be. Usually we are six at table, but you had better make it a practice always to allow for several more. Heath, the large chest goes in Lord Adlam's dressing room. And Theo, you may have the yellow bedchamber overlooking the garden. I will take the blue one. As for your satchel, Tom—"

"Aunt Felicia, Aunt Felicia," a sturdy, tow-headed little boy called from the second-floor landing, "Grandmama collapsed in a heap by her sitting-room door. I think she's dead!"

"Good God," Lady Augusta exclaimed, looking up in horror.

Felicia looked up at him, too, but said with her composure unaltered, "May heaven help you, Freddy Adlam, if this is another one of your horrid tricks."

"No, it ain't, I promise. She's dead! Come see for yourself."

With a sigh of resignation, Felicia smiled at her aunt and said, "The vapors again, I daresay. Will you come up to the drawing room, dear ma'am? It will be a good deal more peaceful there than it is here."

"Aunt Felicia!" The second boy, less fair and four years senior to his nine-year-old brother, sounded distraught.

"Oh, Tom, do forgive me. Your satchel." She thought for a moment. "I fear I do not know precisely where it is, but perhaps if you will remain here in the hall to assist Heath and the rest of the staff in disposing of all this debris, you will soon discover its whereabouts. You know which bags are yours and the children's, so you can be a great help."

"Certainly, ma'am," Tom said, smiling shyly at her. "And if you would like me to take Freddy in hand—"

"Just you try it," Mr. Smart Top," cried the urchin on the stairs. "I'll soon give you pepper!"

"Freddy," Felicia said calmly, "please go at once to Grandmama's bedchamber and tell Mrs. Harroby—her woman, you know—to bring Grandmama's vinaigrette to her sitting room."

"Ain't she dead then?"

"No, of course not. Now, do as I bid you, please."

He ran back up the stairs, and as the two women moved to follow him, Lady Augusta said quietly behind Felicia, "Are you quite sure of that, my dear? I know my sister Selena suffers a great deal from her nerves, but the child might be right."

Turning into a corridor off the gallery, Felicia glanced over her shoulder with a smile. "I should be very much surprised if he is, ma'am, and a good deal less surprised to learn that he jumped out of a corner and startled Mama into a fit of the vapors. Here she is."

She knelt swiftly by her mother, a slender, fragile creature with wispy fair hair and pale skin. Touching her forehead and wrists and observing the pulse beating steadily beneath her right ear, Felicia said gently, "Mama, come, dearest, bestir yourself, for we must get you to your sitting room. Oh, good," she added when Lady Adlam's woman came swiftly toward them from the direction of the service stairs. "Harroby, give me her vinaigrette, if you please."

Lady Adlam moaned faintly when the vinaigrette was waved beneath her nose, and it was not long before she opened her eyes, looking rather startled. "Oh," she said, "oh, my dear Felicia, such a fright! That dreadful boy!"

Helping her to a sitting position, Felicia signed to the hovering Mrs. Harroby to assist them, and they soon had Lady Adlam in her sitting room tucked up on a sofa made comfortable with numerous cushions. "There, Mama, you will do very well now, I think. Harroby can bring you a nice pot of tea to settle your nerves. It was Freddy who startled you, I collect, which is no doubt why he seems to have taken himself off now."

"Such a dreadful little boy," Lady Adlam said. "So odd when his papa was always such a joy to me—a perfect gentleman right from the cradle. Never a moment's concern did Jack give me."

"And if he and Nancy were here instead of in India, ma'am, I am certain that Freddy would behave much better. But Papa did insist upon bringing the children to Town with us, you know, not trusting the servants at Bradstoke to look after them properly, so we must just make the best of it until the next term begins, when the boys, at least, can be sent to school."

Lady Adlam sighed, but she appeared to be relaxing, and with relief, Felicia turned to Lady Augusta. "We will leave her to rest now. Harroby knows just what to do for her."

Lady Augusta was clearly bursting to speak, but she contained herself until they reached the drawing room, a singularly attractive chamber decorated in apple green with white molding and green-and-white striped curtains. A floral carpet muffled her ladyship's footsteps as she moved toward a pair of dark green leather wing chairs near the hearth. She held her tongue only until Felicia had shut the door behind her. Then, as if expelling pent up breath, she snapped, "Never a concern to her, indeed! As if she had not suffered a fit of vapors every time your brother Jack threw out a rash or was half a minute late returning from an outing. And as for his being a pattern-card of virtue, I just wish I might have seen it, that's all. That Freddy is a limb of Satan, but one need not look far to find the tree he was cut from, and that's plain fact. What will you do with him?"

"Send him to school, just as soon as they will take him."

"I mean now, Felicity. You cannot mean to overlook this disgraceful behavior. Spare the rod and spoil the child is what I say, and that young man wants a sound thrashing."

Felicia smiled. "Well, I hope you do not mean for me to thrash him, ma'am. I doubt I could catch him, for one thing, and if I could, I daresay I am not nearly strong enough to hold him."

"Pish tush. Do boldly what you do at all, I say, and do not forget that I have seen you manage more than one mettlesome horse. A child should be nothing, after that. Simply inform him of his fate and command him to assume the proper position."

"Goodness, you sound very fierce, Aunt, as if you had done the thing yourself any number of times. I had not thought you such a violent woman."

Lady Augusta smiled grimly. "Order me some tea, gel, before I forget I am a lady and you discover how violent I can become."

Chuckling, Felicia pulled the bell. "Freddy must have frightened himself thoroughly, for he cannot have expected poor Mama to collapse before his eyes. I daresay he will be a good boy for a time now. But do sit down and tell me all about what is happening in Town."

"Much you care, since you did not even bother to write to tell me you and the others were coming," Lady Augusta said, sitting down in one of the wing chairs.

"But I did write," Felicia protested, taking the opposite chair. "It was quite a long letter, too, ma'am, telling you all about the uproar caused by the children's arrival and Papa's reluctance to leave Longworth—even for his dearest Theo's come-out—and about Mama's failing health."

"I should have been much more interested to read that you looked forward to spending a Season in Town," Lady Augusta said tartly, "or to a demand to know all the latest *crim con* stories. I hope you mean to rig yourself out properly," she added with a disapproving look. "You look as neat as a pin, just as you always do, but that dress don't become you in the least. Makes you look like a drab brown wren, and while fine feathers don't make fine birds, gentlemen rarely look twice at a dowdy dove."

"No gentleman is likely to look twice at me anyway, whilst Theo is about," Felicia said, smiling at her again but aware of a familiar tightening in her midsection at the mild criticism.

Lady Augusta's pale blue eyes narrowed. "Where the devil is your spunk, girl? Had anyone dared to call me a dowdy when I was your age, I'd have snatched her bald-headed! But there you sit, meek as a nun's hen, accepting my words as if they were gospel."

Felicia shook her head. "I know perfectly well, ma'am, that I have little style and less spunk. You have certainly told me so often enough in the past twenty years, but I cannot think why you press me to behave in a manner that I am persuaded you would be the first to condemn. Goodness knows, you roundly condemn Theo whenever she speaks out of turn."

"Your sister, Theodosia, is another matter altogether," Lady Augusta retorted. "The chit may be a beauty, but she has few manners and little elegance of mind. You've got too much of both. Why, I daresay you have never misbehaved in all your life, and whenever anyone else does anything out of the way, you are quick to make excuses for them or take the blame yourself. Always a perfect child, as I recall—and my memory is much more to be relied upon than Selena's—and not so much as a breath of scandal the one year I prevailed upon you to come to Town for the Season. And as I remember," she added shrewdly, "any number of nice, reliable young men made up to you then."

Felicia remembered them, too, and remembered as well that more than one had asked for her hand, though none had really understood her responsibilities. She said only, "I fear I was not much attracted to any of them, Aunt. Most were rather boring and, I daresay, found me just as tiresome."

"That is not natural. Indeed, I cannot think why I like you so well. Milk-and-water misses generally weary me."

Ignoring the tension that crept over her again, Felicia said, "I shall try harder to please you, Aunt Augusta, but I am persuaded you would have been more disappointed had I been the sort of young woman to cause one scandal after another. Not that Theo is that sort, either, of course, for she is not. Oh, good," she added when the door opened and the footman entered bearing a tray, "here is our tea. I will pour it out, Peters, thank you."

When he had departed, Lady Augusta smiled apologetically and said, "A crust eaten in peace is better than a banquet partaken in anxiety, my dear. Forgive an old woman who cares about you, if she occasionally speaks her mind. You may not be the beauty your sister is, but you've got natural style, whatever you think to the contrary, and you have never disappointed me, except insofar as you refuse to look after yourself as well as you look after the rest of your family. You ought to be wedded by now, with a family of your own to look after."

"Why, and so I should be, ma'am, had any gentleman I could love chanced to ask me to marry him. However, none has, and I do not repine, I assure you. I am needed here, and I shall remain so for as long as Papa and Mama require my assistance."

Lady Augusta's eyes flashed sparks, but to Felicia's relief, she tightened her lips and did not speak the words so clearly hovering upon her ready tongue. Instead, accepting her tea, she reached for a sweet biscuit and took a small bite.

Felicia took advantage of the respite to say, "You have not yet repeated a single bit of scandal, ma'am. I cannot believe that you do not have at least one juicy tale to tell."

"Good gracious, child, there is scarcely a person worthy of notice in Town yet. Of course there is his majesty's illness and the usual sort of nonsense one hears about the royal family— the Prince of Wales, in particular, since despite being well and truly married, he continues to make sheep's eyes at Lady Jersey whilst insisting that his one true love is Maria Fitzherbert. Both are old enough to be his mama." She shook her head, frowning, then added, "The Devonshires, too, provide grist for the rumor mills, but they are not nearly so interesting now that poor Georgiana has got fat and is blind in one eye. Forgetful, too, I'm afraid, for she sent me two invitations to her musical evening next Friday. He, of course, has been fat for years. Has gout, still drinks too much, and refuses to pay her debts with Thomas Coutts's Bank, but all that has been so this decade and more, and therefore it is no news to anyone. That cat, Bess Foster, still resides with them, calling herself Georgiana's dearest friend, whilst doing more to please his grace than Georgiana ever did. And Georgiana still gambles, of course."

"That a man, even a duke, can prevail upon his wife to count his mistress as her great friend, and to allow the woman to live with them, seems very odd to me," Felicia said with a sigh. "The duchess's debts must be enormous."

"Well, if you are thinking that that is why she countenances Devonshire's liaison with Bess, you are out, my dear. She truly admires the woman and counts her as her best friend. It is the most amazing thing. I should have murdered Bess, I'm sure."

Felicia hid a smile. "I cannot imagine my uncle ever having had sufficient courage to make you part of a *ménage à trois*."

"I should think not," Lady Augusta said with a snort, "though I will do Charles the courtesy to admit he would have been very much shocked had anyone suggested the notion to him."

Felicia had small memory of the late Charles Hardy, for he had passed to his reward ten years before, but she was sure that her aunt spoke only the truth. She did recall that her uncle had been a small, quiet man with a ready twinkle in his eyes, and that she had liked him very much, but though she knew he had been possessed of great wealth (for both Theo's fortune and her own, as well as Lady Augusta's, derived from that wealth), had she been pressed to remember a single thing he had ever said or done, she would not have been able to comply. Any memory of him was overshadowed by much clearer ones of his outspoken wife.

The two women chatted for some minutes more before Lady Augusta said suddenly, "I hope you do not mean to take second place to Theodosia this entire Season, my dear. Since your expectations, if not your countenance, are certainly equal to hers, you will do yourself a grave injustice if you do."

"But, ma'am, she must have a chaperon, and when I asked if you would sponsor her, you said she ought to wait a year, which Theo refuses to do, so I have decided to attend to it myself."

"Nonsense, my dear. You are entirely unsuited to chaperon that minx, or anyone else. Why, you require a chaperon yourself, if only to ward off fortune hunters, as I had to do when you were with me. But your mother will take you both about, I daresay."

"Mama is by far too frail to be trotting about to all the festivities Theo will wish to attend, Aunt Augusta. That cannot be thought of, as you must have just now seen for yourself."

"Oh, pish tush, I have no patience with Selena's megrims. What can she expect you to do? You are far too young, Felicity."

"I beg of you, ma'am, do not put such a nonsensical notion into Mama's head, for I have assured her that I am quite old enough to be considered a proper chaperon for my sister, and you will distress her beyond reason if you tell her that I am not."

Lady Augusta drew a long breath, clearly forcing herself to think before saying, "Felicity, I cannot allow this. No, do not interrupt me, for I must tell you that you are going about the matter in quite the most shatter-brained fashion. You have not thought. You will be ruining any chance you or your sister have to make a suitable match if you proceed as you mean to do now."

"Why, how so, ma'am?"

"You are not yet one-and-twenty, my dear, and even at that great age, you would not be considered the proper chaperon for a younger woman unless you were married. If Theodosia were the sort of meek and mild girl that one knew would never set a foot out of place, and if you had no mama or other female relative to serve you, certain persons might be reconciled to such a state of affairs. But that is in no way the case at hand. Unless Theodosia has changed her scrambling, wild ways since last I laid eyes upon her, she cannot be depended upon to behave herself, and you do not have the first notion of how to control her. Nor would anyone expect you to. You must promise me that you will put that notion straight out of your head."

"Very well," Felicia said quietly. "I had not thought that it would reflect poorly upon Theo, but if you say it will, I must believe you." She looked directly at Lady Augusta, adding with a twinkle, "Does your concern for us mean that I may depend upon you to lend us your countenance, ma'am?"

"I suppose I must," she said, "or you will be putting yourselves into the hands of someone like Lady Dacres's sister, Leah, who promises much but can produce little, I fear."

"Lady Dacres's sister? Ought I to know her, ma'am?"

"I do not know why you should. Leah Falworthy—she is a widow now—makes much more of the relationship than Fanny Dacres does, though I do not know why she should. Fanny is a pretty chatterbox, whose great claim to fame is a son who has more money than sense. When he had his mama's portrait painted by Sir Richard Vyne, he also commissioned one of his aunt—she begged for it, I'm sure—and she puffs her sitting off now as if she were a duchess, though as I recall the matter, when Vyne refused to give her blue eyes in the portrait, she nearly fell into a distempered freak right there before him."

Felicia chuckled. "I do know who Sir Richard is, ma'am, for as you would know if you had had my letter, I have written to arrange for him to paint Theo's portrait. Papa expressed a desire for one, and since Sir Richard is quite the most famous artist of the moment, it seemed appropriate that he should paint her. They say he is very rude, so I daresay it is as well that Mrs. Falworthy did not throw a fit. From what I have heard of the man, he would have painted her just as he saw her."

"Now that would have been a painting worthy of the Royal Academy Exhibition, I think," Lady Augusta chortled. "Only wait until you see her. A plump little woman who was no doubt once a beauty of sorts, but now she makes her way taking young women into company, many of whom, I regret to say, have no business to be there. But when their papas are rich and their sponsor is the sister of a baroness, what is to be done? Most of them do not see the inside of Almack's, of course. That would be too much."

"Well, Theo will go to Almack's and anywhere else she chooses to go."

"Are you speaking of me?"

Both women turned toward the voice and saw that Miss Theodosia Adlam had found not only her bedchamber but her maidservant and clothing, for she had changed from her traveling dress into an afternoon frock of lace-trimmed pale blue cambric. It set off her deep blue eyes to perfection and matched the satin ribbon that held her golden curls away from her lovely face. She stepped quickly toward her aunt, her face wreathed in smiles.

"Do forgive me, Aunt Augusta, for not greeting you properly when you arrived. I was still trying to find my bedchamber and sort out my things from everyone else's, but now I am ever so organized and ready to play propriety. It is delightful to see you again. Have you got another cup there, Felicia?"

"Certainly, but you will not like this tea. It is China, not India."

"Oh, dreadful stuff. Don't bother then. It is a pity that Jack did not think to send cases of India tea with the children, but now that we are in London, we can set the lack to rights soon enough. What were you saying about me? Nice things, I hope."

Lady Augusta said with a sniff, "A change of scene does not change one's character, I see. It would do you more good to hear the truth, my girl, than merely to hear nice things."

Theo tossed her head and moved to sit on a claw-footed sofa near the window embrasure. "I heard you mention Sir Richard Vyne, Felicia. Has there been any message from him?"

"Not yet," Felicia said. "I wrote to him at his home, you know, for Lady Fellows very kindly gave me his direction, but perhaps the letter had to be sent on to him somewhere else. In any case, he will come to London once Parliament opens, since that is the best time, she said, for him to receive commissions. So I daresay we shall be hearing from him any day now."

"His commissions are very dear," Lady Augusta said. "I hope you do not find the sittings tedious, Theodosia."

"I daresay I shall be bored to tears," Theo said frankly, "but one must endure if one is to be made immortal."

"How true," Lady Augusta retorted dryly.

Felicia said quickly, "Aunt Augusta has agreed to take you about, Theo, whenever Mama is indisposed."

Theo cast her aunt a sidelong look and said pettishly, "I thought you were going to do that, Felicia. I can see no good reason for our aunt to put herself out on my account."

"You would soon enough," Lady Augusta said. "The first time someone made a cutting remark about two young women thinking they had the right to take themselves to parties, you would be wishing you had done the thing properly, I can tell you. And as for you, Felicity," she added, "I never said I meant to take Theodosia about on her own. I shall be glad enough to take the pair of you—even to arrange a proper ball for Theodosia at my house—but only if you promise not to make a May game of the business by pretending to be an old trout past the age of passion. I won't be party to such foolishness."

"But I *am* past the age of passion, ma'am, if, indeed, I ever approached it."

"I tell you I won't have it! Now, you just —"

"Oh, very well, ma'am," Felicia said, laughing. "Here is Theo with her eyes alight at the very thought of a ball, and Adlam House does not even possess a ballroom, you know. I shan't spoil her delight. Nor shall I pretend that I won't like doing the fancy as much as when I was a girl, but nothing will come of that, not with Theo nearby."

"I won't let anyone ignore you," Theo said fiercely. "I am not nearly such a snippet as others make me out to be."

"Of course you are not," Felicia said before Lady Augusta could speak. "You have quite as much family feeling as I do, my dear, and I know you would never be unkind or allow others to be so, but the fact is that one rarely notices what is in the shadows when the sun shines so brightly."

"Stuff and nonsense," declared Lady Augusta roundly. "You just see that you rig yourself out properly, Felicity, and you will soon find that you are not so much in the shade as you think. There are plenty, even amongst London's foolish young men, who prefer quality to quantity when it comes to looks, for beauty is more than what one sees, and ever will it be so. You might even find that Sir Richard Vyne will prefer to paint your elegance rather than your sister's opulent beauty."

Felicia glanced at Theo to see if she would take offense at such a ridiculous statement, but her sister was smiling, no doubt still thinking of the promised ball, so she relaxed, turning their aunt's thoughts in a new direction by asking her advice about which of the many fashionable mantua makers and milliners could be depended upon to rig both young women out in style.

In the week that followed, Felicia was reminded that her aunt knew her business. Their thoughts, and Theo's, were soon filled with all the practical details of preparing for a London Season. The children were left to their own devices, and even Lady Adlam's megrims had to take second place to the necessities of proper wardrobes. Still, there were minor crises to demand Felicia's attention, and Theo managed to ask her at least once a day whether Sir Richard Vyne had yet replied to her letter. And so it was that the following Friday when Peter entered the drawing room to announce a gentleman caller, though she was engaged in writing to inform a friend that an appointment with a seamstress on Tuesday prevented her from accepting her invitation to pay duty calls together, she responded with more alacrity than the interruption might otherwise have warranted.

"A gentleman, Peters? Did he give you his card?"

"No, Miss Felicia," the footman said. "Said he forgot his card case, but he did say to tell you he is an artist."

"An artist? Then it must be Sir Richard Vyne. Show him up at once, and ask Miss Theodosia to join us here in ten minutes, if you please."

"Yes, miss."

But as he turned to leave, the door burst open, and Theo entered, fairly dragging a gentleman in with her.

"Felicia, I found him in the hall parlor and brought him up at once, for he is jolly and amusing, and I knew you would want to meet him. I am certain he must be an even better artist than Sir Richard Vyne."

Felicia stood up, startled out of her composure for once by her sister's behavior, and found herself looking at a tall, well-dressed gentleman with the muscular shoulders and thighs of a sportsman. His dark hair was brushed back from well-chiseled features, and except for the twinkle dancing in his dark brown eyes, he appeared to affect the rather languid demeanor of a man about town.

Regaining her composure with difficulty, she nodded, striving for dignity. "You are not Sir Richard Vyne then, sir?"

"Ah, no," the gentleman replied, glancing away to flick an imaginary bit of lint from his sleeve. "Not exactly." He smiled, an extraordinarily charming smile, then added, "Not at all, in fact."

His voice was deep and as smooth as honey, and to her astonishment, the sound of it caused a very odd, tingling sensation in the depths of her body. He was the handsomest man she had ever seen; yet that was scarcely cause for the weakness in her knees or the unfamiliar humming in her mind. Truly, she thought, the faster pace of London must already be taking its toll on her constitution. She would have to take care not to overdo things or she would soon cease to be any sort of fit companion to her sister.

3

NOT CERTAIN that Vyne might not decide to call in person rather than to write for an appointment as he had said he would do, Crawley had looked up and down Park Lane while waiting for someone to answer the door. Seeing nothing more active than a gray mongrel sniffing the area railing, and pleased to think he was a step ahead of the artist for once, he had given his hat and cane to the butler and announced his purpose as glibly as if he were telling the man the truth. As he spoke, he noticed a towheaded urchin peering over the gallery rail above, but the face disappeared the instant he noted it, and he dismissed the child from his mind.

His assurance wavered when a footman showed him into a small side parlor and requested his name so that his presence might be properly announced, but he recovered swiftly, and the elegance of the chamber soon diverted his attention. Considering that it was merely a room where the servants parked unknown guests, he thought it extremely well-appointed, for its ceiling was nearly as grand as that of the hall through which he had passed, and its furnishings were up to date and obviously fashioned by the finest craftsmen.

He strolled to a tall window framed by blue velvet curtains looped back on gold swags that had been carved to resemble long-necked swans, and found himself looking out at the brick wall and thick overhanging beech trees bordering the east end of Hyde Park. Through nearby Grosvenor Gate, he could see the afternoon sun reflecting off the waters of the reservoir, surrounded by greening lawns. The view was a pleasant one, but he suspected there might be a good deal of traffic here on a Sunday afternoon, or even on weekday afternoons during the

Season, when the *beau monde* turned out in droves to see and be seen in the park.

Turning back to the little room, he noticed several paintings that, thanks to his friendship with Vyne, he recognized as excellent. Definitely a room that spoke of money, he told himself. He had better meet the heiress and stake his claim before the competition caught up with him, for she was going to be in high demand, beauty or no beauty. A distaste for his behavior struck him harshly. Often in the days that had passed since making the decision to stir himself to meet the heiress, such twinges of discomfort had made themselves felt. They were becoming more and more difficult to ignore.

When the door opened behind him, he turned quickly, expecting to see the footman. Instead, a pair of melting blue eyes twinkled engagingly at him from an entrancingly pretty face. The door opened wider, revealing a complete vision of loveliness. Her yellow muslin gown was nipped in beneath her plump breasts with a green satin sash that matched the ribbon threaded through her golden curls. Aside from a bit of embroidery on the flounced hem of her gown, she wore no other decoration. None was required. The thin muslin embraced luscious curves of a splendid body, leaving little to his ever active imagination.

"Oh," the vision said in a soft, musical voice, "I do hope you are Sir Richard Vyne. We have waited so very long for you."

Realizing that his mouth had fallen open, Crawley shut it with a snap and made his leg. "I wish I were," he said, straightening. "You must be Miss Adlam."

"I am Theodosia Adlam," she said sweetly, fluttering her lashes at him as she stepped all the way into the room and shut the door behind her. "My elder sister is Miss Adlam."

So it was Theodosia, not merely Theo, but even as the thought crossed his mind, Crawley looked in dismay at the closed door, knowing full well that he ought not to be alone with her. What was the chit thinking? He might be anyone, a bounder, a throat-slashing villain, anyone at all. "Where the devil is your mama," he asked abruptly, "or this elder sister of yours, at least? You ought not to be alone here with me, you know."

She smiled again and moved closer to him. "Freddy told me you were here, so I came down because I knew no one else would tell me until they had looked you over and decided that you were suitable. I wanted to know if I would like you. I do. You have a nice smile. But did you say you are not Sir Richard?" She added the question as an afterthought, bringing one dainty hand up to her rosebud mouth. "Oh, dear, then of course I ought not to be here. But Freddy said he heard you tell the footman you are an artist, so if you are not Sir Richard, who are you?"

"Who is Freddy?" Crawley demanded.

"My little cousin who is staying with us. My brother, Jack, is in India with his wife, Nancy, and they have no time for children, so their children came to us a month ago, all three of them. But about Sir Richard Vyne—"

"Oh, I daresay he will show up when he has a mind to," Crawley said, hiding his amusement as he thought of what Vyne would say about this unholy charade. "He is dreadfully busy, you know, now that he has managed to make himself all the crack. He certainly has managed to convince people that he is a great painter, has he not? And, of course, having pleased such persons as the queen and Lady Sefton, he has made others desire his services, too. But once I'd learned of your incredible beauty, I thought I could do no less than present my humble self and hope for the best. You will be lucky, you know, if Vyne exerts himself sufficiently to call upon you within a fortnight. He has got rather above himself of late, I fear."

"Oh, has he?" Theo said, the annoyance he had expected clear in her tone. She had responded instantly to his offhand comment about her beauty, and now she smiled approvingly at him. "Have you painted anyone we know, sir?"

He shrugged. "I cannot say for certain, of course, not knowing whom you count amongst your acquaintance, but perhaps you have heard of the Duke and Duchess of Langshire."

"Oh, goodness, yes," she exclaimed, clapping her hands together. "Have you truly done portraits of them?"

"Oh, yes, more than once," he replied blandly, thinking of certain sketches he had drawn for Thorne's amusement at Eton after a particularly blistering letter arrived from the Duke, castigating his son for some misdemeanor or other. "I have also done various studies of the Marquess of Thorne," he added with another gleam of mischief, "and numerous other persons of note." All true, he reassured himself. A good many persons of note had been among his classmates at Eton, where he and Vyne had competed to see who could draw the most ridiculous caricatures. He had also suffered more than once for his talent, either bent over a chair in a master's study, or on the playing fields at the hands of his chums. He had learned to defend himself well in the latter cases, though not, he recalled glumly, in the former.

Theo was nodding her head. "I think Sir Richard requires a lesson," she said. "My sister wrote to him weeks ago, and he has not even had the courtesy to reply, so I think it would do him good to lose such an excellent commission, do not you?"

"Oh, undoubtedly," Crawley replied, adding with a nonchalant shrug and the awareness that this time he spoke only the truth, "Besides, I need the money more than he does."

"And you will do me justice, will you not?"

"As to that," he said gallantly, "I doubt that any mere mortal could do true justice to such beauty as yours."

"Oh, do come now and meet my sister! I know she will like you as much as I do, and then Papa will be compelled to let you paint me. I know I shall love every minute of sitting for you, Mr.—" She broke off, looking adorably confused. "But I do not know your name, sir, do I? What is it, if you please?"

Crawley still had not decided exactly how to present himself. If he gave his true name, it would be all too easy for the Adlams to discover that he was no portrait painter, but if he gave a false name, he stood in danger of being unmasked too soon to suit his purposes. The plain fact was that he wanted to be able to attend such social functions as the younger Miss Adlam attended, and he could not do so without telling her who he was. He decided to play the matter close to his chest, giving only what information he had to give. "You may call me Edward," he said, smiling at her again.

"I daresay I might do so when others are not about," she said with a twinkle, "but I must call you something else when my sister or my aunt is by, and certainly whenever Papa is about."

"Is Papa an ogre then?"

"Oh no, not in the least. Indeed, though he is excessively fond of me, the fact is that he rarely notices anything other than the coins, wines, and Vernis Martin vases that he collects. But he might notice if I were to call any gentleman outside our family by his given name. And my aunt and sister surely would notice. So truly, sir, you must tell me who you are."

"Very well, I suppose I must, but I must also ask you to keep our business to yourself. I do not choose to let all and sundry know that I have decided to accept such commissions. I came to you only because, having heard of your beauty, I could not resist the temptation to put Vyne in his place. But you must promise that if I am granted the opportunity to paint you, you will not go around telling everyone. It is not quite the done thing for a gentleman to paint for money, you know." He made his smile as pleading as possible, wondering if he resembled his sister when he did so. He could feel a look on his face similar to the ones Belinda produced whenever she wanted something from him that he was unlikely to grant her.

Theo nodded quickly. "I do understand. I think such rules are silly; however, you are so clearly a gentleman that I feel I must apologize for mistaking you for a common painter. Pray, sir, what is your name?"

"Crawley," he said, "but I must tell you that Vyne is not—"

"Not Mr. Crawley," she said wisely. "Ought I not to address you as my lord?"

"On no account in the world," he said. "You, my dear, must learn to call me Ned." And audaciously, knowing she would not object, he took her hand and raised it to his lips.

She grinned at him but made no effort to reclaim her hand when he straightened. "We shall just see about that, sir, and you did *not* say you are no lord. Now, come and meet Felicia."

"Felicia?" He was surprised. "I thought . . .that is, I am sure that someone told me your sister's name was Felicity."

"Oh, no doubt it was my Aunt Augusta or one of her

cronies," Theo said, wrinkling her nose. "Aunt still lives in the last century, you see, and will not admit that we have entered upon a new one. She and Papa both continue to refer to Felicia in that outdated style. No one else does so, I promise you, not even Mama. But come now. Felicia will be upstairs in the drawing room, for I know she was meaning to write some letters this morning, and her writing desk is there."

Crawley followed her, aware that his impression of the elder Miss Adlam had undergone a startling transformation. While he had thought of her as Miss Felicity Adlam, he had somehow been able to convince himself that she would be an unequal opponent, a middle-aged spinster with little experience of the world. But a Miss Felicia Adlam could be quite another matter. He could not explain how such a change might have come about in his own mind. It was absurd. Yet he felt his confidence ebbing as he followed the minx up the wide sweep of stairs to the next floor.

He scarcely noted the many paintings lining the stair wall, punctuated by marble busts in niches above every sixth step, or the highly polished mahogany railing of the gallery. His footsteps were silent on the carpet, a magnificent example of Turkey's finest, its colors vibrant on the gallery floor, well lit by the huge window above the front entrance to the house. As he followed Theo to the open doors of the drawing room, he did note briefly that he could see over the wall into the park now through that window, but once inside, he forgot his surroundings again when he came face-to-face with Miss Adlam.

She had been sitting at her desk, talking to the footman, and she turned at the sound of their entrance. Crawley's first impression was of a little dab of a woman in a dun-colored gown, with sunlight from the nearby window glinting on her soft brown hair. His confidence stirred, then faltered again when he found himself being examined from top to toe by a pair of cool gray eyes. He barely heard Theo speak, babbling something about how he was not Dickon but another artist; however, he clearly saw the expression in Miss Adlam's eyes harden as she stood up, nodded gravely, and said, "You are not Sir Richard Vyne, then?"

"Ah, no," Crawley said, confounded by her direct look and

a certain something in the way she looked at him that said she could see straight into his soul. "Not exactly." He cleared his throat, finding it utterly impossible to prevaricate when she looked at him like that. "Not at all, in fact."

"I told you," Theo said impatiently. "He is a much better artist than Sir Richard. He has painted dukes and duchesses, Felicia, and he is here right now. He said Sir Richard has got too far above himself to be bothered with the likes of us. He's too important now, he said. Isn't that right, sir?"

Confronted with Theodosia's limpid gaze on the one hand and her sister's steady look on the other, Crawley suddenly wished he were a hundred miles away. Vyne would murder him for this, if the shrewd-looking Miss Adlam did not beat him to it. "Ah, as to that," he said, forcing calm into his voice but wishing the gray eyes would look elsewhere, if only for a moment, "it is no place of mine to be casting aspersions upon Vyne's character, and I certainly never meant to do so. I apologize, Miss Theodosia, if that was the impression I gave you. It is merely that Sir Richard finds himself extremely busy, as much in demand as he is nowadays, and I fear that he would find it hard to do justice to your great beauty without taking time away from his other work."

"Has Sir Richard actually said as much to you, sir?" Miss Adlam asked bluntly.

"No, certainly not," Crawley replied, feeling himself sinking into ever deeper waters as he strove to sound completely sure of himself. He wished it were possible to equivocate with this woman. He had thought it would be easy, but now he felt like a lying rogue.

He had not thought of it as lying before, but only as an amusing way to meet the new heiress and a fine joke to play on Vyne. Indeed, he had been rather pleased that though he had had to stretch the truth a bit, he had not told any actual falsehoods to Miss Theodosia, and he had expected to continue the same tactics with her sister. But that was not possible. And why it was not, he had not the least notion.

She was certainly nothing special to look at, all mousy brown and gray as she was. The dun-colored gown boasted no particular decoration, and her hair, though elegantly smooth, was not dressed fashionably but merely parted in the center, brushed back from her face, and arranged in two neatly braided coils joined at the nape of her neck. A dowdy, that's what she was, and no mistake about it.

Nevertheless he was aware of an aura of common sense and intelligence radiating from the small figure. She sat down again at her writing desk, calmly regarding him, apparently waiting for him to elaborate upon his statement. She made no effort to speak but waited patiently until he could stand the silence no longer, and opened his mouth to confess the whole.

Before he could do so, Theo said, "Why do you care what Sir Richard has said or not said, Felicia? Papa said he wants my portrait drawn; he did not say it must be done by Sir Richard."

"No, my dear, but you did say you wanted it to be a true Vyne, since that would so much impress everyone. Have you changed your mind?"

Theo flushed, flicking a glance at Crawley. "I may have said some such stupid thing," she admitted, "but I would not at all mind being the one who discovered an even greater artist, particularly since Sir Richard has so unkindly ignored your request to call upon us."

Miss Adlam turned her attention back to Crawley. "Is that true, sir? Has he simply ignored my request?"

It did not occur to him until hours after he had left Adlam House that he might simply have disclaimed any knowledge of Vyne's thought processes. At that moment he simply answered the question as directly as it had been put to him, "No, Miss Adlam, that is not the case."

"Indeed? You are very certain, sir."

"I am. I was present when he received your letter."

"And when was that, precisely?"

Damn, he thought, how did she know the exact questions to ask to put him most in the wrong? But still he could not lie to her. "Yesterday," he said with a sigh.

Theo exclaimed, "Yesterday! But that is impossible, sir. My sister wrote to him more than a fortnight ago."

"I know," he replied, casting an oblique glance at Miss Adlam and noting that there was a silvery glint in the gray

eyes now, "but she wrote to him at home when he was away.
The letter followed him from point to point but did not catch
up with him until yesterday." He had not the least inclination
to describe the great struggle he had fought with his lesser self
when that letter was delivered at Longworth the day after
Vyne's departure. He had wanted to open it the minute he recognized her elegant copperplate handwriting. Basely, he had
kept the letter in his possession until he reached London, de-
livering it to Vyne himself, in order to be at hand when it was
read. He had the feeling now, however, that the silver gray
eyes saw straight through him to the truth. Suppressing a small
shudder, he forced himself to meet her gaze as innocently as
he could.

Theo said, "Still, Felicia, if Sir Richard is as busy as everyone says he is, he might well not wish to paint me, so I daresay we would do better to commission Lord Crawley."

The gray eyes shifted in his direction again, widening in
surprise, and Crawley felt telltale heat suffuse his face. He
could not remember the last time he had actually blushed, and
here he was, doing so like a guilty schoolboy. It would help if
the fool woman would ask him to sit down, he thought, but he
could scarcely do so without invitation or while the younger
chit continued to stand.

Miss Adlam said with emphasis, "*Lord* Crawley? You are a
member of the nobility, sir? You must forgive my sister for
her poor manners. She ought to have introduced you more precisely at the outset. But then, you ought to have announced
yourself more precisely to my footman—unless your title is
spurious."

The last words were spoken more gently than those that had
gone before, and Crawley fought an impulse to loosen his
heavily starched neckcloth, wondering why on earth he had
got himself into such a predicament. The woman reminded
him of his sharp-tongued grandmother, daring to challenge
him in such an outrageous way, but he had asked for it. He had
put himself in the wrong from the moment he had entered the
house. He cleared his throat, glanced at Theo, then back at
Miss Adlam, before saying, "The title is genuine, I'm afraid,
though I have no doubt that certain of my ancestors might take

exception to my claiming it under the present circumstances. I wonder if I might have a word with you alone, Miss Adlam."

She raised her eyebrows, and he realized that he ought not to have suggested such a thing. Somehow the thought of impropriety that had struck him instantly below when Theo shut the door of the little parlor had not touched him here. The thought of impropriety where Miss Adlam was concerned was ludicrous. No man would have such courage.

Attempting to recover lost ground, he smiled at her. "You have clearly taken responsibility for your sister's welfare, ma'am, and I admire and respect that. I would appreciate the opportunity to explain my motives to you privately."

"No," Theo said, "I won't be dismissed like a child! I want you to paint me, sir, and I promised I would not speak of your title, and so I will not. I did not know you meant me to keep it from Felicia, and I would not in any case, because she is my sister and deserves to know, but I will have my way, I promise you, and Felicia will not stop me! If I have to go to Papa on my own, Felicia, and beg him to hire Crawley, I shall, so there!"

He was appalled by the outburst, but before he could think of a response, Miss Adlam stood up and said firmly, "You will come with me, Theo, at once. If you wish to speak privately to me regarding this business, you may, but you must not behave in this manner before his lordship. Come now, and we will speak in the morning room."

To Crawley's surprise, the beauty went with no more than a muttered imprecation, which he did not overhear. Left alone, he strode impatiently to the window, wishing he were the sort of man who could simply depart now that they had gone. He knew he could not, however. He would encounter the Adlam sisters at many social activities during the Season, so he must do what he could now to smooth over the awkward situation. His only hope to escape with pride and reputation even partially intact was to think of some acceptable way to explain himself to Miss Adlam, but what that might be he had no idea.

He looked aimlessly out the window till he saw that it overlooked a barren back garden, then began to pace instead, wracking his brain for a scheme to put himself in the clear, pacing back and forth until he found himself looking idly down at the writing desk. His eyes focused on the last words she had written, and he stared at them in shock. *I cannot go on*, she had written. Swiftly he read the preceding line, but there was nothing helpful there, merely a comment about the household being muddled and the hours of each day too few. He would have read more, but hearing the door latch click, he stepped hurriedly back, turning at the same time to face the door when Miss Adlam returned.

She gazed at him sternly, and feeling his guilty conscience surface again, he wondered if she knew he had seen what she had written. She looked so calm and self-possessed that he found it difficult to imagine that she could be contemplating self-destruction; however, for some reason as yet unknown to him she seemed to carry the entire burden of this household on her slim shoulders, and such a vast responsibility might overburden anyone, let alone one small, inexperienced female.

Felicia interrupted his thoughts. "If you have an explanation, sir, I suggest you get on with it, for I do not have a great deal of time at my command today. My suspicion is that you had some thought of attempting to seduce my sister. If that is the case, you must know now that you have failed."

"No," he said more sharply than he had intended. "That is to say, ma'am, I had no such intention. I confess, I am no artist— not to compare with Vyne, at all events—but my intentions toward your sister are entirely honorable, and I can assure you that neither she nor you has cause to fear me."

"What, precisely, did you intend, Lord Crawley?"

"Marriage," he said, adding hastily, "that is to say, in due time, and only if we should find that we suit one another. I have been foolish, ma'am, but needs must when the devil drives, and the devil has been driving me hard. May I sit down?"

"Certainly, sir, but pray be brief." Seating herself in the chair she had occupied before, she gestured for him to take one nearby, adding, "A declaration ought more properly to be made to my father, of course, but I doubt he would give my sister to a fortune hunter—and that, as I see now, is what you must be. And truly, sir, I have no time to discuss foolishness. I am to take my sister to her dressmaker in precisely half an hour.

He was not doing at all well, he realized. The woman had reduced him to nursery status merely by the way she looked at him. "My only hope is that you can find it in your heart to forgive an impulsive gesture." He said the words only to give himself time to think, for he had not the least notion what to say to her. He was not a *common* fortune hunter, but he could well believe that her father would not accept his request for Miss Theodosia's hand, certainly not when he had just met the girl and had no great reputation to precede him. He smiled again, and was relieved to see this time that his smile was reflected in her eyes. "I confess," he said, "I do not know what to say to redeem myself, though I very much wish to do so."

"I have little tolerance for foolishness, sir. I must say, I should not have thought ill of you had we met under other circumstances. I begin to think this all must be the result of some foolish wager. My young cousin Tom has told me that there were gentlemen on shipboard with them—my brother's children, from India, that is—who were accustomed to bet on how many times the wind would rise before sunset. Was it a wager?"

"There was a wager involved," he said, wishing he could accept such a simple way out. "I enjoy a friendship with Sir Richard, and when we learned that your sister was to have her portrait painted, I bet him I could make her choose myself over him as the artist. But," he added with a sigh, "that is not the sole reason I came today. I am afraid you were right to name me fortune hunter, Miss Adlam. I had not thought of myself in that way, but I did come to see your sister only because I had learned of her great dowry. Now I shan't even win the wager, though I was well on the way to doing so before I encountered you."

"You might easily have lied to me, sir."

"I might, but from some cause or other, I did not."

"I am glad, though I must tell you I think your actions were reprehensible for a man in your position."

Crawley bit back an impulse to tell her precisely—since she liked the word so much—what his position really was, and was relieved rather than annoyed when the footman entered just then, until he said, "Sir Richard Vyne is below, Miss Felicia."

Taking the card from the silver salver the footman held out to her, Miss Adlam read it and looked up at Crawley, her eyes alight with sudden laughter. "You will want to tell Sir Richard the result of your wager, sir. Show him up at once, Peters."

Crawley restrained an urge to command him to do no such thing. He was never going to hear the end of this. Making no attempt to break the silence that fell when the lad had gone, he considered what revenge Dickon might take. His only hope was that he would not be so amused by it all that he would tell her the whole story, beginning with the York Mail robbery and reading her letter. He tried to tell himself it was not so much that he worried about what she would think of him as that she was a gently nurtured female clearly under a good deal of tension already. With all the responsibility she bore, it simply might not be good for her to hear such things as Dickon might tell her. Watching her, he wondered how she could manage to look so calm when both her letters had suggested a mind in great turmoil. He experienced a sudden, overwhelming determination not to add to her troubles, or to allow Vyne to do so.

The artist entered moments later, bowed to Miss Adlam, then turned with an enigmatic look to say to Crawley, "Here before me, are you? I decided to come around directly instead of writing to set an appointment, but I expect you have already convinced this poor lady to suppose that you are a greater painter than I."

Relieved that his friend had said nothing more damning, Crawley smiled lazily at him. "I am indeed before you, Dickon, and I think I might claim victory in our wager, too, for I have got Miss Theodosia begging for me to paint her portrait. However, Miss Adlam knows the truth, so Miss Theo will soon know me for an impostor."

"I see," Vyne said, his expression showing Crawley that he did not see at all but was willing to be led. He turned to Miss Adlam. "I would like to meet your sister, ma'am. I cannot say whether I will paint her or not, you see, until I determine if the exercise will amuse me."

"Indeed?" Miss Adlam's eyebrows rose, and she glanced at Crawley. "Perhaps, sir, you will yet win your wager. My sister will not like being looked over like a prize cow."

Vyne shrugged, glancing around the room. "That is her choice, of course, ma'am. I have seen some excellent work in this house, but you also have a number of commonplace pieces. That Constable over there is certainly not one of his best."

"That is Bradstoke," Felicia said quietly. "We think Mr. Constable captured the feeling we like best about our home."

Vyne shook his head, clearly unimpressed, and Crawley felt impelled to say, "Forgive Dickon, Miss Adlam. He is merely being odious, a thing he does even better than he paints."

Vyne looked at him in surprise. "Was I odious? I did not mean to be." He looked over his shoulder at Felicia and added, "I daresay I am plain spoken, ma'am. My mind is generally on my work, not on such ordinary stuff. Good God," he added, nearly losing his balance when, his attention caught by the movement of the door as it opened, he shifted his gaze, then whipped his head around to stare awestruck at Theo.

Standing framed in the doorway, she looked from one man to the other, then said to Felicia, "Peters told me Sir Richard was here. I don't know what you mean to do, but it *is* my portrait, after all, and I am determined that Crawley shall paint it."

"Serve you right if he did," Vyne muttered, moving nearer the door, still scrutinizing her.

Theo looked daggers at him. "Why, what can you mean by such a rude remark?" she said, raising her chin indignantly.

"Hold that pose for a moment," he ordered, moving to stand beside her, peering at her face. "No, bring your chin down just a hair's breadth. Not like that," he snapped, reaching to grasp her chin firmly in his large hand. "There now, don't move. No, dammit, come into the room. I cannot get around you in the doorway." When Theo, jerking her chin from his grasp, swept past him into the room, he snorted. "Probably wouldn't do, Miss Adlam. Chit's too hot at hand to sit still or take direction."

"I don't want you to paint me," Theo said shrilly. "You are a rude and dreadful man. I want Crawley!"

Crawley knew before he looked at her that Miss Adlam's gaze had shifted to him. He sighed, forced himself to meet her look, and understood it completely. "Miss Theodosia," he said gently. "I fear that I have acted in the worst way imaginable in leading you to believe me a better painter than I am. I can sketch caricatures, but I am not at all the artist Vyne is, and I should be a swindler to pretend for another moment that I am."

"But you are nice, and he is rude," Theo said flatly. "I do not want to sit for him if he is going to treat me the way he has done just now."

He looked apologetically at Miss Adlam, who said gently, "But you do want your portrait painted, do you not, my dear?"

"You know I do. I just do not want that dreadful man to paint it. I do not like him."

Vyne continued to look at her. "Can't say I don't want to paint you, Miss Theodosia. Truth is, I don't see perfect features very often. Be a privilege, I'm sure."

"Don't trip over your tongue, Dickon," Crawley said, amused to realize that his friend really did want to paint her. "The young lady don't want to subject herself to your rudeness, and I cannot blame her. She's much too young and innocent a victim."

"Dash it, I don't want to ravish her," Vyne snapped, grimacing. "I only want to paint her."

Felicia said calmly, "You will have no opportunity to ravish her, sir. Her maid or I will be with her every moment; however, I must warn you that if you are asked to take this commission, you must promise to behave as a gentleman in *every* way."

"Impossible," Crawley said frankly with a mocking look at Vyne. "The only way to guarantee that he does not offend her daily, Miss Adlam, is if someone bigger than he is were to remain in the room with them to protect her from his surly moods."

To his astonishment, Miss Adlam said reasonably, "You are larger than he is, my lord, and you did say that you desired to redeem yourself. If you will agree to such an arrangement, I believe that would suit my sister and me perfectly well."

"Oh, yes," Theo said, smiling brilliantly at him. "The very thing! Oh, pray sir, do say that you will."

Vyne was not nearly so delighted. He looked, Crawley thought, as if he were ready to commit murder.

Smiling blandly at the artist, he did not so much as stop to think before he found himself saying, "It will be a pleasure."

4

SEEING Lord Crawley rise from his chair as both men prepared to depart, and wondering what had possessed her to suggest such a scheme, Felicia stood up, gathered herself, and said with tolerable composure, "Then you will take the commission, Sir Richard. You will work here, of course, for my sister cannot be expected to go to you to sit. When do you want to begin?"

Crawley, giving her another of the odd, rather measuring looks she had noted after leaving him alone those few minutes, said, "You will be well advised to leave the whole business in our hands now, ma'am. We'll return tomorrow at ten o'clock."

"Eight," Sir Richard said brusquely before Felicia could tell Crawley that she had no intention of following such advice. She saw that the artist was still preoccupied, watching Theo. He added, "Ten's not early enough. Light's only good morning or afternoon, not when I've got to make do with a bit of each."

Felicia was not surprised to hear Theo say indignantly, "Then I should much prefer afternoon sittings, Sir Richard, and I should think that my preference must prevail."

Felicia saw Crawley open his mouth to intervene but before he could do so, Vyne retorted, "You are not doing the painting, my girl. I prefer a room on the north side of a house, but if I must paint you here, that cannot be, for this house sits too close to the houses on either side of it. We can either use the west side or the east side, and I prefer the east because it is not so hot on a hot day, and any light in London is clearer in the morning than it is later in the day."

"Well, even half past eight is much too early," Theo insisted. "If I am out late at a party—for example, we are going to Devonshire House tonight—I can scarcely expect to look my best so early in the morning."

"True, Dickon," Crawley said quickly. "Surely—"

"If she wants to look her best, she will not stay out late," Vyne growled. "There is no cause to do so tonight, since I happen to know that it is merely one of her grace's musical evenings. Come on, Crawler. I'm to meet Tom Lawrence and West in Castle Street in twenty minutes. Tied my rig to the area railing, so since I needn't wait for it, I can give you a ride."

Crawley smiled apologetically at Felicia, but she saw that he kept an eye on the scowling Theo as he said, "That would be Thomas Lawrence of the Royal Academy and Benjamin West, its president. The annual Academy Exhibition is to be held the last week in April. Every second year, the members award medals for the finest paintings, and they want Dickon to enter his work. Of course the reason he is in such a devil of a hurry to take me along now is he wants to be sure I don't stay to claim victory on the field, but I too have received an invitation to Devonshire House, and I promise you, Miss Theodosia, I shan't allow him to bully you there or when he begins your sittings." Glancing at Vyne, he added, "I hope you haven't got your brutish chestnuts tied to anyone's railing. They'll have had it down by now."

"Got the blacks. Hurry up, Crawler."

A moment later they were gone, and Theo turned quickly to Felicia, her scowls vanishing. "Wasn't he wonderful?"

"Sir Richard?" Felicia affected surprise. "Why, I thought you detested him, my dear, but that just goes to show how wrong one person can be about another. He is certainly a handsome creature, and with the prettiest manners, too, so I cannot be much surprised that he has caught your fancy."

"Oh, Felicia!" Theo laughed merrily. "What a jokesmith you can be! As if anyone could think that dreadful man handsome, and as for his manners . . .Well, I just hope we may see some before our acquaintance with him is done. Wasn't he dreadful? I meant Lord Crawley, of course. Such a delightful smile, and such a wise way about him. Why, he kept me laughing all the time."

"He kept you preening all the time, like a vain little turtle dove, my dear," Felicia said, not mincing matters, and hoping her sister was not developing a foolish tenderness for the outrageous, albeit charming, Crawley. "You must take care lest your vanity erase some of your beauty. It does not become a young woman to be so sure of her looks, you know."

Theo shrugged lightly. "I did not see that anyone was offended by my behavior, Felicia. And if Sir Richard was, why it serves him right. He is quite impossible."

"True, my love, but do not forget his reputation. You do not want him to paint you as a hag because he takes a dislike to your personality. It would be better, I think, to show him only your graces. A lady does not allow her temper to be swayed by another's action or speech, not if she knows her business."

"Oh, pooh, you sound as if you were quoting one of Aunt Augusta's foolish maxims."

"Her words are rarely foolish, Theo," Felicia said quietly.

"Well, at all events, I shall never be such a pattern-card as you are, Felicia. I gave up the attempt years ago."

"Did you?" Felicia chuckled. "I was unaware that you had ever made such an attempt, my dear. Pray, when was this?"

Fortunately Theo also had a sense of humor. She grinned and said, "Well, if there was no real attempt to emulate you, at least it is true that I gave up long ago the notion of ever being as good as you are. Have you never put a foot out of place?"

"Dear me," Felicia said, dismayed, "if that is what you think, I wonder how it is that we get on at all. I am scarcely a perfect person, Theo. I strive to do what is right, and if you must know the truth, I quite dread being scolded. In point of fact, I have prodigious fear that one day the earth will open up beneath my feet and swallow me, because I have done some awful thing, no doubt right out in public. You have no notion how I envy your indifference to society's stern moral precepts."

"Envy me? But you are forever scolding me, Felicia!"

"Nonsense. If I try to guide your steps from time to time, it is only because I am so much older than you are."

"Just three years, though it often seems like much more, to be sure. But you are not an old cat yet, my dearest." Theo grinned saucily at her. "Madame Bernille will be expecting us soon, will she not?"

Felicia glanced at the little clock on the mantel. "Yes, I told her that we would try to be there by two o'clock, and it is nearly that now. We must bustle about. I already ordered the carriage, so all we must do is tidy ourselves. I hope she has your gown ready, so you can wear it to Devonshire House tonight. It was kind of Aunt Augusta to arrange to take us to her grace's musical evening, particularly since the duchess has pretty nearly retired from society and is so rarely seen abroad nowadays."

"A musical evening sounds boring," Theo said with a sigh, "but perhaps if Crawley is there, it will not be so bad."

"Oh, no, dearest, for everyone in Town will be there."

"Everyone who *is* anyone, you mean?"

"Yes, of course," Felicia agreed. She realized at once that she ought not to speak so, and added, "Do not think I am being snobbish, my dear. I am merely being practical. It is of the utmost importance that you meet as many members of the *beau monde* as possible before the opening of Almack's Assembly Rooms, just after Easter, if you are to be a success. Aunt Augusta will have no difficulty obtaining vouchers for us, but it is important to make a good impression before then, for me as well as for you, since I have not been much in company these past two years."

"Well, I do not much care whether I make a good impression," Theo said, tossing her head. "I am sure I have never made a bad one. Nor have you. You worry too much, Felicia."

"Perhaps," Felicia agreed, rising, "but you do not want to vex Madame Bernille, lest she should rig you out in a gown with weakened seams to get even. Only think how you would feel if your dress collapsed around your ankles at Devonshire House."

Fortunately, Madame Bernille had their gowns ready for them, and Theo's required only a little narrowing at the waist, which the good lady did on the spot. Felicia's gray muslin gown fitted her to perfection, the only alteration being a pink satin sash that Theo demanded on her behalf to replace the lavender one.

"You look as if you were in mourning with that purple

sash," Theo said with a grimace, "and I can tell you right now that if Aunt Augusta condemns that gown, you have only yourself to blame, for I begged you to have the primrose muslin instead, or the Pomona green, and so I shall tell her."

But Lady Augusta, when she arrived to dine with them that evening, magnificently garbed in crimson sarcenet, had only compliments for Felicia. "I declare, I was that tempted to insist that you allow me to accompany you to your modiste, my dear, but I ought to have known better than to think you would rig yourself out in one of those dreadfully thin white muslins that have recently become all the rage. Bad enough three years ago, when you had to wear white in your first and only Season, but there is no rule that says you must do so in your second, and you were wise to select a gown that so perfectly matches your eyes. I like that touch of pink, too. Very dashing!"

Felicia saw Theo regarding their aunt in astonishment. Smiling, she said, "Theo disagrees with you, Aunt. She made me change the ribbons from lavender to pink, declaring that I looked as if I were in mourning with the other."

"She was quite right, too," Lady Augusta said, nodding for once in approval of Theo, and adding, "Some begrudge others what they cannot enjoy themselves, Theodosia. Not that the lavender would not have become her, for it would, but you were wise to insist upon the pink. Now, if everyone else is ready, shall we go in to dinner? I declare, I am quite famished. Oh, there you are, Henry," she said as Lord Adlam appeared in the doorway and stood blinking at her almost as though he were trying to recall her identity. "Is Selena going to join us?"

"Lying down on her bed," Lord Adlam said shortly. "Migraine, I believe Harroby said it was."

"Well, she will make herself truly ill if she does not eat," Lady Augusta said. "You must order a tray sent up to her room."

"Won't touch it," Adlam said, turning toward the dining-room door and clearly assuming the topic was closed.

"But you must insist," Lady Augusta protested, following him. "Tell him, Felicity! A body don't function without food."

"Yours must function well enough," Adlam said, glancing at her over his shoulder but making, Felicia noted uncomfortably, not the least gesture of politeness toward her aunt. "Never guess by that scrawny figure of yours that you eat at all."

To cover Lady Augusta's gasp of indignation and, hopefully, to forestall all-out war between two persons who rarely took the trouble to be kind to each other, Felicia said hastily, "We have arranged with Sir Richard Vyne to paint Theo's portrait, Papa. He means to begin in the morning."

Adlam smiled at his younger daughter as they all took their seats and the servants began to serve the food. "Ought to think it a privilege to be allowed to paint such a rare piece as you are, my dear. Where are you off to tonight in all your finery?"

"Devonshire House," Theo said with a grimace. "We are to attend a musical evening there, Papa, which sounds dreadfully dull, do you not agree?"

Lord Adlam's pale eyes took on a reminiscent gleam. "Quite thought Georgiana had given up entertaining," he said. "Dashed if she wasn't the prettiest girl I ever saw. Your mama was a fairy princess, Theo, but Georgiana Spencer was all fire and light. Used to wear that flaming hair of hers unpowdered, so a man could see her across any room in London. And what a figure! Put all the tabbies in an uproar because she thumbed her nose at their rules and then caught herself a duke before she turned seventeen. Set the whole town by the ears, she did."

Theo sighed. "Like the Gunning sisters. It was so romantic in the old days, not like today, when one is expected to go to boring musical evenings merely because there are not yet any balls or parties to attend. She is quite old now, is she not?"

Lord Adlam look astonished. "Old? Good gracious, she is six years younger than I am, and the Gunnings were long before our time, so I don't know what they were like. But had Georgiana been a collector's piece, I'd have paid any price for her."

Lady Augusta said sharply, "Utter nonsense. You needn't think her life has been a fairy tale, Theodosia, for it hasn't. She married a man as opposite to herself as anyone could be. Where Georgiana was a giddy and emotional young girl, William Cavendish was a cold fish bored with life. She tried to teach him her enthusiasm for music, but I doubt if you will see him tonight, for she never succeeded."

"There were worse things than that to interfere with her happiness," Lord Adlam said tartly.

"Not things we need discuss in present company," Lady Augusta retorted, silencing him.

But Theo said, "As if I did not know about the most scandalous *ménage à trois* in London! The Duke and Duchess of Devonshire have had Lady Elizabeth Foster living with them for years, and both still claim her as their very best friend and her children as orphans taken in out of charity. Still, I should like very much to be all the rage, just as Duchess Georgiana once was."

Lady Augusta retorted, "Georgie was not merely all the rage. She was notorious, and while men often mistake notoriety for fame, it is not at all the same."

Observing her sister's appreciative grin, Felicia knew their aunt was doing little to alter her opinion of the Duchess of Devonshire, but the conversation did help reconcile Theo to the visit to Devonshire House. The appearance of the house itself, with its sumptuous Kent reception rooms, its spacious torchlit gardens, and the high stone wall guarding it from the lesser folk in Piccadilly, made her eyes widen in appreciation. Their first view of the duchess was another matter.

Georgiana stood leaning on her cane beside the younger, prettier, and healthy-looking Lady Elizabeth Foster, who drew first one guest, then another to her attention with the air of a kindly nursemaid whose charge was rather backward. The Duchess of Devonshire, in her forty-fourth year, retained little of the beauty that had graced her earlier years; but though her figure was corpulent, her complexion course, her neck immense, and the patch over her blind eye unfortunately rather noticeable, her smile was still one that lighted the room and made her guests feel as if they had been embraced. When Lady Augusta presented her nieces, Georgiana greeted them with delight in a surprisingly youthful voice.

"Felicia, I remember you well. We met several years ago, I believe, but I have seen nothing of you since. Shame on you, Augusta! You ought to have had her to visit you often."

"Well, and so I would have done if she had only agreed to come to me," said Lady Augusta roundly, "so I'll listen to none of your scolds, Georgiana. There is much to be said for

the fact that my nieces have not yet achieved so much famil-
iarity with life amongst the *beau monde* as to have learned
contempt for it."

"Oh, goodness," Georgiana said with a chuckle, "they will
be very out of the way, then. Do you intend to be an enthusi-
ast, Theodosia? When I was young, I certainly was, but everyone around me pretended to be bored all the time."

"Not everyone," Lady Elizabeth Foster said, smiling.

"Oh, not the men," the duchess agreed.

Felicia could tell by Theo's expression that she had not
made up her mind whether to like the duchess, but the younger
girl clearly saw where their interests lay, for she smiled and
said, "I don't pretend much, your grace. I say what I think."

"She generally don't think at all is what she means to say,"
Lady Augusta said sourly, "but that will do her no harm in
your eyes, I suppose. You were never one to look before you
leapt."

"No, I was not," the duchess replied. With a gimlet air she
looked Theo over carefully with her good eye and sighed.
"You are much prettier than I ever was, you know."

Seeing Theo flush deeply and realizing that her generally
outspoken sister was for once at a loss for words, Felicia said
gently, "I am sure that cannot be, ma'am, for we have heard
that you were the queen of them all."

"Well, I can tell you that I was nothing of the sort, and Bess
and Augusta would agree if I were not standing here beside
them. Not beautiful the way you mean, at all events, but the
best way to prove that is to show you. Augusta tells me, Theodosia, that you are to have your portrait painted by Sir Richard
Vyne, so I daresay you would like to see his work and compare it to that of other fashionable portrait artists."

Lady Elizabeth said quickly, "I do not think you ought to
tax your strength, Georgiana, by wandering about."

"Oh, piffle, Bess, I shan't die of it, you know. I'm good for
years yet, and I shall enjoy showing off my lost beauty. You
stay here and greet our remaining guests, if you will. Augusta
and the girls will look after me perfectly well." Not until they
were well away did she let out a sigh of relief and say, "There
now, we have escaped. A dear friend, Bess is, but she and
Devonshire would wrap me in cotton wool and never let me

stir. To be truthful, I hate receiving, knowing that every next
guest merely wants to see how much old Georgie has deterio-
rated since the last time he laid eyes on her. I shall enjoy our
little excursion much more than pandering to their curiosity.
Come this way. We'll begin in the dining room, for the ones I
particularly want to show you are there. There are pictures all
over the house, of course, for there is no proper picture gallery
here."

They followed her through a magnificent series of state
rooms, adorned with splendidly decorated and gilded ceilings,
entablatures, doorcases, and carved marble fireplaces, all with
the bold architectural relief typical of William Kent's work.
Every room was hung with paintings, so many that once Felicia found herself wondering if there really were any walls behind them. In the dining room Georgiana stopped before a
painting of a rather plain woman, playing with a red-headed
baby whose bare toes peeped out from beneath its long white
dress. The woman was dressed informally with her hair unpowdered, and sat on a settee. The baby had its hands raised
over its head and looked about to burst into laughter at any
minute.

"That was painted by Sir Joshua Reynolds the year after my
daughter Georgiana was born," the duchess said. "There is an
earlier one by Gainsborough, there on the wall to your left,
and the one alongside it was painted by your Sir Richard,
Theodosia."

"He is *not* my Sir Richard."

"Theodosia, try for some proper conduct!"

The duchess laughed. "Do not scold her, Augusta. I ought
not to have phrased it like that. I simply meant it was a Vyne."
She looked at it critically. "I admit, that portrait is quite my favorite one. Vyne is the best of today's three great portrait
artists, you know, and looking at that, one can see why he
beats Hoppner and Tom Lawrence all hollow."

Felicia smiled at the painting and saw that the other ladies
were smiling, too. The duchess, caught at her writing desk,
was looking over her shoulder at the artist with a delightful
mixture of mischief and guilt. Though she was clearly older in
that portrait than in the other two, Vyne had caught her charm
and personality much more clearly than the other artists had,

and Felicia saw instantly why men had once thought her beautiful.

"Do you see what I mean?" the duchess demanded. "I was not a beauty at all, certainly not one to compete with Theodosia."

Lady Augusta said severely, "Beauty is as beauty does, Georgiana. Your charm is worth a good deal more."

A familiar masculine voice behind them said, "Their skill was not sufficient to capture your beauty, Duchess. Mine was."

Felicia turned with the others and saw Sir Richard, Lord Crawley, and a third man, plumper and with lighter hair than the first two, approaching them. Crawley, shooting her yet another of his odd measuring looks, suddenly smiled, and the room seemed instantly warmer and, despite its size, rather crowded.

Vyne was saying, "Why, that blind old fool Reynolds did a better job of capturing the baby's chuckles than her mama's delight in playing with her, which I am convinced must have been perfectly clear to him. He just couldn't catch it on canvas."

The duchess said genially, "I quite forgot I had invited you tonight, Dickon. Indeed, I appear to have invited quite a number of persons to whom I do not recall sending invitations. How do you do, Crawley. And you are Langshire's nephew, Dawlish, are you not?" she said to the third gentleman. "Allow me to present you to Lady Augusta Hardy, Miss Adlam, and Miss Theodosia Adlam. Do not tell me the music has begun and frightened you all away," she added when the gentlemen had made their bows.

Felicia, feeling Lord Crawley's keen gaze upon her again, fixed her attention upon Vyne, who said in a tone gentler than she had heard him use before, "I could not resist showing Crawley and Dawlish around, particularly since they have not been in the house before and had no more wish than I did to sit chatting with Crawley's mama and sister and their group of cronies. This is by far the best collection of pictures in London, after all."

Crawley said, "I am honored to have had the pleasure of

seeing them, ma'am. But you are shivering, Miss Adlam. Did
you bring a shawl? May I send a footman to fetch it for you?"

Felicia started. She had indeed been feeling chilly in her
muslin, and her wrap had been left in the ladies' withdrawing
room before they had been received by the duchess. She
looked at Crawley, found him smiling warmly at her, and said,
"I did not bring a shawl. I suppose I ought to have done so."

"Certainly you should have," he said.

"Fiddlesticks," Theo said in a tone sharp enough to warn
her sister, at least, that she did not like any of the gentlemen
paying heed to someone else. "We shall be quite warm enough
once the music begins and we are seated with all those other
people. Truly, I did not know so many had already come to
Town."

"Nor did I," said the duchess. "I told Bess this was to be a
small, select group, but she must have added more names to
my list. Oh, and here she is now, come to collect me I daresay.
Yes, dearest, here we are, still looking at pictures. Is Madame
Fournier ready to begin? A remarkably talented opera singer,"
she added in an aside to Lady Augusta. "She will please you
very much, I am certain."

"They are all ready," Lady Elizabeth said gently, "but they
cannot begin until you return."

Felicia heard Vyne say in an undertone, "Then stay here,
Duchess, for I doubt Fournier will please me so much. Is she
not the scrawny one who sent the Prince of Wales running
from Covent Garden a week since? Said she reminded him of
a screeching cat."

Dawlish said thoughtfully, "Might have been the Italian one
instead. Squawks like a chicken, that one does. Doubt her
grace would ask a screeching cat to sing for her friends,
Dickon."

"Prinny has an excellent ear for music," the duchess said,
"but he does not always appreciate a true soprano, you know."

The men looked at one another in such a way that Felicia
was forced to stifle an urge to laugh, for the thought that had
leapt unbidden into her mind was not one she could repeat in
polite company. One simply could not say that the prince had
long since shown an appreciation for well-endowed females,

sopranos or otherwise, that had nothing to do with their singing talents.

Even as that thought crossed her mind, however, Crawley said, "Prinny's appreciation is scarcely founded upon the range of a lady's singing voice. Had either the Frenchwoman or the Italian been better padded in certain places, and a trifle older, I daresay things might have been different at Covent Garden."

Lady Augusta looked disapproving, but the duchess laughed merrily, and Felicia struggled to contain her own amusement.

"I believe you have contracted a cough, Miss Adlam," Crawley said. "You must go at once to the music room, where it is sure to be warmer." He held out his arm in a compelling way, and not wanting to look at him for fear that unseemly merriment would overcome her customary composure, she responded to the gesture only when Vyne performed the same office for the duchess. She was certain that Crawley ought to have escorted Lady Elizabeth, but she had not the least desire to draw more notice to herself by saying so.

When they reached the music room, Crawley presented the Adlam sisters to his mother, her friends Lady Westfall, Lady Dacres, and a plump woman who proved to be Lady Dacres's sister, Mrs. Falworthy. They also met Miss Belinda Crawley, her friend Rosa Westfall, and another young lady, Miss Caroline Oakley.

Felicia liked all the young ladies and was glad to see that Theo liked them, too. Dark-haired Caroline was a quiet, well-behaved young woman who reminded Felicia of herself in her first Season, and Belinda's merry grin and Rosa's laughing ways made them a pleasure for anyone to know. As the evening progressed, Felicia became certain that Theo had found, if not kindred spirits, at least a few friends in whom she might confide.

Felicia thought Lady Crawley and Lady Westfall a pair of amiable chatterboxes and Lady Dacres a snob. The latter's son, a tall, handsome young man with jet black hair and dark blue eyes, joined them midway through the evening, and Felicia saw Belinda color up to her eyebrows and glance at her brother. But Dacres paid more heed to his aunt and to Miss

Oakley than he did to Rosa or Belinda, so it was left to
Dawlish to look after them when refreshments were served.

Felicia had met a number of pleasant young men like
Dawlish during her first and only Season—all well-spoken,
polite, and rather boring. When Belinda and Theo complained
that they could not understand the Frenchwoman's words, it
was he who very kindly explained her songs to them, keeping
his voice low enough so that he did not irritate anyone who actually had come to hear the music. Such persons were few, for
as Felicia had seen at once, the main interest of the evening,
aside from having a good look at the reclusive duchess, was to
see and be seen and to catch up on all that had happened since
everyone had left London at the end of the previous Season.

"Will you walk with me?"

Felicia started and turned to find Crawley behind her. When
the others in their party had disappeared toward the refreshment room, she had stayed behind, standing to ease the strain
of having sat still for more than an hour.

When she did not respond at once, he said, "The doors to
the garden terrace are open, and the garden is lit with torches,
which must be a magnificent spectacle. Moreover, it is warm
in here, just as your sister said it would be, but if you are still
cold, we can stroll through the reception rooms instead."

"I do not know that I ought to go anywhere at all," she said.
"If my sister were to come back, she might wonder where I
had gone."

"Your sister is surrounded by a host of admiring young
men," he said. "I could not even get near her. Besides, I want
to talk with you, so do not disappoint me."

"I should like to see the garden," she said, thinking that it
might be her one and only chance to do so. From all she had
heard about the duchess, such evenings as this had become
rare.

"Since her grace is not likely to do this again soon," he said,
"I own, I am glad of your choice."

"I wish you would not do that," Felicia said.

"Do what?" His hand felt warm in the small of her back as
he guided her toward a set of double doors, the gold curtains
of which had been looped back with red cords. The doors
stood open.

"The way you seem to say the words that are in my head is most unsettling to my nerves," she said, looking up at him.

He smiled, and so close was he as they moved through the doorway that his smile seemed to heat the very blood in her veins. His voice was low. "Am I doing that? I did not know."

"N-no, how could you?" She collected her wits with difficulty. "It is most uncanny, sir, as if you were reading my mind. But of course, such a thing is not possible."

"No," he said. "I wish it were."

"Do you?" She continued to look up at him. He was so much taller than she was and, she thought, very handsome, especially when he smiled at her as he was smiling now. His right hand was still at her waist, guiding her, its warmth passing easily through the muslin to her skin. It was a large hand, certainly twice the size of her own, and it felt comfortable there.

"If I knew what you were thinking," he said, "I would know whether to count you as a friend or a member of the opposition."

"Opposition?" She tilted her head a little. "I do not understand you, sir. How might I oppose you?"

"Why, it would be simple. You have only to betray my folly in the way I introduced myself to your notice, and I shall find myself at *point non plus* in no time."

"Oh, yes," she said with a sinking feeling, "you did mention that you wished to fix my sister's interest, did you not? I had forgotten, I'm afraid. But surely, you will not pretend that you fell in love with her at first sight."

He did not answer at once. Noting that he glanced briefly away from her, she half expected him to insist that that was the case, but he said abruptly, "No, I'll not say that. Indeed, if we are to talk of pretense, Miss Adlam, I'd prefer that you tell me why you must always pretend to be so damned composed."

"I don't pretend!"

"Oh, yes, you do, and I must tell you it accomplishes little other than to make me want to discover what will disconcert you."

"You talk nonsense, sir."

"Do I?" He glanced swiftly about, and she realized that for

that moment, at least, they were alone on the terrace. Before she had time to discern his intent, he pulled her close and kissed her. When she struggled, as much against a surge of unexpected desire as against the unspeakable outrage, he let her go at once.

She raised her hand to strike him.

"Not too hard," he warned. "The mark will show."

Her hand fell. She said with what she hoped was a scathing chill in her voice, "If you brought me out here in order to pique Theo's interest, and hope I will tell her of this, you have sadly misjudged me, Lord Crawley, for I will do no such thing. Nor will I ever allow my sister to marry a mere fortune hunter."

"Oh, not so mere, Miss Adlam. Witness your precarious hold on that composure of yours. In point of fact, I brought you out here because I wanted to do so, and for no other reason; however, it does occur to me now that it is entirely possible your sister is not the only heiress in the Adlam family. Am I correct?"

Felicia moved away from him and said coolly, "It can make no difference for you to know my circumstance, sir. You would not for a moment make me believe you were interested in me, not after your reaction to my sister. And your efforts will prove fruitless with her, as well. Theo is bit impulsive perhaps, and a trifle . . .well, a bit—"

"Vain?" he suggested helpfully, apparently not the least bit offended by the animadversions she had cast upon his character.

She glared at him. "She is also very shrewd, sir, and not the least likely to give her heart to one who seeks her fortune. Indeed, I should prefer it if you do not visit our house again."

"Do you intend to play gooseberry then?" he asked, smiling again. "I can promise you that your sister and Vyne will be at each other's throats within ten minutes of his arrival."

Felicia thought about that, and also about the fact that Theo would be furious if she barred Crawley from the house. Finally, she said, "I suppose you can still be of help, and I daresay you can do no harm. Indeed, sir, it might well teach you a good lesson," she added, wanting badly to have the last word.

She was denied it. With a mocking smile, he said, "We shall see, Miss Adlam. We shall certainly see."

5

WHEN Felicia and Crawley returned to the music room a few minutes later, the others were in their seats and Madame Fournier was taking her place to sing again. Ignoring Crawley, who promptly began to flirt with Theo, Felicia sat down beside her, striving to look composed despite her outraged sensibilities. She paid little heed either to the music or to the low-voiced conversations around her, and had she been asked later, she would have been hard pressed to name a single song Madame Fournier had sung. But the evening ended at last, and by the time they reached Park Lane, she had herself in hand again and had decided she had been making entirely too much of quite a small matter.

Watching her lovely sister accept the footman's hand to descend from the carriage, Felicia was certain Theo had not the least idea that Crawley meant to fix his interest with her. She had chattered all the way home about the people she had met at Devonshire House, but there were as many young women's names mentioned as young men's, and Felicia was glad of it.

Lady Augusta, leaning out to say good night to them from the carriage, which would carry her on to her house in Upper Brook Street, said earnestly, "You have been quiet, my dear. One has nothing to complain of in your behavior, of course, but you must exert yourself more in future to join the conversation, lest you be thought a trifle too haughty."

Felicia, caught unaware by the mild stricture, said rashly, "Surely we were meant to listen to the music, ma'am."

"Pish tush. There is a time and a place for everything, Felicity, and the beginning of the London Season is not the time to ignore those who can do you the most good."

"I shall know better next time, Aunt Augusta. Come, Theo, we must not keep these horses standing. It has grown chilly."

Theo did not even wait for the carriage to drive away before saying, "It was unfair of her to take you to task, but you were very quiet, even for you. Is anything amiss?"

"No, no, nothing," Felicia said, hoping the powers above would forgive her the deception. She had little fear that Theo would fall victim to any fortune hunter, for the girl had a strong sense of her own worth and would no doubt demand high payment for her hand, but Felicia was persuaded it would serve no good purpose to tell her she had already made such a conquest.

They went up the shallow steps together, and Peters, who had preceded them in order to apply the knocker, moved aside when the door opened, and they stepped into the hall to discover Miss Ames, looking disheveled in her cream-colored nightcap and robe, peering myopically down at them from the gallery railing.

"Oh, thank heaven, Miss Adlam," she exclaimed. "I have only just this moment left her with Mary, but I must beg you to come up at once. I quite simply do not know what to do for her!"

"For whom?" Felicia asked, stripping off her gloves. "Has Mama been ailing? No doubt she missed our company this evening."

"Oh, no, miss, nothing of the sort. It is Miss Sara Ann." The governess appeared to realize that it was not at all the thing to be carrying on a conversation from the gallery rail, within the hearing of several servants in the hall. Primming her lips, she straightened and stepped back rather quickly, as though she wished to disappear into the hall.

Felicia said to Theo, "I will attend to this. You go to bed so that you will not look like a hag in the morning. Do not forget, Sir Richard is to be here at eight o'clock. He did not seem to be the sort of man who will be unpunctual."

Theo grimaced. "No, he will be here if only to torment me. You did not go with us to the supper room, Felicia, so you cannot know how rude he was. The least objectionable thing he said was when he pointed out a picture on the wall and said it was the one time the artist ever dipped his brush into paint that he did not make a royal muck of his work. Belinda Crawley said she thought that was by way of being a compliment, but I ask you!"

Felicia smiled. "Nonetheless, my dear, you will admit that the portrait he painted of the duchess was a splendid one."

Theo shrugged. "True, but if he thinks he can continue ordering me about, or even talking to me in that stupid, superior manner of his, I shall soon pin his ears back, I promise you."

"I would not risk annoying him until your portrait is done, however," Felicia said with a smile. Then, at the sound of a hiss from above, she looked up and said, "I am coming, Miss Ames. Come on up to bed, Theo, and think pleasant thoughts so you will be at your best in the morning."

They went upstairs to the gallery together. Then Theo went on up to her bedchamber and Felicia went to speak to Miss Ames.

"Is Sara Ann sick?"

"Oh, no," the governess said quickly, "but she's had the most dreadful nightmare, and nothing will calm her. I even resorted to scolding the poor child, telling her a lady does not indulge in such tantrums. It wrung my heart, for I can see that she is overwrought, but I did not know what else to do. Mary is sitting with her now, so that I might come to tell you."

"Excellent," Felicia said. "Mary comes from quite a large family and will no doubt know just what to do for her." She was able to indulge this belief only for the few short minutes it took them to go up to Sara Ann's bedchamber on the next floor. The moment Felicia walked in, she knew she had more to deal with than a simple nightmare.

Sara Ann was sobbing gustily against the plump chambermaid's bosom, and Mary looked up at the sound of the door's opening with a look of helpless bewilderment.

"I don't know what to make of it, miss. She's just been a-sobbing and a-sobbing like her little heart was breaking, and if I try to set her back against her pillows, she screams as if ten devils was after her. First she said it was robbers, then murderers, and when I told her that them as does such stuff knows better than to set foot in a gentleman's house, she just started sobbing like what you hear now."

"You may go now, Mary," Felicia said quietly. "I will attend to her. Fetch me a glass of water with a tablespoon of hartshorn in it. Then you may go to bed. Miss Ames, you may also go. No, Sara Ann, you must not begin shrieking again," she added, putting a hand on the child's shoulder when, with a doubtful look, the maid began to disengage herself from the child's frenzied clutches. "I am with you, and I will not go away till you give me leave, but I cannot abide shrieking, so you must be quiet and concentrate on collecting yourself."

"Are you sure?" Miss Ames asked in a tone so low that Felicia nearly did not catch the words. "I do not mind staying. I am very concerned about her."

"I know, but I think she will do better if I am alone with her. We must discover what caused her distress, you know."

"Well, if you can do that, it will be something," the governess said with a sigh. "Goodness knows, I tried."

For a time it seemed that she, too, would fail, for by the time Mary returned with the articles Felicia had requested, the little girl still had not spoken sensibly. When she quieted enough to allow Felicia to ask her a question, the reply was another flood of tears. And when that happened a second time, Felicia fell silent, holding her as Mary had done, stroking her tangled blond hair, and rocking her. At last, when Sara Ann had been quiet for several minutes, except for an occasional sob, Felicia tried a different tack.

"Have you fallen asleep, little mouse?"

"No." The word came in a whisper.

"Shall I tell you a story? I know some very good ones that Aunt Augusta used to tell me when I was small. She was quite a good storyteller, in fact, though her remarkable affinity for fables did become rather tiresome after a time. There was always a moral, you see, and one always felt as though one ought to benefit from hearing the tale. There were times when I felt utterly at a loss, because I simply hadn't understood the moral and did not know what I was expected to learn."

"But Aunt Augusta would . . ." The words died in a sob.

"Oh, she would have explained them to me, certainly," Felicia said in a tone of agreement, as though the child had finished her sentence, "but I never asked for an explanation because I thought she might be angry with me for not understanding. I know now, of course, that she would never have been angry in such a case, but when one is a child, one frequently does not trust grown-ups to behave sensibly."

There was silence.

"Would you like to hear a story?"

The small head against her bosom nodded.

"What kind do you like best? Animal or people stories?"

"People." Sara Ann straightened a little, getting more comfortable, and Felicia pulled a pillow forward, plumping it. "You can lie back against the pillow if you like."

"I like it here. Tell me more about when you were little."

Felicia shifted on the small cot, trying to make herself comfortable, and dredged her memory for an entertaining reminiscence. She hoped the dawn would not find her still in the same position, but she did not have the heart to leave Sara Ann in her present state. She began by telling her about the first time she had fallen off her pony and had to walk home. A watery chuckle greeted the revelation, and Felicia went on, feeling more confident that she might yet calm the child enough to sleep. She had been focusing all her attention on Sara Ann, so she was surprised when she finished the tale to look up and see Tom standing in the doorway, watching her.

Sara Ann, confused by her sudden silence, sat straight, and seeing her brother, said, "Come in and hear the story Aunt Felicia is telling me about how she learned to ride a horse. You know Aunt Theo has told us Aunt Felicia is the very best rider in the family—even better than Papa—but it was not always so."

"I heard most of it," Tom said as he stepped farther into the room. He was in his nightshirt, with his cap still on his head, and he reached up self-consciously to pull it off. "What was all the ruckus before?"

Sara Ann hid her face against her aunt's breast, and Felicia said, "She cannot talk about it yet. Perhaps later."

He nodded, his brow furrowing. Then he said, "She oughtn't to be keeping you up till all hours, ma'am. I can sit with her."

Feeling Sara Ann stiffen against her, Felicia said, "What is it, dear? Surely, you are not afraid of your brother."

A hiccup was followed by a sob before Sara Ann muttered, "Why don't our mama and papa want us, Aunt Felicia?"

"Oh, darling, you mustn't think that," Felicia said, dismayed. "It isn't that they don't want you; it is just that there are so many advantages for you here in England that they cannot provide in India. You will get a much better education, for one thing. And things are cleaner here and healthier for you. And when you grow up, you will want to take your proper place in society, just as your mama did. But she and your papa will have returned long before then, of course. They just want to be certain you do not lack anything in the meantime."

"We lack *them*!" Sara Ann sobbed. "I want my father!"

Felicia looked at Tom and, seeing her own surprise reflected on his face, said, "I had expected her to cry for her mama, I suppose. I hope you will forgive me if I find it difficult to imagine your papa inspiring such despair."

Tom's eyes had narrowed, and he moved forward now to kneel beside her, reaching out to take the little girl gently by the shoulders and turn her to face him. "Why do you want Papa, Sara Ann? Why him, especially?" When she did not reply, he went on in the same tone, "It is Freddy, is it not?"

Silence. The little girl was not even breathing.

"I thought so," Tom said. "What nonsense did he tell you?"

Felicia stared at him. "I ought to have thought of Freddy."

Tom nodded. "He likes to discover how people will react to what he tells them. What did he say, love?"

It took them a good while, but at last they found out.

"Robbers and murderers hiding in the house," Tom repeated in disgust. "What a thing to tell her! And making her think it was all because Papa wasn't here to protect her. By heaven, Aunt Felicia, only give me leave, and I'll make him sorry. In fact, I mean to go and drag the little scoundrel out of bed right now."

"No, Tom," she said hastily. "I am too tired to deal properly with him now. Let him sleep, and I will speak to him in the morning. He must be made to understand that this will not do. Sara Ann," she added firmly, "London is filled with watchmen who watch out for murderers and robbers, so they cannot get into our house. Also, the doors are locked and we have our own servants to look after us. I have sent Mary to bed, which I see now was a mistake, but tomorrow she can set up a truckle bed here in your room, and tonight Tom may stay with you. Will that do?"

The child agreed with little persuading, and Felicia, having shown Tom where to find quilts to put down for himself, went wearily to her own bedchamber, assured her tirewoman that she still intended to be up at the crack of dawn, and fell into bed.

She could not sleep. Her thoughts were in turmoil, and while they began with her brother and his wife, and her own unspoken indignation that they had so easily shipped their children off to veritable strangers to raise, it was not long before she found herself thinking about Crawley and the resentment she had felt when she realized he had been cultivating her acquaintance for the good it might do him in his pursuit of her sister. Some people simply did not consider other people's feelings. Jack and Nancy had not, and certainly Crawley had not. Nor had Freddy.

She forced her thoughts to what she would say to the boy in the morning. She would have to speak sternly to him, for he deserved a good scolding, but somehow, she kept imagining herself scolding not a boy but someone taller, dark rather than fair, with powerful shoulders and muscles in his thighs that showed distinctly beneath his well-cut knitted breeches, someone who had the most delightful smile and practically perfect teeth.

Turning over, she muttered imprecations to herself and forced her thoughts back to Freddy, but so unsuccessful was the exercise that, though she slept very little, by morning she still had not the least notion of what she was going to say to him.

Maintaining her customary calm facade before her maidservant was not difficult, for Felicia had had years of experience, but the clatter of curtain rings against the rod, followed by glaring sunlight spilling into the room, nearly caused her to speak sharply when the woman asked what she would wear.

"The russet with the brown ribbons will do, and I shall twist my hair into a knot." She looked at the little clock on the mantelpiece. "Nearly half past. Is Miss Theo up yet?"

"Yes, miss. Her maid went and shook her awake nigh onto half an hour ago, knowing how long it would take to stir her out. She's already had her chocolate and her toast, so she'll do. I let you sleep a bit longer, because I knew you ain't one to dawdle over yours. There it be, on the table yonder."

"Thank you," Felicia said, scrambling into the dress that was being held out for her and turning to let the woman do up the fastenings. "I should like you to waken Master Freddy, if you please, and tell him to come here. I can do my own hair."

"Lawks, miss, that limb o' Satan's been up this hour and more. Out into the garden to play with that pesky mongrel what's taken up residence in the areaway, and like as not around to the mews to pester the stable boy. He's a lad as likes the horses near as much as you do yourself."

"Oh, dear. I must speak to him, and I have little time before Sir Richard arrives. Go and ask Mrs. Heath if everything is ready in the northeast parlor for Miss Theo's sitting."

"Yes, miss. I'll see to that, right enough."

Hurrying with her hair, Felicia drank a few sips of her chocolate and went downstairs. On the gallery landing, she paused, noting that the door into her father's bookroom, opposite the drawing room, stood ajar. It was not like the servants to forget to close it, since that was the sort of thing guaranteed to send Lord Adlam into one of his rare fits of temper, and it was too early for his lordship to have left his bedchamber.

She saw at a glance that Peters was at his post in the front hall and knew that no one had arrived yet. A noise from the bookroom decided her, and she stepped quickly across the landing to the open door.

Freddy stood near the huge cherrywood desk with his back to her. His head was bent, and she could not see his hands, but his attention was clearly focused upon whatever he held in them.

Felicia stepped into the room. "I want to talk to you, young man, about—" She bit off her words when he turned. He held a pistol in his hand, and for one terrifying moment, the weapon was pointed directly at her.

"Hello, Aunt Felicia," he said cheerfully. "I found this in Grandpapa's desk drawer. Why does he keep it there, do you think? My papa keeps all his guns locked in a gun case."

Distracted by noises of arrival from the hall, but fighting both to concentrate and to keep her voice from betraying her terror, Felicia said, "Then you know you are not to touch a gentleman's pistol, Freddy. Turn away from me, if you please, and put it down on Grandpapa's desk at once."

He eyed her speculatively. "I just wanted to see if it was loaded. Do you think it is?"

His casual attitude was more frightening than if he had been defiant. Felicia swallowed carefully. "Do as I tell you, Freddy. Guns are very dangerous."

"Are they?" He turned the weapon over in his hands, and for another dreadful instant she saw the opening in the barrel. Then, with a mischievous smile, he said, "I'll just see if it's loaded, shall I? I can aim it out the window if it makes you nervous. And then, if it *is* loaded, it will do no harm."

To her amazement, he simply turned away from her and began to walk toward one of the tall windows overlooking the garden.

In a few quick steps and without so much as a thought for her own danger, she reached forward to grab his shoulder with one hand, and snatched the pistol away from him with the other.

"Be careful," he cried. "It's—"

The gunshot echoed through the house, and Felicia stared down at the pistol she held. A puff of smoke floated near the barrel opening, and at her feet a charred round hole appeared in the carpet. She looked at Freddy and said in a harsh voice she did not recognize as her own, "Go to your bedchamber at once. I dare not trust myself to say the things I wish to say right now, but do not dare to put so much as one toe outside your room until I have given you leave to do so. Do you understand me, Freddy?"

"Yes, Aunt Felicia." His face was white with shock, and he turned away with none of the bravado he had shown earlier.

Still fighting to keep from shrieking at him in a voice that would have done Sara Ann proud, Felicia could not even look at him, and turned away just as the library door crashed back on its hinges. The next thing she knew, she was caught from behind in a viselike embrace, and the pistol was wrenched from her hand. In the next instant she was jerked around to find herself face-to-face with a furious Crawley.

"Just what the devil do you think you are about?" he demanded. "Nothing can be so dreadful that it warrants taking your own life. Nothing! Do you hear me?" He shook her. "Answer me! What were you thinking? Are you injured?"

Since the words made no sense to her, she had a sudden feeling that she was losing her mind before the sight of Freddy, standing wide-eyed just beyond his lordship, steadied her. The boy stood to one side of the doorway where he must have been passed unseen when Crawley burst into the room.

"Unhand me, my lord," Felicia said quietly. "I am not injured, nor did I intend to fire the pistol."

"Nonsense," he snapped. "You cannot expect me to believe such a faradiddle. I know you have been contemplating putting a period to your existence—"

"A period to what?"

"You know perfectly well what I said."

"But how could you—"

"How could I know? I saw the note you wrote, of course. Do you not recall that you left me alone yesterday while you spoke to your sister? I chanced to see it then. I know I ought not—"

"I wrote no note," she said, her voice steadier now, though she was no less bewildered. "You are talking nonsense, my lord. I had begun to ask how you could possibly think such a thing of me. I took that pistol from Freddy because he was going to fire it out the window, and it went off in my hand. I daresay it must have one of those hair triggers that men seem to think so desirable, though not, I believe in one's ordinary pistols, only in duelling pieces. Or have I got that bit backward? I do not know much about guns."

Freddy said diffidently, "P'raps I ought to have told you right off that it was loaded, Aunt Felicia."

Crawley had been staring doubtfully at Felicia, but at the sound of Freddy's voice he whipped around, looked balefully at him, and said in a voice fierce enough to send shivers up Felicia's spine and make the boy take two steps backward, "Did I hear you admit that you knew that pistol was loaded?"

Freddy nodded.

"Come here."

Freddy hesitated. Other members of the household had reached the doorway, but Peters responded at once to Felicia's signal to shut the door, and after the snap of the latch, there was not another sound to be heard.

"Now," Crawley said.

Reluctantly, Freddy moved toward him. Felicia watched, feeling paralyzed, as if she were not part of the scene but was watching it from a distance. Crawley did not stir, but he seemed to her to grow larger as the boy moved nearer. Not until Freddy stood directly before him did he say in that same awful tone, "Has your father not told you never to play with guns?"

Looking at his feet, Freddy nodded. Another silence fell until he looked up, saw that Crawley was still waiting, and muttered, "Yes, sir."

"Do you know why you are not to play with them?"

Another nod, followed a moment later by another mutter.

Crawley glanced over his shoulder at Felicia. "Is your father at home, Miss Adlam?"

"He does not come down from his rooms until after noon."

"Then I'll save him some trouble," Crawley said. Going down on one knee, he put Freddy over the other and gave him several smacks hard enough to make him yell. Then, standing him on his feet again, he said grimly, "Don't let me hear that you have touched another pistol until you have been taught to use one properly, and don't let me see you again today if you don't want a second dose of the same excellent medicine I just gave you."

The boy fled, leaving the door open behind him, and Felicia, having come to her senses, said, "Lord Crawley, I must protest. You were too harsh. That poor child has been wrenched from his family and does not yet know all that is expected of him here."

"Nonsense, I doubt I was harsh enough. Wrenched or not, that lad knew he had done wrong and deserved every lick. Good God, don't you realize you might have been killed? It would have saved you the trouble of attending to the matter yourself, which is certainly what I believed to have been your intent. Yesterday I convinced myself that I was imagining things, but then, this morning, to be greeted by a pistol shot as I entered the house—"

"Yes, I can see that that must have distressed you, sir. What

I cannot understand is how on earth you came to believe that I ever had any such sinful thought in my head."

"I read your letter," he said simply.

"You mentioned a note, but truly, sir, I cannot recall writing any such thing."

"There was certainly a note," he said. "I saw it myself. You had written that you could not go on."

"Very melodramatic, but I assure you I never wrote—" She broke off as a sudden memory refuted what she had been about to say to him, and a gurgle of laughter escaped her lips.

Crawley frowned. "You find humor in such a situation? I'd advise you to have a care, Miss Adlam."

"You are generous with your advice, sir, but I am persuaded that you, too, will be amused when I tell you. Yesterday when you arrived, I was writing to tell a friend that I could not go on Tuesday to pay calls with her."

"Not go on . . ." He stared at her in disbelief for a long moment, and then his eyes began to twinkle. He chuckled, low in his throat at first, then louder, until he was holding his sides and gasping with laughter.

6

CRAWLEY stopped laughing at last, aware of a deep sense of relief and a lightheartedness that he had not felt in a long time. He saw that Felicia was regarding him in much that same way that she might have looked at someone she suspected had taken leave of his senses, and for the second time he noticed the way the sun glinted on her soft brown hair. He noticed as well that she had a nice, very womanly shape.

Her breasts were still rising and falling rapidly in reaction to what had taken place in the last few minutes. At least he assumed it was reaction to the combination of Freddy's mischief, being grabbed by himself, and her indignation toward his treatment of the boy afterward. She probably thought him a monster, but he would be damned before he would apologize for smacking the brat. She had nice breasts. He hadn't really noticed them before, either.

"Lord Crawley."

Startled, he shifted his gaze back to her face and saw that though her eyes were still twinkling, she looked perplexed. Collecting himself rapidly, he said, "Sorry, my thoughts were diverted. You ought to wear blue, Miss Adlam. The color would suit you much better than that russet does. And you should effect a softer style with your hair. That severe style makes you look a bit governessy, if you don't mind my saying so."

The twinkle faded, but she said calmly, "Not at all, sir. It would be the height of bad manners for me to criticize you on your choice of observations, would it not? Particularly since we do not know each other very well."

Feeling much as he had been accustomed to feel when he

had displeased his nurse, nearly a quarter of a century before, he sternly repressed the feeling, summoned up his most charming smile, and said, "Perhaps you ought to sit down. The past few minutes have been a great shock to your sensibilities."

"Meaning that I would be more amenable to criticism had I not been shocked, I suppose," she said. "Well, perhaps you are right. I daresay I am a trifle undone by Freddy's behavior, and yours too, for that matter. I cannot believe that you assumed I would do away with myself only because you misunderstood an unfinished sentence in a note to my aunt. Either you have an extremely overactive imagination or—" She broke off, then said, "Well, that must be it, for I can think of no other reason for leaping to such an excessive conclusion."

Feeling a strong need to justify himself and an even stronger sense of being drawn to justice, he said reluctantly, "There was a bit more to it than that. I had not meant to tell you this, for it does not redound to my credit, but I find it is worse to allow you to believe me a complete fool. The fact is that I read your letter to your aunt."

"Yes, we have already established that fact," she said patiently. "Look here, sir, this conversation is pointless. Indeed, it is well past time that we should be going downstairs."

"Vyne is setting up his things, and your butler told us that Miss Theo has not yet come down from her bedchamber. Vyne sent a message up, telling her to make haste, but you will know better than I do how much good that will accomplish."

"Not much, I'm afraid."

"Then we have time to talk, and I would like to clear up this misunderstanding, though clarity will do little, I fear, to redeem me in your eyes. Do sit down, please."

"Very well," she said, suiting action to words and gesturing to him to do likewise, "but you must be plain, sir."

He remained standing. "Do you mind if I shut the door? This is not a tale I'd like to hear repeated in the clubs, and all it would take is one servant overhearing me. If you fear for your reputation, of course, I will leave it open."

She smiled. "You need not concern yourself with my reputation, sir. My servants will not think ill of me for taking ten minutes alone with you in my father's library. Nor will they talk out of turn, for that matter."

"Nonsense. You are naive beyond reason if you think any servant worthy of such trust, ma'am."

"Perhaps you are right," she admitted, surprising him, for he had begun to think she delighted in contradicting him. "In point of fact, I was thinking as I would about our servants at Bradstoke, but of course, several who serve us here are new, and I know little about them. But do shut the door if you like, and then sit down and explain yourself. I am convinced that although Theo might keep Sir Richard waiting a short time, she will not keep him waiting long. She is no fool, and it has been made clear to us both that he is perfectly capable of going upstairs to fetch her if she tries to play tricks with him."

He agreed, but he did not want to talk about Vyne or Theo. When he had taken his seat, he said abruptly, "It was not yesterday's letter to which I referred, but one you wrote sometime ago, advising your aunt of your intent to come to Town."

Instead of the shock he expected to see, her face registered relief. "That letter! But Aunt never received it. How—"

"The mail coach carrying it was attacked by robbers."

"Robbers?"

"Yes, and lest you leap to the unwarranted conclusion that I was one of them"—he saw by her expression that that was just what she had been thinking—"let me inform you, my girl, that I was not. Vyne, Dawlish, and I intervened, and I saved your letter from being ground to dust beneath a horse's shoe. They had emptied the mailbags into the road, you see."

"I suppose the direction must have been made illegible, and that is why she never received it."

"A good part of the *letter* was illegible," he retorted, "but there was a comment about being at your wits' end and seeking relief in a watery grave. I do not recall the exact words—"

"I do," she said, chuckling, "but they do not bear repeating. I meant that merely for a jest, sir."

"Not a pretty one," he said grimly.

"No, I suppose it was not."

"You must see now how I was led to my conclusion. I confess, my first impression was that the original comment was meant to be humorous, but then I saw what heavy responsibilities you bear here. Still, when I chanced to see that second note, your composure convinced me I was mistaken. But last night I decided the serenity is but a mask you wear, and this morning, to hear the pistol shot and find you . . ." He spread his hands.

She nodded. "I do see how it was, and I suppose your shock is in a great way responsible for the harsh way you treated poor Freddy, too, but I still say—"

"Don't say it! I have not the least desire for you to believe I smacked that lad out of shock or fright. I smacked him because he deserved smacking. You know he did."

He was learning to read her expressions well, and he could see now that her emotions were mixed. She said, "My Aunt Augusta would agree with you—indeed, she has said precisely the same thing on more than one occasion—but I cannot bear to see a child hurt, sir, and Freddy is only nine."

"What do you intend to do with him?" he demanded.

"Why, he must go to school, of course. We are waiting for the next term to begin at Eton."

"Eton!" He grinned. "Do you know anything about the headmaster at Eton, Miss Adlam?"

"Only his name," she said. "He is Dr. Keate, I believe."

"Yes, a great man! He has quite a reputation, and no doubt will be the making of young Freddy." When her frown disappeared, he checked his next words, seeing no good reason to inform her that Keate was also known as a famous flogger. He was beginning to see that Miss Adlam was very tenderhearted, an admirable quality unless carried to excess. He would not distress her. In any event, Freddy would soon learn his own way, as most boys did, and the place would do him good. "I went to Eton myself," he said conversationally.

"Did you, sir? I never went to school. I had governesses, of course, but I think I should have liked a school. When Sara Ann is old enough, I mean to find one for her if she wants to go. If not, of course, I will be delighted to keep her at home."

"You will no doubt be married long before then," he said.

She raised her eyebrows. "Perhaps I shall, but I do not see why or how that could affect what becomes of Sara Ann."

"She is the responsibility of your papa and mama, surely."

She laughed. "Oh, no, sir. Even my brother, Jack, never

thought such a thing, though he might have been forgiven for doing so, since he has not seen them for nearly fifteen years and cannot know how frail Mama has become or how fixed in his own world is Papa. The children are as much mine at the moment as if I had borne them myself, sir, and any man I marry would have to accept that fact. Unless, of course, Jack and Nancy should return to England and take the children to live with them."

"You sound as if you welcome the responsibility. But surely, you are too young and inexperienced—"

"I love it," she said, interrupting him. She went on with more enthusiasm than he had yet seen in her, describing Tom and Sara Ann in glowing terms, and telling him some of the more amusing things Freddy had done, and how greatly the children had enriched her otherwise mundane life. She had clearly forgotten Miss Theo and Vyne, for a time at least.

He made no attempt to remind her, but listened with amused tolerance, thinking that when she was animated, she was almost as pretty as her sister, and wondering why it was that she was so nearly on the shelf. She was so earnest, so vibrant, and her eyes had softened. They were lovely. Lazily, he let his gaze drift over her, taking in the soft womanly curves and wondering how long it would take him to bring her around his thumb, to—

"Lord Crawley."

He looked up and saw at once that something was wrong. Her tone of voice had changed, and the expression in her eyes was no longer gentle. He was reminded again of his old nurse, even of his strictest schoolmaster. That thought startled him. She was not in the least like that master. He must be losing his mind.

"You were not listening, sir."

"Certainly I was," he said, dragging his thoughts back to what he could recall of her conversation. To prove that he had not been inattentive, he said, "The children sound delightful, but I fear you are going the wrong way about raising them, for they would all do better not to be coddled. Tom ought to be in school right now, not encouraged to wander about London on his own without proper guidance, as it sounds like he has been doing, and as for young Freddy—"

"I am sure you believe your advice to be excellent, my lord," she replied politely, rising to her feet, "but my sister must have gone downstairs by now, and as you said yourself last evening, it will not do to leave her alone with Sir Richard."

Before he could get to his feet, she swept past him to the door, opened it, and went across the landing to the stairs. Feeling as if he had been soundly slapped, and well aware that he had taken a large misstep, he followed swiftly in her wake but made no attempt to stop her.

Felicia could feel her cheeks burning and knew it had been a great mistake to open herself so much to his lordship. He was clearly not interested in her thoughts or her opinions. He had made that perfectly clear when he began telling her just what was wrong with them. Since it was extraordinary for her to reveal herself in such a way, she could not imagine how she had come to do so with him, a mere fortune hunter—moreover, a fortune hunter interested primarily in her sister. But he had only to smile at her, and she found herself telling him her innermost thoughts. She had even told him how indignant she was that Jack and Nancy had so casually sent their children to England, insisting she could never have done such a thing. Since their having done so was not thought unusual by the rest of her family or her friends, Felicia had looked right at him then, waiting for him to disagree with her. Instead, she had seen at once from his expression that he was not listening to her. But when she challenged him, not only had he denied his abstraction, but he had promptly begun telling her she was doing all the wrong things.

She could not think why it annoyed her so much that he should behave so, since he was nothing to her and she rarely expected people to be interested in such things. Focusing her attention upon the northeast-parlor door, she turned her thoughts to Theo and Vyne, so when she entered the room to find that the curtains had been ruthlessly swept back from the windows and the furniture shoved higgledy-piggledy all to one side, she smiled serenely at the sole occupant of the room and said, "Has Theo not yet come down, Sir Richard? How naughty of her! But she rarely gets up so early, you see, and so you must not be angry with her."

Vyne scarcely acknowledged her entrance, for he was carefully setting a chair in place in the center of the room, glancing behind him as he did so to take note of the way the light fell upon it from the windows. Looking up, he said, "It is of no concern at the moment, Miss Adlam. I can do nothing else until I decide upon the light. Oh, Crawler," he added, seeing Crawley enter behind her, "grab two of those side chairs for yourself and Miss Adlam, will you?" Then, when Crawley had moved to obey, he glanced back at Felicia and said, "I sent one of your footmen to fetch her, so she will not be long."

Felicia was not so certain of that, but before he got the chair in the exact position he desired, Theo swept into the room, looking magnificent in a Parisian robe of pink silk, trimmed with coquelicot and black velvet. Her sleeves and bodice were adorned with black lace, and she wore a matching pink silk turban with one long end trailing carelessly but most becomingly over her shoulder. The costume was the height of fashion, but since Theo's blond curls were half hidden by the headdress, Felicia was not as displeased as she might otherwise have been to hear Sir Richard say curtly, "Take that damned thing off your head."

"I will not," Theo retorted. "Papa said I may wear whatever I like, and the turban goes with this dress. And since certain people"—she glanced pertly at Felicia—"will not let me wear it to parties, saying I must wear insipid white muslin instead, I shall wear it for my portrait. And you, sir, are being paid to paint, not to order persons about. So pray, tend to your painting, and don't try to tell me what to do."

Felicia turned anxiously to Sir Richard, fearful that he might reply in kind, and wondering how she might stop him, but to her surprise, he was just watching Theo, frowning as he did so. He said nothing for a time, walking all the way around her and looking her over from head to toe. Finally, he said, "Sit in that chair. I want to see how the light strikes you."

With a toss of her head and a smugly triumphant smile, Theo walked over and sat down, smoothing her skirt and twitching the end of her turban into a position that better pleased her.

"Sit still," Vyne muttered.

"I have not got my skirt quite right," Theo told him.

"It doesn't matter. I haven't got that far, nor will I today. I want to set a few poses and draw some sketches, but that is all. Tomorrow you can change that ridiculous dress."

"I will not," Theo snapped. Turning to Crawley, she batted her lashes and said, "You like this gown, do you not, sir?"

"Certainly," Crawley said, smiling at her. "A delicious confection, and very fashionable."

She said to Vyne, "You see!"

"He can't see the dress," Vyne said scornfully. "He's too damned busy trying to imagine you without it."

Theo gasped, and Felicia bit back an unladylike gurgle of laughter, thinking that the artist was no doubt right, though he ought never to have said such a thing. She turned to see if Crawley would deny the accusation.

He said blandly, "A man would have to be blind and without a drop of red blood in his body to fail to attempt that feat once he had seen Miss Theo; however, I can assure you that all I see now is that magnificent gown. Truly, Miss Theo, that dress is so marvelously elaborate—with all that poppy red and black velvet trimming, you know, that one does see only the gown, so you need not fear my imagination. It would take one more active than mine to get past all that decoration to the lovely girl beneath it."

Felicia opened her mouth to say that that was no doubt precisely Vyne's point, but she saw at once that Theo had fallen silent and was giving thought to Crawley's words. Casting a glance at him, she wondered if for once she had misjudged him. But when he smiled at her, she looked quickly away again. Wrong or not, she told herself, she was still not ready to face that smile without losing her equilibrium. Did the man always have such confidence? He must know that he had infuriated her earlier, not to mention the night before. Yet there he sat, smiling as if he had never done a thing out of turn, and the great wonder was that it was as if he had kissed her again.

Vyne ordered Theo to turn her head, and Felicia forced her attention back to her sister, fearing for a moment that there would be more rebellion. Theo's mouth did tighten dangerously, but Crawley said, "I cannot think how one can follow your instructions, Dickon, for it must be impossible to sit like another person tells one to sit. I don't know how she does it."

Theo threw him a smile. "It is not so hard," she said, relaxing and tilting her chin up a few degrees. "This is what you mean, is it not, Sir Richard?"

"Turn toward me now from the waist," was his only response, but she obeyed without comment, and continued adjusting her position as he directed until he was satisfied.

Felicia glanced again at Crawley, but he did not return her look this time, apparently having eyes only for Theo. Felicia turned away, wondering why she should feel disappointed. Surely, he had done just what she had asked him to do, which was to keep Vyne from distressing Theo. That he had done it by charming Theo into obeying Vyne ought not to surprise her, let alone unsettle her, for she knew perfectly well that such tactics were the best ones to use. Why then should it annoy her that Crawley had used them?

The respite was a brief one, for Theo's ability to sit perfectly still was not nearly great enough to suit Vyne's wishes. "You're moving," he said.

"I want to move. I have been sitting like this for hours."

"You have been sitting five minutes by the clock."

"That cannot be so!"

Felicia said pacifically, "It has been a little longer than five minutes, Sir Richard."

"Don't talk. You distract me."

"I ought to have got Papa to commission Mr. Lawrence to paint my portrait," Theo declared. "No doubt he is a gentleman."

"No such thing," the artist retorted. "Tom's the son of a Bristol innkeeper and damned proud of the fact. Now button your lip. I am trying to sketch your head at the angle I want."

"Mr. Lawrence *must* be kinder than you are," Theo said waspishly, though Felicia noted with surprise that she did not alter her pose. "I *do* wish he were painting me."

"Serve you right if he were. Not only would you find yourself sitting for his numerous pupils as well as for Tom, but his manner is too facile to suit anyone of taste. It lacks dignity, and his choice of colors is downright blatant."

Chuckling, Crawley said in an aside to Felicia, "Dickon and

Tom Lawrence are much the same age, you see, but Lawrence became a student at the Royal Academy at eighteen. They didn't take Dickon until he was nearly twenty, and he was two years behind Lawrence both when it came to being admitted as an Academy associate and then as a full member."

Vyne, overhearing him, snapped, "Tom gave up his crayons for oils only a year before they let him into the school."

"But he had his own studio in Bath when he was twelve, Dickon. At the same time you were playing cricket at Eton and getting yourself sent to the headmaster's study for drawing naughty caricatures on the walls of our dormitory."

Vyne laughed, and Felicia was amazed to see how much his countenance changed. His eyes lighted up, and he seemed almost handsome for once. She saw that her sister was also looking at him in astonishment. He said, "I had forgotten those drawings. How I smarted for them! No, Miss Theo, you have moved again. Look toward the window but turn your shoulders toward me. Yes, that's it. It will not be much longer now."

Theo muttered, "I am sure this must be a most unnatural position for anyone to take. It cannot look well."

Crawley chuckled. "You have a mirror, Miss Theo. Surely, you must know what a beauty you bring to any pose."

Theo laughed, and Felicia saw Vyne begin sketching even more quickly. She had been watching him carefully, and it seemed to her as if his pencils had wings. She was no novice herself when it came to sketching, for she had been well taught and possessed most of the accomplishments expected of young ladies of fashion. She enjoyed sketching, too, albeit not nearly so much as riding. But she knew she could never draw as fast as Sir Richard. He ripped off the page and dropped it to the floor, but his pencil never stopped moving. Curiosity overcame her at last, and she stood up, moving to see what he had done.

"Stay back," he growled, his gaze flicking back and forth from Theo to his pad. He did not spare a glance for Felicia.

"I would like to see what you have drawn," she said.

"I don't show my sketches," he said, still drawing.

"But surely . . ."

The pencil stopped moving, and he glared at her. Then his

gaze swept over Theo and Crawley as he said, "Understand me, all of you. I do not show work in progress. You will see what I have done when I have done it, and not before. Indeed, Miss Adlam, I will trouble you now to give me the key to this room, and your word that no one will attempt to enter it when I am not here. I will take my sketches away with me today, but once my easel is set up, I shall not want to move it between sittings. I must be assured that it will be safe from prying eyes."

Theo said indignantly, "You cannot keep *me* from seeing what you are doing, Sir Richard. It is my portrait, after all."

Vyne snapped, "Since Adlam is paying me, it is his portrait, but only the finished work is his. I cannot imagine why anyone would wish to see anything less than that."

Theo looked mutinous, and even Felicia felt that Sir Richard was taking the matter a trifle too far, but Crawley said, "You will not make him change his mind, ladies, so do not try. Have you the key by you, Miss Adlam?"

"No," Felicia said with a sigh, yielding, "but I will fetch it directly." She went to do so, and when she returned, she found the gentlemen ready to leave. Theo bade Sir Richard an extremely civil farewell and Crawley a much warmer one, but the moment they were gone, she said irritably, "I cannot think why you allowed that dreadful man to bully you so, Felicia."

"He does have the right to expect his work to be kept safe," Felicia said.

"But the parlor will become dreadfully dusty," Theo pointed out. "Surely, you must mean for the maids to tend to it."

"That is a point," Felicia said, smiling at her, "but you needn't think you fool me, miss. You do not care a rap for a tidy parlor. You only want to see what that man is painting."

Theo grinned. "True, and I will, too. Don't think for a moment that he will keep me out once he has begun to paint me."

"We shall see. What are we doing tonight? I declare, my mind must be disintegrating, for I have quite forgot."

"Aunt Augusta is taking us to Drury Lane," Theo said, "to see Mrs. Jordan as Maria in *The Country Girl*. I would much rather see a comedy, but it is to be Mrs. Jordan's first appearance of the Season, and Aunt said we must not miss it."

"Since it is your first play, I think you will enjoy it."

"Perhaps, but I shall like my first ball—at Lady Crofton's house, next week—much more," Theo said. "I shan't like going to Queen's House, however. I am sure it will be utterly boring."

"Queen's House?"

"Oh, of course, you cannot know about that, because the subject came up after you went out to fetch the key."

"Tell me."

"Sir Richard and Crawley began talking about Mr. Lawrence again, and Sir Richard asked if Crawley had seen the portrait Mr. Lawrence painted of Queen Charlotte."

Felicia smiled. "I suppose Sir Richard criticized it."

"No, he didn't. In fact, he said it was remarkable and Mr. Lawrence's best work to date, which quite makes one want to see it, does it not? But he decided we are all to go on Thursday, that date being most convenient for him. I said that I was not certain you would agree, but then he did not even ask you, so I'll wager he thinks we will simply go when he wishes to go."

"Very likely." Having had more than enough of Sir Richard, Felicia said, "What do you mean to wear to the theater tonight?"

"One of my dreary white muslins, of course."

"I do not know why you despise them so. They are extremely becoming to you. I never looked half so well in white as you do, or in any other color," she added with a chuckle.

As Felicia had known she would, Theo immediately protested, assuring her that she could look very well indeed if she would but put off the drab colors she preferred and be more daring. "This gown would become you even more than it does me," she said frankly. "I have been thinking about what Crawley said, and I cannot like a dress that is more like to be looked at than I am."

Felicia laughed. "As that would never happen, my dear, I shan't even bother to dispute the matter. I don't like the dress on you, but only because you are too young to wear such high fashion. I won't say you must never do so, however."

"Well, you need not, because I have already decided to wear my pink muslin for the portrait instead," Theo said. "It is much plainer, but the color is quite good."

"Yes, it is one of the gowns I like best on you." They discussed fashion for some minutes more before Felicia excused herself to attend to household matters. She realized an hour later that she had forgotten all about Freddy, and went to the schoolroom to inform Miss Ames of what had occurred.

She found the governess alone with Sara Ann, and having been informed that Tom had gone riding in Hyde Park with one of the grooms, soon discovered that Miss Ames already knew the pistol had been discharged and that Freddy had been in the bookroom at the time, and had drawn her own conclusions. Felicia therefore was able to keep her explanation brief.

When she finished, Miss Ames said firmly, "He deserves to be severely punished for such a trick, particularly after his prank last night. I hope you do not mean to let him off with no more than a scold and a day in his room."

"He has been well punished," Felicia said. "There is no need to do more. As for last night, Sara Ann has agreed that if Mary sleeps on a pallet in her room, she will not be frightened by anything Freddy might tell her. Is that not right, darling?"

Sara Ann nodded, but her eyes were wide, and she said, "Did you really punish him, Aunt Felicia? I am glad."

Gently, Felicia said, "A lady does not find joy in someone else's sorrow, Sara Ann."

"Well, I am still glad," the little girl said stoutly.

Felicia left it at that, since the sentiment was not at all difficult to understand, and went about her other duties.

Tom returned from his ride in high spirits and said with a congratulatory note in his voice that he was delighted to hear that young Freddy had finally come by his just deserts.

Felicia stared at him in dismay. "Good gracious, you have only just come in. How can you know anything about it?"

"The groom told me, of course," the boy said. "I went out early this morning, just as soon as Mary came in to look after Sara Ann, as a matter of fact, so I missed the excitement. Bad luck, I thought, when I first heard there had been a shooting and that Freddy was in on it, but then Peters came out to tell his cousin—that's the chap who serves me as a groom, you see—that Lord Crawley had really given it to Freddy. I mean to thank him just as soon as I meet him. That little varmint has been asking for a drubbing this month and more. Well done, I say!"

It took time for Felicia to convince him that the less said about the incident the better it would be. After that there were the usual minor crises to fill her day, not least of which was her father's sudden agitation upon discovering that Spain had formed the intention to declare war on Portugal.

"I cannot think why he is so taken up with the news in the *Times*," she said that night as they sat in Lady Augusta's box at the theater, waiting for the drama to begin. "He rarely concerns himself with anything other than his vases, coins, and wine, but now he can talk of nothing but whether Spain will declare war. I could understand such concern if he were fretting over the king's health like everyone else, or the French, but not this."

The elderly gentleman sitting with them for the simple reason that Lady Augusta insisted upon male escort to such events as the opera or the theater, leaned forward and said earnestly, "It is not at all out of the way for a gentleman to speak of military matters, Miss Adlam, and the fate of Portugal must be of concern to all of us. Its safety is vital to us."

"I could murder you," Theo informed Felicia roundly some hours later when they had said good night to their aunt and her talkative companion. "How could you have been so misguided as to make a gift to old Major Brinksby of a topic he could use to bore us through every interval of the night?"

Felicia chuckled ruefully, "I certainly did that, did I not? But you were no help, you know, when you insisted that Sir Hyde Parker must be a made-up name."

Theo giggled. "That did set him off, but how was I to know that a man with such a name as that could be an admiral of the fleet? Even Aunt was bored, but she could find no better news with which to divert him than that she had again received duplicate cards of invitation—to Lady Sefton's rout on Saturday and to Lady Crofton's ball next week. Though it is odd that such a thing could happen three times, as it has, one cannot wonder that she did not succeed in diverting the major. The rout will be all chatter, of course, but at least the ball will not be boring. I quite look forward to it, Felicia."

That last week of March passed quickly in a whirl of engagements, including, much to Felicia's surprise since it was instigated by her sister, a lecture given at Somerset House by the president of the Royal Academy. Lady Augusta, pleased by Theo's evident desire to attend cultural events, rashly suggested attending a concert of ancient music, but the suggestion was summarily rejected. After the lecture, Theo could think only of the Crofton ball.

But when they arrived at Lady Crofton's huge mansion in Berkeley Square the following Wednesday evening, greatly to their astonishment, their entrance was barred at the door.

7

LADY AUGUSTA stared in outrage at the liveried porter who barred their way. He stared right back, looking down his nose at her in an extremely haughty fashion.

"Who do you think you are, to stop *me*?" she demanded.

"I am most dreadfully sorry, madam, but that is not a proper invitation card that you have shown to me."

Felicia did not think he sounded sorry in the least. He sounded rather as if he were enjoying himself hugely. She glanced around, feeling very much exposed and wondering what the people coming up the steps behind them must be thinking.

Lady Augusta said crisply, "Of course that is a proper invitation card. Why, I have known Catherine Crofton these forty years and more. She has never given a party to which I was not invited. Indeed, so intent was she upon my coming to this one that she actually sent me *two* invitations."

A stout little man wearing a wide brimmed black felt hat emerged from behind the porter to say abruptly, "Two invitations, mum?" Imperiously he held out his hand to the porter. "Let me cast my gazers over that one, lad, if you please."

Felicia stared in amazement with the others at the little man, who seemed entirely at home in the noble mansion despite being most peculiar in his dress for the occasion. Besides the broad-brimmed hat, he wore a very tight suit of yellow-green knee breeches, a canary yellow coat, and short gaiters. After a moment he doffed his hat, plopped it back on his head, and said to Lady Augusta, "You have not answered the question, mum. Was the other one just like this?"

"I do not know who you are to question me in such a manner upon Lady Crofton's doorstep," Lady Augusta said grandly, "but I believe the other one was exactly like that one."

"I should be sorry if that were so," he said, making her a profound leg. "John Townshend at your service, mum. Bow Street. Providing a bit of security for the countess, don't you know, just as I do for the Prince of Wales. This card don't bear her device, I'm afraid, as you can see if you will take a look-see."

Lady Augusta looked at the card. "How very odd," she said. "I never noticed that, but Catherine always uses engraved cards, with the Crofton crest in the top right corner. But I do not recall if the other card was engraved or plain like this one."

"Then I am afraid—"

"There you are, Lady Augusta!" With an inexplicable sense of relief, Felicia turned at the familiar voice and saw Crawley hurrying toward them across the hall. He said with his charming smile, "It is quite all right, Townshend. One of the guests mentioned receiving two invitations, and Lady Crofton immediately sent for her guest list to give you. She did not do so before because she assumed—incorrectly as we see now—that knowing the difference between the forged cards and the correct ones would be enough. I can assure you that you will find Lady Augusta's name on the list, along with those of her nieces."

The names were found, and as they made their way up the grand stairway toward the ladies' withdrawing room, to leave their wraps, Felicia watched with amusement while Crawley exerted what she thought must have been every ounce of his considerable charm to soothe her aunt's ruffled feathers.

They gave their cloaks to the withdrawing-room attendant, and as they walked to the ballroom, Felicia heard her aunt say grimly to Crawley, "I do not see why that dreadful little man did not insist upon having a guest list from the outset. But then, even a fool is wise when it is too late to do him any good."

"And he who is doubly deceived is doubly cautious."

She looked at him, nodding wisely. "That is quite true, my

lord, but do you mean to say that Catherine has had this dreadful prank played upon her before now?"

Felicia saw that he had the grace to look chagrined, but she did not miss the twinkle in his eye when he said, "Well, no, ma'am, not that I know about, at all events, but that maxim is a favorite of mine and seemed somehow to fit this situation."

Lady Augusta fixed him with a basilisk eye. "I believe you are a rogue, sir. Do you dare to mock an old woman?"

"No, ma'am," he answered promptly.

Swiftly Felicia moved nearer and said, "How did they come to think that there might be forgeries tonight, sir?"

He gave her a mocking look that told her he knew she had intervened to avoid hostilities, and said, "It has happened at other *ton* parties, evidently, so Townshend warned her ladyship that she might expect some tonight. He asked her to give a real invitation card to her porter to compare with those shown by her guests, just to see, you know, if such a thing did occur, but he was no doubt as surprised as anyone else when it did, for he believed in one case, at least, that ill feeling toward the host had prompted the business. The man in question is one of those shouting for Mr. Pitt's resignation, you see."

Theo said in a tone of exasperation, "Please, sir, no more war or politics. We have had a surfeit of both, I assure you, for not only has Papa been rattling on for days about possible war between Spain and Portugal and whether English wine merchants will be able to get their wines out of Lisbon, but Major Brinksby accompanied us to the theater last week and to the Royal Academy lecture as well. Not that anyone told me people are demanding Mr. Pitt's resignation," she added naively, "How very odd."

"Not so odd when one considers his position on the Catholic question," Crawley told her. When she curled her lip at him, he chuckled, and said, "Oh, very well, Miss Theo, no politics." He grinned at Felicia, adding, "Your sister doesn't approve, either."

Felicia saw no need to respond either to the remark or the teasing look that accompanied it, and she turned to greet Lord Dawlish, who approached with Miss Crawley on his arm.

Crawley asked lightly what Belinda had done with Dacres. "Weren't you with him when I left to go downstairs?"

Belinda flushed and said airily, "He is showing Miss Oakley the state apartments. They are open for the evening, of course, and she has not been here before. I have seen them a number of times, so I allowed Dawlish to bring me to find you."

"Where is Mrs. Falworthy?" Crawley asked. "I have not seen her tonight, but if Miss Oakley is present, she must be here."

"Mrs. Falworthy is indisposed, so Mama invited Caroline to come with us, as you would know had you taken the time to escort us here yourself, Ned dearest." There was a twinkle in Belinda's eyes now, but Felicia thought she discerned an edge in her tone, and wondered what Crawley might have done to provoke it.

He apparently had not heard anything amiss, however, for he laughed and tweaked one of his sister's curls. "With three of you in the carriage, you needed every bit of room for yourselves. You'd have had none to spare for my long legs."

"Perhaps not," she admitted. "We had Lady Dacres, too, if you must know. But Dacres managed to accompany us, Ned. He said he could easily walk as fast as the carriage could make its way through the crowded streets." She glanced away at the rapidly filling ballroom. "This is certainly a crush."

"So Dacres accompanied you, did he?"

Felicia thought she heard satisfaction in his tone, and listened with growing fascination, especially since Belinda, having sounded as bored as ever Theo could, when she first mentioned Dacres, seemed a trifle anxious now as she replied, "Yes, he did, but I think it was only because Caroline was there. I am afraid he is making a dead set at her, Ned."

Crawley sighed, turned as though to speak to Felicia, only to turn back when Lady Augusta said tartly, "Who is Miss Oakley if one may be so bold as to inquire? I recall meeting her at Devonshire House, but I do not know the family."

"No, ma'am," Belinda said. "She is a protégée of Dacres's aunt, Mrs. Falworthy, who has agreed to introduce her to the *beau monde*. I believe Miss Oakley's father is something in the City."

"Good God," Lady Augusta said. "A Cit's daughter. What can Leah Falworthy be thinking of?"

"Not merely any Cit's daughter," declared Sir Richard Vyne, emerging through the growing crowd to join them. "Couldn't help overhearing," he added apologetically. "Know Oakley. He's a patron of Tom Lawrence's, fairly drips with filthy lucre. Dacres could do worse, Lady Augusta, I promise you."

She shook her head. "But for Leah Falworthy—the sister, I remind you, of Fanny Dacres—to chaperon such a girl to parties like Georgiana's and this one! It simply will not do. One is judged by the company one keeps, you know."

Crawley said, "But such things are frequently done, ma'am. Consider the Duchess of Devonshire and Banker Coutts's daughter. The duchess took her everywhere, I'm told."

"That was different," Lady Augusta insisted. "Georgiana was forced to bring the Coutts girl out. Thomas Coutts had lent her the money to pay all her gambling debts, and she could not afford to repay him. Devonshire refused to do so," she added grimly.

Vyne shrugged. "Still, it has been done, ma'am. They are forming sets for the first country dances, Miss Theodosia. May I hope you have not already promised your hand to someone else?"

"You may hope, but not prosper," Theo said, raising her chin. "I have been promised to someone else for a week."

He bowed and left them, and Lady Augusta said, "False confidence is the forerunner of misfortune, Theodosia, and self-conceit leads to self-destruction. You had best have a care with that man. He has a temper."

"Well, I have one too, Aunt, and if he wanted me to save him a dance, he has had every opportunity to ask me long before now. I cannot think what a painter is doing at a ball, anyway."

Dawlish said, "There is nothing particularly odd in Dickon's being here, since Crofton is his cousin."

Theo exclaimed in astonishment, and Felicia, glancing at Crawley, saw confirmation of the fact in his smile. She said, "I suppose we thought he must have got his title for painting the queen's children, or for some other, similar accomplishment."

Belinda laughed and said, "Oh, no, did you think he was an innkeeper's son like Mr. Lawrence? He is nothing of the sort.

It is why he will not take pupils as the others do. He paints to please himself, and does not much care what others think. Has he enraged you too, Miss Adlam? I own, he has frequently provoked me, but Ned tells me I am too easily aroused and that I must take better care to govern my sensibilities."

"I have no cause to dislike him," Felicia said, smiling.

"Well, I do," Theo declared. "The man is a monster, and I mean to pay him out before I am done with him."

Dawlish said, "I would not recommend it, would you, Ned? Dickon generally don't pay heed to aught but his oils and canvas, but Lady Augusta is dashed right about that temper of his. It's worse than Thorne's, and I, for one, take care not to arouse it."

"Oh, pooh," Theo said. "I am not afraid of him."

Crawley said, "Do you really have a partner for the first country dance, Miss Theo? Because if you do not—"

"Oh, but I do," she said with a startled look, turning at once to look around the crowded room. People who did not mean to take part were moving away from the center now, and as the musicians began to play a spirited tune, a young man hurried toward them. "Oh, there he is," Theo said, smiling radiantly.

Felicia, recognizing one of her sister's admirers from the Devonshire House evening, watched them hurry off with Dawlish and Belinda to take their places in one of the sets. Then, seeing that her aunt had taken possession of two empty chairs near the wall, beside Lady Crawley and Lady Dacres, she turned to join them. Crawley stopped her with a touch of his arm.

"Will you dance, Miss Adlam?"

She looked up at him, feeling what was rapidly coming to be a familiar mixture of emotions. She yearned to dance with him, but she wished he had not made it clear that she was his second choice. "I had not intended to dance, sir," she said at last.

"Nonsense, of course you will. I must say, I am glad to see that you took my advice with regard to your gown. That one suits you much better than any other I have seen."

She looked down at the bright blue silk Etruscan robe she had allowed Theo to coax her into wearing that evening. It was trimmed with white satin ribbon, brown cord, and yards of lace, and it was indeed a pretty thing, but she thought it much more suitable to someone with Theo's coloring rather than her own. She had flatly refused to wear the fancy headdress that Theo recommended, deciding instead on a simple lace and muslin cap ornamented with a blue satin bow and a matching silk rose.

"I did not wear this to please you, sir," she said.

He grinned. "Will you dance with me?"

"You are asking me only because Theo refused you." The words were out before she had known she would say them.

He did not seem much shocked by her outspokenness, saying only, "Theo did not refuse me, nor did I ask her to dance. I merely inquired as to whether—"

"You meant to ask her."

"Did I?" His smile was warm, and the look made her wonder if perhaps he had not meant to ask Theo after all. She wanted to know, but she did not want to press for a more direct answer. He said gently, "The music has begun, and we shall annoy all manner of persons if we intrude upon one of the sets now, so I will either escort you to your aunt if you insist that I must, or I can show you the state apartments. Have you seen them?"

"No, but I begin to think they merely provide an excuse for gentlemen who wish to take ladies away from their chaperons."

"Very true, but Crofton House does not boast much of a garden— certainly nothing to rival Devonshire House—so we must make do. And the state apartments here are splendid. Tell me, Miss Adlam, do you mean to go with us to Queen's House tomorrow to see Lawrence's portrait? Though we have seen little of you at the sittings this past week, I am persuaded that Miss Theo must have told you about Dickon's plan."

"She did. She also said she did not wish to go, and since no one has mentioned it to me since then, I was not certain Sir Richard still intended for us all to do so."

"He can scarcely force either of you to go if you do not agree," he said. "Nor would I allow him to. But perhaps you did not know that the Queen's House galleries have been shut up to the public since the king was taken ill. Few people have had the privilege of seeing any of the paintings. Kew Palace, which is much his majesty's favorite residence, is being re-built, so he has had no choice but to remain at Queen's House, since the journey to Windsor was not to be thought of."

"You are very conversant with the king's business, sir."

"No more than any other citizen who reads the *Times*. His majesty's doctors provide daily bulletins, you know."

"I did not know. I rarely see the papers unless my father chances to comment on an article and give it to me to read."

"Well, you ought to read them more—very interesting." He guided her toward a pair of tall double doors as he spoke. "Much news about the royal family, and Parliament, not to mention that interesting rascal Bonaparte."

She chuckled. "Don't mention him to Theo. That is just the kind of subject she detests most to hear gentlemen talk about."

"So she has said more than once. Your visits to the theater and the Academy lecture must have been disastrous."

"Not so bad as that, but Major Brinksby is a trifle long-winded on the subjects of Lord Nelson, the British fleet, and the burgeoning war between Spain and Portugal."

"So Dickon and I have heard, at length."

"Oh, dear, I hoped her sittings had been going better. She has not complained much since that first day."

"Perhaps you should not avoid them."

"I do not avoid them. I have been sending her maid with her as I said I would. I have any number of more important things to do, sir." She did not look at him as she said this, fearing he would see the truth in her eyes, that she had not wished to sub-ject herself to watching Theo flirt outrageously with him while bedeviling Sir Richard.

"I never took you for a coward, Miss Adlam."

Her gaze flew up to meet his. "But I—"

"You knew perfectly well that the fur would fly, and so it did when she showed up for her second sitting in that pink dress. I am surprised she did not tell you all about it."

"But that is a lovely gown," Felicia said, surprised to hear that there had been any difficulty, for Theo had not said a word about it, and neither had her maid. "At least, I presume she wore her muslin, and not the pink gown from the first day."

"Oh, it was a different gown, but Dickon wants her to wear

white, and he told her so. The little vixen has claws. Called him a mere painter again. I had no notion when I agreed to act as gooseberry, that I might be putting my life on the line."

"You knew exactly what you were doing, my lord."

"Are you attempting to divert me, Miss Adlam?"

"Is there any purpose to this conversation?"

"Certainly. I asked if you intend to accompany us to Queen's House tomorrow, and I even tried to make it sound more enticing by pointing out that the general public is not yet admitted to the galleries. Dickon will get us in privately."

"A tempting offer, to be sure."

"It is. He will very kindly tell us a great deal more than we want to know about the pictures we see, and we shall all come away far more knowledgeable than any of our acquaintances."

She laughed. "You are absurd, sir."

"Will you go?"

Certain though she still was that he wanted her to go only so that Theo would go, she could not resist the pleading look in his eyes. She nodded, then looked around in dismay when she realized they were alone. "I have not heeded where we have been walking, sir. Is this one of the state apartments?"

"I'm sure I don't know," he replied, watching her. "I should think it must be, though. Do you think Lady Crofton would decorate the servants' quarters in pink and gilt with dozens of claw-footed sofas lining the walls?"

"But—"

"I have not the slightest notion where we are, my dear, but I have no intention of kissing you again merely because we find ourselves alone. Shall we go back the way we came?"

"If you please," she said meekly, telling herself that the endearment had been a mere slip of his tongue, and pretending she was relieved to know he would take no more liberties.

She made much of looking about her and commenting on the decor of the grand rooms through which they passed until they met Dawlish in the room adjoining the ballroom. She thought he looked a trifle harassed.

Crawley said, "What have you done with my sister, Mongrel?"

"Left her talking about forged invitations, like everyone else, and making a cake of herself over Dacres. You ought to put a stop to that," Dawlish added bluntly. "He ain't the man for Belinda. Besides, Miss Theodosia has entered the ranks now. When Vyne came up and asked her again if she would dance with him, she put her hand on Dacres's arm as calmly as you please and said she had promised the dance to him. Quite sure she hadn't, but Dacres didn't turn a hair. Walked off with her as though he had taken the prize at Newmarket."

"Oh, dear," Felicia said. "She ought not to do such things, but Sir Richard does seem to bring out the worst in her."

"She certainly ought not to do such things," Crawley said. "I still have some small hope that Belinda might snare Dacres. Lord knows, she seemed likely to do so all last Season, but from some cause or another it came to naught."

Rather sharply, Dawlish said, "Came to naught because the chit don't like him. She's bound to try to win him for your sake, Ned, and for no other reason. Says you need the money. I told her it was no such thing, that all you needed was some resolution and a few months to tend your property, but—"

"That's enough," Crawley said.

Reddening, Dawlish looked unhappily at Felicia. "Sorry, Miss Adlam. Spoke out of turn. Your servant." Bowing hastily, he turned and walked away.

Crawley, placing her hand on his arm and moving toward the ballroom, said calmly, "Mongrel's a rattle. Pay him no heed."

"He is a kind and pleasant gentleman," Felicia said. "Indeed, sir, I think he is a very good friend to you."

"True, but he talks too much."

"I hope you are not pressing your sister to wed merely to please you, sir."

"Of course I am not. I care for her a good deal."

"Have you told her so? I, too, have noted her lack of strong feeling for Lord Dacres, you know, so perhaps you ought—"

"She knows I care. Look here, Miss Adlam, I have twice asked you a question, which you have not yet answered."

"I will go, sir," she said. "I thought I had said so."

"Then I shall return you to your aunt, for I daresay your next partner will be wondering what has become of you."

"I suppose the truth is that you don't enjoy hearing my opinions as much as you like offering your own to me."

"Not at all," he said coolly.

"Then, no doubt, you simply wish to join the throng of admirers surrounding my sister," she said with a sigh.

"In point of fact," he retorted, "I am going to take your advice and dance with my own sister."

She was not sure she believed him, and tried to tell herself it did not matter whom he danced with, but she could not deny a sense of relief when she saw him enter a set for a reel with Belinda. Sitting beside Lady Augusta, she turned her thoughts resolutely homeward. There had been no nightmares for several nights, but she wanted to look in on Sara Ann as soon as they got home, to be sure she was sleeping peacefully. Having spoken at length with Freddy to explain why he must not frighten his sister, Felicia had been reassured by his chastened demeanor, but she had learned in the short time the children had been with them that Freddy's demeanor was not always to be trusted.

Her partner for the next set soon came to fetch her, but though she danced every dance after that, she did not dance again with Crawley. They did not stay very late at Crofton House, for Theo came to her shortly after supper, when the guests had begun to return to the ballroom, and said angrily, "We are to go home now, if you please."

"Well, I for one am glad of it," Felicia said. "Is Aunt Augusta too tired to stay longer?"

"Nothing of the sort. I'll have you know it is Sir Richard who commands it, not our aunt."

"Sir Richard!"

"Yes, and you may well look astonished, for I was nothing less myself. The nerve of the man, Felicia, ordering one about as though one were a child. How am I to enjoy my first Season if I am to be packed off to bed at such hours as this? Why, every other person here means to attend at least two or three other parties before they retire. Crawley and the others have already gone on to another ball, and I wanted to go with them, but Sir Richard said I must not. He said I have not been looking my best these three days past and will look a hag in the morning, *and* that he will sketch me just as I look. Sir Richard said—"

"Enough," Felicia cried, holding up her hand. "Each time

you say his name, you make him sound like some sort of disgusting insect you would like to trample beneath your feet."

"Well, and so I would! The man is insufferable. When I was dancing with Dacres, he cut in just as though he had been my husband, for I am sure that no one but a husband ever dares to do such a thing. And when I objected, he said merely that he had wished to dance with me, as if that settled that. But I like Lord Dacres. And he is wealthy, not a mere painter!"

"He is very handsome, too," Felicia said, determined to calm her before she drew the attention of everyone else in the room, and seeing no good to be gained by pointing out that Vyne, as they had discovered that evening, was rather more than a simple painter. "Dacres seems much taken with you, dear, but it would not do to be setting your cap for anyone just yet, before you have had time to see more than half the gentlemen in London."

Theo sighed. "That is just the trouble, for Crawley told me you have agreed to go to Queen's House tomorrow, when I had hoped we might beg off by saying we ought to stay at home with Mama."

"Mama will not mind. I sat with her yesterday and today, as well, and we only promised her one or two afternoons a week."

"Yes, but if you go to Queen's House, then I must go, too, because I quite see that it would not do for you to go alone with two gentlemen—three actually, for Dawlish expressed a desire to see Queen Charlotte's portrait, and Sir Richard most obligingly said he might go with us if he liked."

The sarcasm in her tone as she added the last bit did not augur well for the expedition, Felicia thought, biting back a sigh. She said, " I see that you are distressed, my dear, but I cannot cry off now; moreover, I cannot understand what my decision has to do with your meeting eligible young men."

"But for goodness' sake, Felicia, surely you can see that the more Sir Richard gets his way, the more he will assume that such a state of affairs will continue. If he is not thwarted occasionally, he will become insufferable."

"Very likely," Felicia agreed, "but in this instance he is perfectly right, you know. If he is to paint you looking your best, you must look your best. It is not fair to expect him to paint what he does not see."

"I cannot think why not," Theo snapped. "Goodness knows every other fashionable artist does it all the time."

"Perhaps they do, but Crawley has said Sir Richard paints what he sees, and does not pander to vanity. In point of fact, I begin to wonder if all his present concern is only for his work. That would not be cause enough to interrupt your dance with such an eligible man as Lord Dacres."

Seeing by Theo's thoughtful expression that she had given her something to think about, Felicia urged her toward their aunt so that they might take their leave. She had begun to think the ball tedious, and was anxious to be going.

At home, she hurried upstairs to look in on Sara Ann, and was reassured to find the child deeply asleep, with Mary snoring gently on a pallet beside her cot. A thought struck her as she left the room, and she took a moment to peep into Freddy's, but he was sleeping soundly, too, and looked, in the glow of the lamp she held up in the doorway, more like an angel than the little devil he was. She smiled as she turned away, for despite everything, she rather enjoyed Freddy's spirited approach to life.

8

G ENTLEMEN, place your bets."
Crawley placed chips on the four and the eight and coppered the queen. Then, absentmindedly reaching for the drink at his elbow, he watched the dealer discard the soda, as the top card in the pack was called, turn up the next card, and lay it on the table beside the box. It was the queen of hearts. Crawley collected his winnings from Lord Thomond, who held the bank, then a moment later, watched him collect his other chips with a new turn of a card. Crawley sighed. His mind was not really on faro, but he did prefer winning to losing.

"Penny for your thoughts, Crawler," said the fop beside him, pushing his flower-decked hat back on his head and peering owlishly at Crawley through wire-rimmed spectacles.

"Women, Corey. I was thinking of women."

"God bless them," Viscount Corey said, raising his glass.

Obligingly, Crawley drank, but he was far from echoing Corey's sentiments. Placing his next chips carefully between the six and five, and the ace and deuce, and coppering the latter, he murmured, "Do you understand women, Corey?"

"Good God, no," the fop replied in dismay. "Does anyone?"

"I suppose not."

"What's amiss?"

But Crawley was not so far gone with drink or abstraction that he could speak of his troubles in so public a place. He smiled at his friend and shook his head. "Nothing to speak of, Corey, nothing at all to speak of."

They played in silence for some time after that, and the pile of chips in front of Crawley diminished considerably.

"Wondered where you had got to, Ned. Ought to have suspected Brooks's right off. Dipping deep or playing deep?"

Startled at the sound of Dawlish's voice so close behind him, for he had fallen into a reverie again, he turned and looked at him for a moment before saying, "What's o'clock, Mongrel?"

"Nearly four. Saw the ladies safe home an hour ago and been looking for you since. Expected you to accompany us from Crofton House to the Sefton's party. Your mother drew attention to the fact that we'd misplaced you before we got there, but Dacres's mama was so concerned lest they might have received a forged invitation to the Sefton party, that I could not abandon them."

"Where was Dacres?"

"Oh, he was there, right enough, but if you'll pardon my saying so, though the man may have money, he don't have much sense in his cockloft. I wouldn't want *my* sister to marry him."

"You haven't got a sister."

"No, but all the same—"

Crawley glanced at the interested fop beside him and muttered, "Leave it, Mongrel. This is no place to be saying such things. Not that you need worry about Corey, of course."

"No, no," the fop said hastily. "Never."

"Because," Crawley went on in the same conversational tone, "if I should hear that Dacres had got wind of this conversation, I should know in a moment who spoke out of turn."

"Not me," the fop insisted. "I wouldn't. That is, I couldn't, because I never heard a thing. Assure you!"

"Ah," Crawley said, "how reassuring that is, Corey. Are you in a push to get home, Mongrel? I will do myself the honor of accompanying you if you like."

"A dashed good notion," Dawlish said. "Good night, Corey." When they had made their way down the grand stair, bade the porter a civil good night, and found themselves in St. James's Street, he said as they began walking toward Piccadilly, "Sorry about that. Must have had a sip or two over the mark at Sefton's. Only came here because I thought you might be with Thorne—he's in town, you know."

"So I heard. I, too, thought I might find him here."

A short silence fell before Dawlish said abruptly, "Thought you had talked to Belinda."

"Well, you thought wrong," Crawley replied. "I did dance with her, but she chattered sixteen to the dozen about a lot of people, including Dacres. She thinks he is interested in Caroline Oakley one moment and in Theodosia Adlam in the next."

"And why do you suppose she tells you such things."

"Chatter, Dawlish. What do you think?"

Dawlish sighed, pulling his coat tighter against the chill of the night. "Not my business to think, of course—"

"Glad to know you realize that."

"—but it appears to me that you've shifted the burden for saving your groats onto your sister, and I don't like to see it. Think of her as my own sister, don't you know, and have done since the first time I visited Longworth with you from school. Tiny thing she was then, with long chestnut curls down her back, and stockings always falling down around her ankles. Taking little puss, I thought then. Still do."

Crawley glared at him. "Don't get any damned silly notions in your head, Mongrel."

"Oh, don't put yourself in a pucker. I told you I think of her as a sister. More important than that—she thinks of me as just another brother. And even if she didn't, though I wasn't born without a shirt and my uncle's a duke, I do know you ain't interested in my pedigree but only in snaring a Midas for her. I liked you better before you inherited, Ned, and that's a fact. Here is your street. I'll see you tomorrow afternoon . . .That is, if I may still accompany you and the others to Queen's House," he added with a more doubtful air.

"Don't be foolish," Crawley said, clapping him on the shoulder. "Of course you must come."

Dawlish nodded, started to turn away, took a deep breath, and turned back, blurting, "She is trying to let you know, as easily as she can, that she thinks Dacres is even more intent upon marrying money than you are for her to do so, that's all!" And with that he turned and strode off down the street.

Crawley stared after him for a long moment, then shook his head, and turned toward home.

He did not sleep well, for not only had Dawlish made him think about Belinda and Dacres, but he was vexed about his own behavior with Miss Adlam. He remembered her saying that Vyne brought out the worst in her sister, and wondered if she did the same to him, if in fact her original letter might not—in some way he did not yet understand—have sparked an irresistible urge in him to make a cake of himself. Tossing and turning did no good. He could not convince himself that it was any doing of hers. He had done it all to himself. He was a fool.

The following morning he resisted his valet's strenuous attempts to waken him until the fellow said loudly that if he did not mean to go to Adlam House that day, he ought to have said so the night before.

Crawley opened one sleepy eye, blinked at the glare in the room, and said, "Shut that damned curtain, Belsham, and give me whatever it is you give me when I have had too much to drink."

"But, my lord, you were not in the least inebriated when you came in last night. Nearly stone sober, I should have said."

"Then you are a fool, for I cannot have been sober. Get me the stuff. If it does nothing else, it will wake me up."

By the time the man returned, he had got out of bed and put on his dressing gown, an elaborate creation of bright red silk with purple cording. The sight of it made him react much as the sun's glare had done, but he was feeling better now that he was upright. He truly did not know if he had had too much to drink the preceding night. He rather thought not, for his memory was perfectly clear. Particularly with regard to his discomfort over Dawlish's parting words.

Damning Vyne for making it necessary for him to be up so early—though he had begun to suspect he wasn't needed to keep peace between artist and subject anymore—he let Belsham shave him and help him dress in tan breeches and a dark coat, smoothed his snowy neckcloth into place, and went down to the breakfast parlor. He had expected to have the room to himself, but to his immense surprise, he found his sister there before him.

"Good God, Bella, what ails you that you are up so early?"

She smiled. "Nothing ails me, Ned. I couldn't sleep, so I got up. That is all."

She looked cheerful enough, he thought, moving to help

himself from various dishes a footman was setting out on the sideboard. "I'll have coffee," Crawley said. He could still taste the awful concoction Belsham had mixed for him. Though he suspected it consisted of little more than whiskey and hot pepper, his head was clearer than it had been, and there was something in his sister's casual air that troubled him.

He sat down, waited until he had his coffee, then dismissed the footman and said, "Open the budget, love. What's troubling you that you felt you had to see me this morning?"

She was silent for a long moment, and he did not press her. At last, looking down, she said, "I cannot think why you must believe I have motives for doing quite natural things, Ned. One cannot sleep, so one gets up and eats breakfast. That is all."

"Rubbish. Last Season, there was not a single occasion that I can recall when you got out of bed before noon."

"Lady Jersey's alfresco breakfast," she retorted promptly.

"You were late," he reminded her. "Moreover it did not begin until two in the afternoon. Such so-called breakfasts never do begin before noon."

"Well, then, the day we rode to Richmond Park."

"Bella, cut line."

She flushed. "Oh, it is nothing. Now that I see you, I can think of nothing that I need tell you. Don't provoke me! I must suppose you went to your club last night after you left us."

"Yes."

"I thought so. Did you lose very much, Ned?"

"I cannot think why that should concern you."

"Did you?"

"I lost more than I won," he said.

"Everyone loses," she said with a long sigh. "What happens to all the money that gets lost?"

"Well, Mr. Thynne retired from Brooks's because he won only twelve thousand pounds in two months. Needless to recount, the other members are hoping he does not decide to return." When she did not respond, he said coaxingly, "Come now, that was meant to make you smile. What's amiss?"

"I do not think I can bring Lord Dacres up to scratch," she blurted. "Oh, Ned, I have tried, truly I have, but it is of no use whatsoever. I had thought, when it was only Caroline that he was interested in, that I still had a chance, for her papa is in trade, you know, and they say that even Mr. Sheridan was not let into Brooks's because his papa was an actor. Dacres would simply hate it if he were forced to resign from his clubs—"

"He would not be asked to do so," Crawley said. "Sheridan got in at the end, you know."

"Yes, but only because the Prince of Wales kept the man who always blackballed him away long enough for the others to vote."

"We are not talking of Sheridan, however. Nor do I much want to talk about Miss Oakley."

"Oh, I know, but she is not the problem now, anyway. Theo is. He is simply mad about her, Ned."

"Any red-blooded male in London who has seen her is mad about her," Crawley said with a grimace.

"You, too? Oh, Ned, I'm so sorry!"

"Well, you needn't be," he said. He meant it. It did not bother him in the least that Dacres wanted Theo Adlam. But he had no wish to explain himself to her. Instead, he said firmly, "In my belief, Bella, you are quite as pretty as Miss Theodosia."

"Oh, Ned, you are kind to say so, but—"

"No 'buts' about it. The only difference between the two of you is that she is accustomed to hearing herself praised and you are not, which has given her a confidence you do not feel, but I promise you that if you were to carry yourself as she does and look at the world with the same sort of confidence, you would find that you could be just as popular as the lovely Miss Theo."

"Do you really think so?"

"I do. Now, hush, and let me drink my coffee, for I must make haste if I am to get to Adlam House before she murders Dickon or he murders her."

Belinda laughed. "I cannot believe you are still playing nursemaid, Ned, for that is what it sounds like to me, and you have not yet missed a day. Although I suppose that if you are in love with Theo yourself, there is no real mystery about it. If you weren't, I should certainly wonder.

Indignantly he said, "It's been little more than a week and only two hours each day!"

"Very true, but you are generally not so much to be relied upon. You will not mind my saying that, I know, for you quite frequently say the same thing yourself."

Maybe he did, but he did not like hearing it from her after the soul searching he had done in the night, and since one day of hearing Miss Theodosia Adlam snipe at Vyne had put any thought of wedding her straight out of his head, he wondered why he did feel so obligated to continue his job as nurse-maid—for Bella had hit the mark there. It was exactly how the pair of them made him feel, and since the first day, he had not even had the benefit of Miss Adlam's company to keep him from becoming bored.

When Belinda jumped up, kissed him on the cheek, and took herself off, he wondered if his telling her she was as pretty as Theo had done any good. He had hoped that if she felt more confident, she would begin to concentrate on her own interests instead of his. While he would not turn down a wealthy suitor, he certainly did not want her marrying only to please him.

Realizing he had no time to waste, he finished his meal and left for Adlam House. When Heath admitted him, the next person he saw was Miss Adlam. She looked worried, and he instantly wondered if she had feared he would not come today. In that instant, he realized that the reason he felt such an urgency to keep his word was simply because he had pledged it to her.

Felicia was relieved to see him. She had been certain that he, of all people, had not retired early the previous evening. Had Theo not said that he and his party had gone on to other events? It was absurd of her, she knew, to be counting on a man like Crawley to keep peace between two such temperamental persons as her sister and Sir Richard, for he was clearly irresponsible. Even his friends seemed to agree on that point.

"Good morning, sir," she said. "I am glad to see you."

"Did you suppose I would not come?" he asked, smiling at her. "You might well have wondered, had you known what a chore my man had to rouse me this morning. Have they begun?"

"No, Theo has not yet come down, and Sir Richard is a bit

cross about it, but he said he wanted to look his sketches over in any event. There . . . there is a small complication, sir."

"Complication? Is something amiss with the children?"

"No." She smiled more naturally. "I am not surprised that in the short time you have known us you have come to think them my primary concern, but Sara Ann and Freddy are with Miss Ames, and Tom has found himself a tutor."

"The boy found his own tutor?"

"Yes, was that not resourceful of him?"

"I doubt the fellow can be much good if the boy found him. You ought to have told me he wanted a tutor. I might have been able to ferret out a proper one for him."

"That is kind of you, though I do not know why you should. You are already doing a great deal more than we have any right to expect by attempting to keep peace between my sister and Sir Richard. And I think Tom has found the very man. He has been going about the neighborhood on his own, you know, exploring the park and the streets as far as St. George's Square. And he found his man at St. George's Chapel, for he is one of the curates there. He and Tom got to talking, for Tom is the friendliest boy, you know, and due to his odd upbringing is quite experienced in talking to strangers. He told the man he was planning to enter Eton when the new term begins, and it turns out that this man does a good deal of work with other boys preparing to enter, to see that they are not behind boys their age when they do."

"Who is this fellow?"

"Well, I don't know, precisely. His name is Chambers, and I know of no family with that name, but there can be nothing out of the way about a curate of St. George's, surely." She realized she was holding her breath, waiting to hear what he would say.

"No, I suppose not. It seems Master Tom has done well, which means he cannot be the reason for that frown I saw, so perhaps you will be so good as to explain. I might warn you that I have already had to cajole one young lady into confiding in me this morning, so do not expect me to coax you, for I shall not."

She chuckled, relieved beyond measure that for once he had accepted her reading of a situation without argument. "I collect that you refer to your sister, sir, and I hope that means you have encouraged her to know better what you want from her."

"Miss Adlam, what do *you* want of *me*?"

"Only for you to discover if Sir Richard can finish Theo's portrait in time to unveil it at a ball my aunt wishes to give for her," Felicia said in a rush.

"When is the ball to be? If you tell me 'in a fortnight,' I can assure you I won't even ask him, for he will never finish the thing in less than a month."

"Well, he will have a bit longer than a fortnight, for Theo is to be presented at the queen's drawing room a week from Thursday, and she cannot have a ball until after that. But Aunt Augusta wants to arrange it for the twenty-fourth of April."

"About three weeks, then," he murmured. "I do not know if I can persuade him to finish so soon."

"Well, if you will not ask him, then I am sure I do not know what we shall do, for Theo is persuaded that he would refuse even to consider such a thing if she were to ask, and if I do so, he will suspect it is at her instigation, will he not?"

Crawley smiled. "I will see what I can do. Wait. I have just remembered something. This is the year the Royal Academy awards gold and silver medals for excellence. They do so every two years, you know, and Dickon and the other two portrait artists will be vying for the gold. He has said nothing about what he intends to enter, but I'd wager a large sum that at least one entry will be your sister's portrait. And the exhibition begins the last Monday in April. There will be a big dinner the Saturday before the opening, and all the entries have to be judged before then, for that is when the awards are announced."

"Then we have only to ask him if he means to enter the portrait for the exhibition," Felicia said.

"Let us ask him now. If we wait for Miss Theo, the answer we get may be different, for he does seem to enjoy teasing her."

Accordingly, they went to the northeast parlor to confront the artist. He looked up expectantly when they entered, and Felicia was certain he was disappointed to see only them, but there was nothing to suggest that in his crisp tone of voice.

"Good morning," he said. "I am nearly ready to begin, so I hope Miss Theodosia does not mean to keep me waiting long."

"Oh, no," Felicia said. "It is not quite half past eight, sir, and you know she never comes down before then."

"I know." There was a twinkle in his eyes when he said the two words, so Felicia decided they need not equivocate with him, and did not wait for Crawley to frame his question.

"I have a small difficulty with which you can help me, Sir Richard," she said, flushing when she saw Crawley's lips twitch with amusement.

"My pleasure, ma'am," Vyne said. "What can I do?"

"Finish Theo's portrait in time to unveil it at the ball my aunt is to give next month. It was Aunt Augusta's notion," she said quickly when he frowned. "She thought it would make the ball a truly memorable occasion, and she would like to include in the invitation that the portrait will be unveiled."

He was silent long enough for her to fear he was going to refuse, and she glanced anxiously at Crawley. When he smiled, she looked more hopefully back at Sir Richard.

He too had glanced at Crawley, and he said now, "I have no doubt, ma'am, that you have heard about the Royal Academy Exhibition, and that I have been asked to submit my work for the judging. I should be an utter fool not to consider submitting your sister's portrait. Once it has been submitted, it cannot be taken from Somerset House until after the exhibition is ended in May, but there is no rule to prevent its unveiling before submission. What is the date of this ball?"

She told him.

He nodded. "It can be done, certainly."

"Crawley feared you could not finish so soon."

"Which shows only how little he knows. The biggest problem is that certain bits must dry before others may be painted, and since your sister is wearing a white dress, that necessitates some careful planning. White takes longer than any other color to dry, you see, and cannot be painted over a dark color that has not yet dried; however, I am not painting a large canvas—only three feet by five—so such difficulties can be surmounted. Lawrence is painting a portrait of the Princess of Wales for the exhibition," he added as an apparent afterthought.

"There is no contest there," Crawley said, chuckling. "What is Hoppner doing?"

"I haven't the least idea. Where is the chit? I am ready for her, and I dislike wasting time."

Theo came in a few minutes later, and upon hearing that the portrait could be finished in time for its unveiling to take place at Lady Augusta's ball, became quite cheerful. After her remarks the previous evening, Felicia had dreaded the possibility of a scene, but it was apparent that her sister meant to be pleasant to all and sundry.

Sir Richard and Crawley left at ten, promising to return at one o'clock for the promised expedition to Queen's House, and Felicia realized when Theo said only that it looked to her as if it were coming on to drizzle that she had reconciled herself to the inevitability of its taking place.

It did indeed begin to rain before the gentlemen returned to fetch them, a gentle shower dampening the streets and changing the sound of passing carriage-wheels on the cobbles. When Felicia, in the morning room, heard barking and then the sounds of a vehicle drawing up outside the house, she looked out to see Crawley jump down to the pavement, and saw, too, that Freddy was perched up beside the coachman with the gray mongrel from the areaway sitting proudly between them.

Crawley explained the minute he saw her. "Young rascal was playing with that blasted creature two blocks from here, and called to us from the pavement. Nothing to do but stop and take him up with us, but he would have nothing of sitting inside when he discovered the dog wasn't welcome. Said it was probably musty anyway—an aspersion on my mother's town carriage that is quite unwarranted—and that they would sit by the driver. From the increase in our pace that began shortly afterward, I think my coachman was rash enough to let him hold the ribbons."

"Good gracious!"

"My sentiments exactly. Is your sister ready, or are we expected to wait an hour or so for her pleasure?"

Felicia said calmly, "Such sarcasm does not become you, my lord. I sent to warn her that we would not wait for her, so I believe she will be down directly."

"She is down now," Theo called from the landing. "I hope your carriage is right at the door, sir, for this pelisse, though quite in fashion, is ridiculously short and will no doubt do nothing whatever to protect me from the rain, but it is better than letting my gown be soaked through."

"That chip straw hat will soon droop, too," Felicia said. "You ought to have worn one of your bonnets, my dear."

"Too dowdy for words, Felicia. You, my dearest one, look like a little brown wren in that vast cloak."

"A very pretty brown wren," Crawley said.

Surprised and flushing with pleasure, Felicia turned to thank him, but her delight faded when she saw that he looked nearly as surprised to have said the words as she was to have heard them. He signed to the footman waiting with an umbrella to hold over the ladies as they made their way to the carriage, and Felicia followed Theo and went past him and out the door.

"Aunt Felicia, look at me," Freddy called to her from the box. Water dripped from his chin, and his long eyelashes were stuck together in clumps, but he was grinning from ear to ear. "Fletcher let me take the ribbons for nearly a whole block!"

"Did he, my dear? How thrilling for you, but you must come down now, because you are getting soaked to the bone, and we must go. Tell the coachman 'thank you' and let Peters help you down."

"I don't need help," the little boy said scornfully as he handed the wet dog to the reluctant footman and swung agilely down from the box. He cast a wary look at Crawley. "I hope it was all right, sir. Me taking the ribbons, I mean.

Crawley smiled. "If Fletcher let you take them, he must have thought you looked as if you could handle them. I will take you out one day in my curricle, and show you how to handle the ribbons in style. How would you like that?"

Freddy seemed unable to speak, but he nodded fervently, his eyes sparkling with delight. Finally, he said, "Tomorrow?"

Crawley laughed. "We'll see. Now, in with you, so your aunts don't concern themselves for the rest of the afternoon with whether you will catch your death of cold before we return. And leave that dog outside."

Freddy assured them that Cook would look after Scraps and that he was going in straightaway to see if he could not find

Tom and Sara Ann to tell them of the delight in store for him the following day.

Crawley, climbing into the coach behind Felicia, said with a chuckle, "I suppose that means I must take him at once or he will pester the life out of all of us until I do."

Vyne called impatiently to the driver to get on with it or they would be late to Queen's House, and Theo said with an edge to her voice, "I think it was very kind of you to make the offer, my lord. Freddy is excited, of course, and one is delighted for him, but some persons can think only of wretched paintings, and don't spare a second thought for anyone save themselves."

Vyne said, "If that barb is meant for me, which I strongly suspect it is, it falls short of the mark, my girl, for if we do not make haste, they will think we are not coming and will go about their business. And if you think it is no great thing to gain entrance to Queen's House when the galleries are shut to the public, then you may soon find out how wrong you are."

Felicia, sitting next to Theo and across from the two gentlemen, gave her a quelling look, whereupon Theo tossed her head and looked pointedly out her window.

Vyne ignored her and said conversationally, "The Raphael cartoons which were used to amuse everyone so much have been taken away to Windsor, but there are still a great number of fine pictures, and since no one else of the public has been admitted yet this Season," he added with a sharp look at Theo, "I rather thought you would like to be amongst the first who are."

Theo turned then, and Felicia saw that her brow was furrowed thoughtfully. Vyne had clearly gained a point, but she feared Theo might take up the gauntlet, and was grateful when Crawley drew Vyne into a more detailed description of what they might expect to see, and what they particularly ought to look out for.

9

The queen's palace, called Buckingham House for the simple reason that it had been built, one hundred years before, by the then Duke of Buckingham, was located at the western extremity of St. James's Park. Just before the turnpike that separated Piccadilly from Knightsbridge, the carriage turned into a gravel drive, to pass between the extensive gardens behind Queen's House and the Green Park.

Vyne, in a pedantic mood, explained that the house had been purchased forty years before by the king, then settled on the queen by an act of Parliament, in the event that she survived his majesty. "Somerset Palace was used to be her dower house," he said, "but once the embankment was enlarged and what is now Somerset House expanded to house the Royal Academy and certain government offices, a new dower house was required."

"History," said Theo with awful emphasis, "is not a subject that I find particularly interesting. Do you, Lord Crawley?"

Crawley said, "Look out to your left, Miss Theo. From this angle one can look straight up the Mall. Does it not look like a long forest of dutiful trees? See how neatly they are lined up, like soldiers on parade?"

"Damp soldiers today," Theo said, smiling at him. Then, looking out again as the carriage turned into the circular drive in front of the handsome brick house, she said, "Is that not Birdcage Walk yonder, the other side of St. James's Canal?"

Crawley agreed that it was, and as the carriage door was pulled open by a Buckingham House lackey, added that it was a pity the inclement weather prevented their strolling beneath the trees there after they had seen the gallery.

"This way," Vyne said, ignoring the exchange. "Take my arm, Miss Theodosia, so that Crawley can aid your sister."

Felicia, though grateful that someone had recalled her presence, had begun to suspect Vyne's motives and suspected he had used her merely as an excuse to divert Theo's attention from Crawley. There was no sign of disappointment in his lordship's expression, however, when he turned with that perilously charming smile of his to offer his arm to her. The lackey put up the steps, the carriage drove off, and they followed Vyne to a side door in the south wing of the palace.

Felicia found much to admire both in the noble apartments through which they passed and in the vast art collection. She had visited the gallery once before, during her first Season, but she had no idea then what she was supposed to admire, or why, and had been a little bored. With Vyne as their escort, the visit was magical, and she was fascinated by his explanations of the works they saw. Even Theo, she noticed, forgot to be at all waspish to the artist, and for once, seemed to hang upon his every word. Not until they heard rapid footsteps approaching from behind and turned to see Dawlish hurrying toward them, did Felicia recall that he had planned to meet them there.

"Sorry I'm late," he said, gasping his words. "Didn't think the fellow at the door was going to let me in."

Vyne glared at him. "He oughtn't to have done so. I told you what time you were to meet us here."

"I know, I know. I was detained."

"Just what could be so important to make you risk offending the Buck House people," Vyne demanded, "or me, for that matter?"

"Well, it was Belin—" He broke off, cast an anxious glance at Crawley, then said quickly, "Bellingham, that's who. Accosted me outside Brooks's, demanded directions to Eaton Street, then didn't heed me when I gave them. Had to repeat myself any number of times." He shook his head, saw that Crawley was frowning nearly as heavily as Vyne, and tugged at his cravat. "Dash it, I said I was sorry. Can't ask a man to do more than that."

Felicia, feeling uncomfortable tension in the air, tried to think of something to say to ease it, but Crawley spoke first.

"Being helpful again, Mongrel?"

"That's it," Dawlish said on a note of relief.

Theo said innocently, "I thought you were going to say it was Belinda who kept you, sir. Isn't it funny how one thinks one name will come out and then another one does?"

Dawlish cleared his throat. "Dashed funny, Miss Theo."

"Are we here to look at pictures or to talk nonsense?" Vyne demanded. "Here are a number of West's pieces, Miss Theo, for he is Limner to the King as well as being president of the Royal Academy."

He went on to describe West's methods and strengths, but though his commentary was surely as interesting as it had been before, Felicia found herself watching the other men instead of listening. She had noted that Crawley kept glancing at Dawlish and that Dawlish was careful to avoid his gaze, so it came as no great shock that when Vyne drew the still fascinated Theo a little ahead of them and Felicia began to follow, Crawley caught Dawlish by the arm, and she heard him say, "Look here, Mongrel, what's amiss? I know as well as Miss Theo does that you nearly said Belinda back there. Is there something I ought to know?"

Felicia, encountering an embarrassed glance from Dawlish, stepped quickly away and tried to pretend fascination with one of West's paintings, but she could not help hearing him mutter that he thought Crawley had forbidden him to mention Belinda. "Just trying to follow your orders," he added lamely.

Reluctantly, telling herself that curiosity was a most unbecoming sin, Felicia forced herself to move on.

Crawley, with one eye on her retreating figure, retained his hold on Dawlish's arm and said in a low but furious tone, "Dammit, Mongrel, if something is amiss with my sister, I want to know about it. I talked with her this morning, tried to give her something to think of besides pleasing me, and had reason to believe I'd succeeded."

"Well, if that's what you thought, you were wrong. The last thing you ought to have done was to mention last night's losses."

"But I didn't." Even as he spoke the words, however, he remembered that Belinda had asked about his losses. "Damn," he said. "I did tell her, but she ought to have known they were of no great consequence. I hope you told her so."

"Couldn't," Dawlish told him. "Don't know myself what they amounted to. Couldn't tell her you don't gamble too much either, because the fact of the matter is that you do. My belief is that it's time and more that you looked to your estates and to the welfare of your mother and sister."

"Oh, is it?" Crawley demanded in a dangerous tone.

"Yes, it is," Dawlish retorted, standing his ground. "I know you expect me to back down, Ned, for I generally do when you or Dickon begin looking like you'd like to murder me. Stands to reason, both of you being better marksmen than I am. But you won't, either of you, call me out. Wouldn't do you any good if you did, for all that, because I wouldn't go."

Crawley was silent, struggling with his emotions, but finally, reluctantly, he smiled at Dawlish and released his arm. "I suppose you are right about everything, but the fact is I'm not cut out to be a landowner. I know nothing about it and should make a mess of it if I tried."

"Couldn't make more of a muck of it than it is already." Dawlish pointed out, smoothing his sleeve. "Look at Thorne. He knew next to nothing about the estates he will inherit either, because the duke left everything to stewards and bailiffs for so long and never bothered to teach him anything, but Thorne has learned because he has made it his business to do so."

"Thorne is interested in farming and in all manner of things that I find tiresome," Crawley said.

"Wouldn't if you took the time to learn about them," Dawlish said flatly. "How will you feel to see your mama bear-leading young ladies through next Season like Mrs. Falworthy does now? I don't say she means to do any such thing," he added hastily when Crawley stiffened. "All I say is, if you don't take the reins soon, she may be reduced to doing something of the sort. She can't afford another Season on that jointure of hers, you know."

"All the more reason for Bella to find a husband. It needn't be Dacres, as I hope I made clear to her, but the plain fact is that the best way for any female to look out for herself in this day and age is to marry well. As I told her this morning, if she were only a bit more con—"

"Your problem is that you somehow grew up thinking you can get your own way just by telling others what you think they ought to do," Dawlish said curtly. "There's Dickon, looking for us. He'll want our heads on a platter if we dawdle longer."

He turned away before Crawley could reply to the astonishing accusation, and moved to join the others. Crawley saw him offer an arm to Felicia, but to his surprise, she shook her head. A moment later, Dawlish moved on with Vyne and Theo, but Felicia did not go with them. She seemed to be waiting for him. His spirits lifted a bit, and he walked to meet her.

Felicia watched him approach, thinking he had looked angry and now sad, and wondering why his moods should affect her so. It was almost, she thought, as though he transmitted his feelings to her. However, a moment later, when he responded to her smile, she noted that his did not reach his eyes and, for once, found little in it to cheer her.

"Bored?" he asked.

"No, merely concerned. Is something amiss with your sister?" Hastily, lest he suspect her of eavesdropping, she added, "I ask because you have devoted so much time to us this week that your family may quite reasonably be feeling neglected."

"Don't trouble your head about that. It is only Mongrel—that is, Dawlish—pushing himself in where he is not wanted."

"Oh." She eyed him speculatively as she placed her hand on the arm he held out to her and let him guide her in the wake of the others. After a brief silence she said, "You are most fortunate in your friends, sir."

"Am I?"

"Yes. I have noted many times that despite your teasing, you all share a concern for one another that is most enviable. Surely, if his lordship is troubled about you, he has cause."

"He's a damned busybody," Crawley muttered, glancing ahead as though to judge whether Dawlish could overhear.

Felicia, seeing the look, said gently, "He is merely trying to be helpful, you know."

"His besetting sin is that he tries to help everyone," Crawley said bitterly, "but if he thinks it will help me to isolate myself on an estate in Nottinghamshire when I would far rather be here in London, he is out of his mind."

"Your own estate, I collect."

"Quite."

"I see."

"No, you do *not* see! What can you know of the burdens of an estate like mine? Although, to be perfectly fair, I don't know them either, because my father was used to look after every detail. He wanted me to learn his ways, of course, but whenever I did any of the work, he would just do it over, so I stopped wasting my time, thinking I could always learn later. And he made not the least objection, saying I should enjoy myself, so I did. I think it was quite unfair of—" He broke off, looking at her in astonishment. "Forgive me. I can't think what came over me to make me talk in such an uncivilized way to you."

"I provoked you, no doubt. I quite frequently do provoke people, though I cannot think why. I rarely mean to."

"It's because you are always so self-controlled," he said bluntly, "and so competent about everything you do that you make me, at least, feel like an oaf. Indeed, I believe I was crazy to think of marrying your sister. I ought to marry you."

His obvious surprise—and annoyance—at his own words compelled her to speak before he could retract them. "I expect that means you have discovered that my fortune matches Theo's and believe I would be of more help in setting your affairs to rights," she said coldly, certain of only one thing, which was that he was not serious in suggesting marriage to herself. Wanting to slap him, but sternly collecting her wits, she added, "I cannot think why, if your estates are such large ones, sir, that you do not exploit them—in a perfectly practical spirit, you know—to lure some more unsuspecting heiress to wed you."

He blinked, then said curtly, "You mistake my character, Miss Adlam. No more than I welcomed the burden of vast estates left me before I was ready to inherit them, am I so lacking in conscience that I would try to convince anyone they were worth marrying me to possess."

She had made him angry again, and she was sorry for it, but

this time she heard what she had missed before. "I begin to see the truth, sir," she said gently. "It is not at all unusual, you know, to bear anger when a parent dies suddenly and unexpectedly, leaving one with responsibility one feels unprepared to assume."

He glared at her. "Nonsense, what can you know about it?"

"Little perhaps about such a death, but I know a good deal about responsibility, sir, and about having it thrust upon one before one is ready to assume its burden."

He opened his mouth, then shut it.

She waited.

He grimaced. "I suppose you do at that, and I ought not to have snapped at you, but you don't dislike your responsibilities, Miss Adlam. Indeed, you assume more of them than you need assume because—for some reason I have yet to fathom—you enjoy them."

If he only knew, she thought. But she would not let her guard down with him again, not so much so, at all events, as to tell him he was wrong to believe her so sure of herself. She was nothing of the kind, but since she could not say so, she said instead, "One does what one must, sir. We all must accept what is given us in life. A child may be forgiven for running from his responsibilities, but it is a measure of maturity that an adult knows when he must face up to them."

He flushed angrily, and she realized at once that in her attempt to avoid betraying herself, she had snatched from her aunt's long list of maxims merely for something intelligent to say. That her choice had been unfortunate was perfectly clear, but whatever he might have said in response she would not know, for they were interrupted even as he opened his mouth to speak.

"Here you are, you two!" Theo cried, coming toward them with Dawlish and Vyne a short distance behind her. "Sir Richard has said it is time for us to depart, Felicia, if we are to have time to dress and dine before Aunt Augusta arrives to take us to the opera tonight. He also says he does not like the opera, Crawley, so I hope you mean to attend. It will be very flat if no one we know is there. Afterward, of course, we will go on to Lady Thomond's rout, even if *some* people think we will not get enough sleep if we do. Only think how dreadful if we discover that our invitations are more of those awful forgeries!"

Felicia saw that Crawley had himself in hand again long before Theo stopped chattering, so she was not surprised when he said matter-of-factly, "I suggest that you look in today's *Times* for a published guest list for the marchioness's rout. I believe I saw one or two such lists in the morning papers."

"Oh, what a good idea!" Theo exclaimed. She went on chattering, drawing Dawlish into the conversation from time to time until they were outside again, when Dawlish took his leave. Then Theo devoted herself wholly to Crawley, much, Felicia realized, as if to underscore his attentiveness for someone else's benefit. Vyne did not comment. He had fallen into a brown study, leaving Felicia alone with her thoughts until they reached Park Lane, where the gentlemen bade them good day.

"Let us go and look at the paper," Theo said. "I doubt it is necessary, of course, for Aunt Augusta has often mentioned how well she knows Lady Thomond, so we must have been invited."

The list was there, and to be sure, their names were on it, but a moment later, Theo cried, "Felicia, no one else we know is on this list! Oh, how I wish now that we had never sent our acceptances, for Aunt Augusta will insist that we go, and from what I see here, all the marchioness's guests are in their dotage except you and me. How dreary it will be!"

Her dismay was augmented an hour later when she received a message from Miss Crawley. "Only listen to this," she exclaimed, rushing into Felicia's bedchamber, where she was attending to her toilette for the evening ahead.

"What is it, dear? You are not dressed yet, and you really must not keep Aunt Augusta waiting, for you know she does not like to be late to the theater or the opera."

"No, I know, and I will hurry. But, Felicia, Belinda and Caroline Oakley both received invitations to Lady Thomond's rout. I was sure they had done so, but they must have been forged, and Belinda writes that Lady Dacres and Mrs. Falworthy have decided to get up an impromptu gathering at Dacres House for a number of friends they know who also received fake invitations. She begs us to go to their party instead of to

Lady Thomond's. Oh, do say we may! It will be much more amusing, I am sure of it."

"It may well be," Felicia said calmly, "but we cannot go, Theo. It would be very bad manners to miss the marchioness's rout merely because she did not invite our friends. You may be certain Aunt Augusta will insist upon it even if I did not."

Lady Augusta did insist; however, she also pointed out that there was no particular reason that they could not go on to Lady Dacres's party afterward. "For you know, my dears," she said comfortably as they settled themselves in the carriage that evening, "one goes to a rout only long enough to see and be seen. Then one is expected to go on to other entertainments. Indeed, since we are to go to the opera first, where the performance begins at seven, all our friends may have left Thomond House before we arrive. We need not stay long, but they who neglect old friends for new ones are rightly served when they lose both."

"Well, they are your old friends, not ours," Theo said.

Felicia felt the familiar clenching sensation in her stomach and hoped her aunt and sister would not soon be at daggers drawn, but for once she could think of nothing to say to divert them. Her thoughts had flown ahead to the opera house, where she wondered if they would see anyone they knew, who might decide to accompany them to Lady Thomond's, even though his name was not on the guest list. He might decide to take his chance, knowing that rarely was an eligible gentleman turned away from any party, and she wanted very much to see if he was still angry with her.

The magnificent theater on the west side of the Haymarket was brightly lit and crowded with music lovers. When they had taken their seats in Lady Augusta's box in the second tier, Felicia opened her fan and, waving it gently before her, looked as casually as possible around the five tiers of elegantly ornamented boxes, the spacious pit, and the ample gallery. Although she saw several persons she knew, she did not see the one tall, broad-shouldered figure for whom she searched.

"What a pity," Lady Augusta said suddenly, "that dancing has begun so greatly to prevail here as to threaten to triumph over the more refined and noble art of music. Nowadays, to allow for the performance of the ballets, operas which originally consisted of three acts have been reduced to two, and a ballet is often extended to even greater length than any act of the opera."

"But just think of the pleasure the opera dancers give to the audience," declared a familiar male voice behind them.

Felicia turned around more quickly than dignity warranted and dropped her fan. The one place she had not expected to see Crawley that evening was in Lady Augusta's box. He bowed over her ladyship's hand with his customary aplomb, then with warm smile for Felicia, he picked up her fan and gave it back to her before greeting Theo.

"Thank you," Felicia murmured.

Theo laughed. "Oh, how glad I am to see you, sir! But you are very naughty to talk about opera dancers to Aunt Augusta, is he not, ma'am?"

"Very naughty," she agreed, looking sharply at Felicia, then back at Crawley to add, "We would be grateful to have your company, sir. You will see your opera dancers much better from this box than from the pit, which I daresay, is the sort of ticket you purchased. As you see, Major Brinksby failed me tonight, and I do like to have a gentleman escort, for one simply cannot depend upon the lower orders to keep to their places. Why, not long ago, some villain actually leapt from box to box, pulling young ladies' hair and making a nuisance of himself."

Crawley chuckled. "I would be glad to take a seat here, ma'am, since you are so kind."

Theo said instantly, "Sit by me, sir, so you can explain the Italian to me if I become confused."

Felicia was glad when he obeyed. Clearly he was no longer angry with her, but there would be no chance to talk much before the interval, and to be sitting silently beside him all that time would be most uncomfortable. The performance began soon after that; however, when the interval came, Theo continued to monopolize his attention, and Crawley made no effort to check her. But at last it was over, and Lady Augusta seemed to assume that he would continue to accompany them to the Marquess of Thomond's great house in Berkeley Square. He did not decline.

The carriage delivered them, and they went inside to discover their old friend Mr. Townshend of Bow Street standing guard in the hall. He nodded. "Don't have to cast my gazers over your card, ma'am," he said. "Saw the name on the list and remembered you very well, indeed. How d'ye do, young ladies."

He made no objection to Crawley's presence, clearly assuming that as part of Lady Augusta's party, he had a proper invitation, but nodding toward a bench near the side wall, where two well-dressed ladies sat looking miserable, he shook his head and said, "Had to send for their carriage, they did. Most inconvenient for all, I say it is. Here we have two pleasant-spoken ladies coming up to the door as nice as you please, with an invite that wasn't sent them by her ladyship. Can't have that, I told them, but the older one wailed that their carriage had already drove off, which of course they do, you know. Expected of 'em, ain't it? Can't just wait at the curbstone. So I says we'll send for it and they can wait here. Couldn't put them into the street, now could I?"

Felicia, glancing at the two, was grateful that guest lists were now being printed in the *Times,* and made a mental note to insist that her aunt hand theirs in to be published. That there might be any awkwardness attached to such an act did not occur to her until they had greeted Lady Thomond and Lady Augusta informed her of the unfortunate pair awaiting their carriage in the hall.

"Oh, isn't that too bad," her ladyship said, "and it just goes to show that allowing one's guest list to be published is not worth the time and trouble to do so. It is so delicate a matter, Augusta. You cannot imagine!"

Felicia, greeted in turn, said, "My aunt is arranging a ball for my sister, ma'am. Pray tell us why printing the guest list is such a delicate matter. We thought it an excellent idea."

The marchioness laughed. "You can have no notion, my dear. We are not commoners, after all, that we must peek and preen over who agrees to attend our parties. In the usual way of things, one counts one's replies or has one's secretary count them, and a guest list is made up from the replies, for no one wishes to advertise that she has invited the Duke and Duchess of Langshire unless they have accepted the invitation. Otherwise our enemies choose to believe such names are put down to augment our importance and take great delight in commiserating with us if an invitation appears to have been rebuffed."

"But surely, ma'am—"

"Oh, now do not say that one has only to print the list of acceptances, for then what happens if the duke and duchess decide to come and have not, for some reason or other, written to accept? Not that they would do such a thing, but few young men these days remember to reply at all, you know. So what is one to do? I told Townshend that he should admit all single gentlemen unless he knew they were villains, and ask to see invitations from anyone else whose name was not on the list, unless they were persons of rank who are known to him. As I said, very awkward."

Lady Augusta said firmly, "I do not believe in allowing one's name to appear in a common newspaper, except when one is born, marries, or dies, and that is all there is about it. Advertising one's guests—and I hope you will forgive my saying this," she told the marchioness, "I find common and distasteful. We shall have Townshend, of course, and that will simply have to do. Lovely party. Come girls, we must mingle. Oh, and you too, of course, Crawley. Mind that lady's train, Felicity. You nearly stepped upon it."

Crawley's hand caught her arm at nearly the same moment that Lady Augusta spoke, and she looked at him gratefully. "I must have been air-dreaming. Thank you." She added quickly, "I'm sorry I displeased you this afternoon."

He let Theo pass them before he drew her into a quiet corner and said, "I should like myself better if I could say you did not displease me in the slightest, but the fact is you put me in a temper and made me feel ashamed of myself all at the same time. I came tonight purposely to tell you that you had every right to say what you did to me. My friends have all said much the same things to me, and I was a villain to take snuff over it when you echoed them. Perhaps I shall make more of an effort now to put my affairs in order."

"Will you, sir?" She did not believe him for a minute, but she was grateful that he had made the effort to apologize.

He smiled wryly. "I make no rash promises. Has Theo told you she and Dickon had a tiff this afternoon at Queen's House?"

Felicia shook her head.

"Dawlish told me. She tried to tease Dickon into agreeing to let her look at her portrait, now that he has begun to paint in earnest. He told her not even to think about it, that she would not see it until it was finished. I'm afraid she intends to try her hand at outwitting him."

"She does," Felicia said, accepting the change of topic since she saw nothing to be gained by pressing him for any promises that he might fail to keep. "She told me at the outset that he could not keep her from seeing her portrait."

"I'd advise you to talk her out of trying anything foolish," Crawley said. "To say that Dickon would be displeased is to put it mildly. It would send him into a flaming rage."

"That would be too bad, sir, but I do not know how you think I might prevent such a thing. I do not carry so much influence with my sister as you seem to think."

"Then I'd advise you to increase your influence," he retorted.

Felicia bit back the response she would have liked to make, since even the thought of taking him to task in so public a place made her feel a little sick; but her pleasure in his company dimmed and she found herself wishing he would not so casually advise her in matters he knew so little about, particularly when he so consistently scorned to take advice from anyone. Her displeasure lasted only until they were ready to depart for Lady Dacres's party, however, altering without warning to disappointment when Crawley said a previous engagement prevented him from accompanying them to Dacres House.

10

CRAWLEY'S appointment was at Langshire House. He had sent a hasty message late that afternoon to his friend, the Marquess of Thorne, asking him to meet him at the ducal mansion, because he wanted advice and did not want to be interrupted.

The tall, dark-haired marquess greeted him with a handshake and a laugh. "You look mighty serious, Ned, and when your man ran me to earth at my solicitor's, he said he had been commanded to search the whole town if necessary, beginning with the clubs. I've not set foot in Brooks's above twice since I arrived, I'm afraid, for I've been commanded to keep to business this trip, and if I don't get home soon, Gillian will be suspecting opera dancers at the least. So tell me what the devil's amiss, or should I just ask how much money you need and save us some time?"

"Nothing's amiss, Josh, and I don't want money, though I don't blame you in the least for thinking I do. In point of fact, I think I am beginning to grow up, and I'm finding the experience a painful one."

"I remember that feeling," Thorne said with a wry grimace. "Come and tell me all about it."

They adjourned to his comfortable sitting room, where Crawley, far from telling him all about it, found it difficult to tell him anything other than that he had decided to look into finding a steward whom he might trust.

"Thought you might help me, Josh. You must have told me a hundred times that if I took the reins at Longworth, I should be able to re-establish my fortune. Well, I want to do just that, but I'm not such a fool as to think I can do it alone, and my last man was a scoundrel of the first order. I need someone I can trust to show me how to go on."

"I know just the fellow," Thorne said. "My father's bailiff has a son who's been helping him, but the lad would like to find a position of his own. Honest as a saint, with a lot in his brain box to make him useful. I'll send a message to Langshire, if you like, telling him to meet you at Longworth straightaway."

"I'm not going to Longworth yet," Crawley said, "but I'll write my people there and tell them to expect your man. He can learn all he needs to know by examining the records and looking the place over. I can't tell him much, after all."

Thorne frowned. "But you can't just send a man to do the work without any supervision, Ned. I thought you said you were ready to attend to business."

Crawley felt warmth in his cheeks but managed to keep his tone even as he said, "I do mean to do so, but I can't leave London just yet. I have matters to attend to here; moreover, as I told you, I doubt there is anything I could do to help the lad. Prefer to give him sufficient time first to take his measure of the problem."

Thorne sighed. "Very well, I'll send for young Penning. That's his name, Joseph Penning. You'll need to write a letter of authorization for him to take to Longworth, so they'll know he is the right man, and you must also send the same authorization to whomever is looking out for your affairs now, so that Penning will be welcomed when he arrives. Do not forget." He shook his head, looking stern. "I fear you have not grown up quite as much as you think you have, Ned."

His cheeks burning now, Crawley held his temper in check with difficulty. He wanted to tell Thorne he was wrong, but he couldn't. He wasn't altogether certain it was the truth. At last he said only, "I'll need paper and pen, Josh, if I am to write that letter so you can enclose it with yours."

"Very well, but I wish you would reconsider."

"I cannot. I gave my word I would see that Dickon finishes Miss Theodosia Adlam's portrait before her aunt's ball, and I also promised to teach a mischievous young man to drive a team in form. I can't disappoint them, can I?"

"Excuses, Ned. Oh, don't eat me." Thorne got up and pulled the bell. "I'll get you your damned paper and pen."

They played piquet afterward, and since Thorne forbore to lecture and Crawley won nearly a hundred pounds, his spirits improved considerably; however, by the time he reached his own house several hours later, they had sunk again. His mother and sister had not yet come in, so he adjourned to his library and rang for wine, sitting before the crackling little fire, his feet propped on the fender, to think.

He could not imagine why, when he had not had the least intention of bothering with estate business until autumn (before the hunting season began) that he had suddenly taken it into his head to tackle matters at Longworth now. Certainly Dawlish had only irritated him by begging him to do so, and Dawlish was one of his closest friends. So why, he wondered, should comment by an annoyingly overcompetent female stir him to such lengths as to have sent him to Thorne for help?

He had left the library door open, and after a time he heard the porter walk across the marble floor to the front door. A moment later the door opened, and he heard his sister's voice.

She swept into the library, followed by Lady Crawley. Getting to his feet to greet them, he found himself thinking that Belinda looked particularly well that evening, in a gown of pale pink muslin trimmed with turquoise satin ribbons that matched her eyes. Another ribbon was threaded through the chestnut curls framing her pixie face, and her eyes sparkled with pleasure. She flitted her fan at him and said with a laugh, "Where did you disappear to, scoundrel? We hoped you would at least come to collect us." Turning before he could respond, to gaze at her reflection in the glass above the mantel, she tilted her head to one side and went on gaily, "It was a pleasant enough gathering, I'm sure, but we were simply forced in your absence to insist that Dacres escort us home. Was it not kind of him to do so?"

"Look here, Bella," he said sharply, "I thought I had made it plain to you that you need not try to bring Dacres round your thumb. If he has fallen tail over top for Miss Oakley or Theo Adlam, there is no reason for you to make a cake of yourself."

She put her face close to the glass and frowned. "I hope that is not a blemish forming. How vexing! Just when one wants to look one's best." Then, looking over her shoulder at him, she added in an airy tone, "I would have you know, dearest one, that Dacres danced three times with me this evening and only once with pretty little Theo. He did dance twice with Caroline, but she will not dance with any man more than that because she is too afraid someone will disapprove, but of course, no one minds what I do, for they have all known me forever." Tossing her head, she sent him a challenging look, and turned to her mother. "Really, Mama, you look worn to the bone. You must go straight up to bed. I'll go up with you. Ned is not at all amusing tonight. No doubt he had another bad night at the tables."

She took Lady Crawley's arm and had begun to urge her toward the door when Crawley said grimly, "Bella." His tone stopped her, but she did not turn.

"She will be along shortly, Mama," he said.

Lady Crawley gave him a look he could not interpret. He thought she looked relieved, but was not certain why she should be and dismissed the notion once she had left the room. He said, "Shut the door and sit down, Bella. I want to talk to you."

She tossed her head again. "I cannot think why you would wish to do so, for I am merely following your advice. I do not feel at all in the mood for more conversation tonight. It has been a long day, and I wish to go to bed. You were right, by the bye. I had not thought it would be so, but it is. I had a wonderful time tonight. Good night, dearest."

She stood on tiptoe to kiss his cheek and was gone before he thought to stop her. He could not remember any other time that she had disobeyed him. What on earth, he wondered, had come over her that she should do so now? A yawn midthought caught him unaware, and he looked at the clock on the desk. Nearly three. He had promised to take Master Freddy out for his first lesson the next day, after yet another session of playing nursemaid. He had better, he decided, try to get some sleep.

The next morning, when he arrived at Adlam House, he drew his curricle in behind another carriage. Since it was little more than half past eight, he wondered who could possibly be calling so early. When he recognized the device on the door panel as Lady Augusta's, he grew more curious yet.

Bidding a civil good day to the little mongrel, standing guard in his usual position, he went up the steps. Having given his gloves and hat to the butler, he turned automatically toward the parlor, but Heath stopped him. "Miss Felicia would be much obliged if you would step up to the morning room, my lord."

"Certainly," Crawley said, turning toward the stairs. He heard Theo's angry voice before he reached the landing, and the sound quickened his steps.

"He is a villain, I tell you, and I want someone else to do my portrait!"

Felicia wanted to shake her abominable sister. "Theo, please lower your voice."

"Every truth has two sides, my dear Theodosia, and you may criticize others only when you have done some good thing yourself. Pray, do collect yourself."

"I don't want to collect myself, and I will shout if I want to," Theo cried at the top of her lungs.

"Good morning, everyone," Crawley said cheerfully, stepping into the room through the open doorway.

Felicia made no attempt to hide her relief at seeing him. "Good morning, sir," she said. "I fear you have come to attend a Cheltenham tragedy."

"Where's Vyne?" he asked resignedly.

She could not blame him for his tone, but she gave him a quelling look as she opened her mouth to tell him.

Theo snapped, "He has gone, and I hope he never returns! "He is a beast, Crawley, and that is all there is about it."

"What did he do now?" There could be no mistaking the exasperation in his voice.

Felicia managed to speak this time before Theo could do so. "I am afraid he was provoked, sir. No, Theo, hush. Indeed, you have both spoken and done entirely too much this morning. Had you ever before troubled to come downstairs at eight o'clock, you might have learned that Sir Richard always arrives before then. And had you known that, you might not have been caught in the act." A bark of laughter from Crawley made her add coolly, "You may well laugh, sir, for there is no doubt some humor in the situation somewhere; however, I must tell you that I do not see it at the moment."

"A bad temper carries with it its own punishment," Lady Augusta said with unruffled calm.

"Aunt Augusta," Theo began dangerously, "If you say—"

"Be silent," Felicia said.

"I won't! Not if I have to stay here, at all events." And with that and a flounce, she swept past Crawley out of the room.

Felicia sighed. "Do sit down, sir. I should like to know what you think is best to be done next."

"What is this? Are you *asking* for my advice?"

"If you please."

"I should advise you to slap that young woman soundly."

"Hear, hear," Lady Augusta said with a fierce nod.

Felicia bit her lip, feeling that it would be unwise at this juncture to admit that she was sorely tempted. Instead, ruefully she said, "I do not require advice in regard to Theo, sir, as I think you know perfectly well. But you know Sir Richard much better than I do. Will he come back? He has said he will not."

Crawley sat down in a chair near to hers and said more gently, "Perhaps you had better tell me exactly what happened. I collect that she tried to get a look at the portrait."

The memory of it made her wince, but she said with what she thought must be admirable calm, "Theo is determined to see it, and Sir Richard refuses to allow her to do so."

"I am well aware of that," he said. "Do not forget that I spend two hours with them each morning. I believe I have heard most of her demands and nearly all of his refusals."

"Well, today she took matters into her own hands," Felicia said. "Recalling that I had given Sir Richard my key to the parlor, and having already determined that there was no way by which she might otherwise break in—"

"Yes," he murmured, "particularly since the front areaway prevents her from simply climbing in one of the windows."

Certain that it was unnecessary to tell him that her sister, however unprincipled, would never make such a public spectacle of herself, Felicia repressed a shudder at the mental image and said firmly, "Quite so. At all events, she remembered that Mrs. Heath—our housekeeper, you know—has a complete set of keys to the house. Theo simply asked her for the key to the parlor, and Mrs. Heath not knowing any better, gave it to her."

"I see how it was," he said. "Theo didn't do the thing in the middle of the night like a sensible person would have done. Instead, she came down just a bit earlier than usual and got caught in the act. I suppose Dickon was not polite about it."

Lady Augusta laughed harshly. "I walked into the house right behind him, Crawley. The parlor door stood ajar, and I actually saw him grab her just as she was reaching for the cloth over the portrait. I thought for a moment," she added with a look of unholy relish, "that he meant to strangle her."

Felicia was watching Crawley closely, but this time he showed no inclination to laugh. Instead, eyes narrowed, he looked straight at her and said grimly, "My advice holds, but I'll see what I can do to smooth things over with Dickon. I think you can trust him to return simply because he has promised to have that damned painting—forgive me, Lady Augusta—"

"No matter, dear boy. I have heard language before, I assure you. Moreover, I quite agree with your sentiments."

He smiled at her, then said reassuringly to Felicia, "He has promised to show it at the Academy Exhibition, and since Lawrence has defied him to show anything as good as his portrait of the Princess of Wales, it has become a matter of honor, I believe, but I will do what I can to make certain of it."

Felicia sighed. "I should not burden you with my troubles like this, but I do hope you can smooth things over with him."

"Troubles shared are troubles halved," Lady Augusta said.

For a brief moment Felicia had yet another urge to slap someone, and wondered why she, who had never had such urges in her life before, should suddenly be having them so frequently. She chanced to look at Crawley and saw that his eyes were twinkling. He did not smile, but she knew he was amused. Nonetheless, the expression was one of such understanding that it warmed her to the bone, much as a caress would have done. For a long moment, she could not look away. Her gaze was pinned to his, as if some power beyond her own were controlling it.

"It is no burden," he said suddenly.

She heard his voice as if it came from a great distance. Blinking, she fought to collect her wits and, rushing her words, said, "Thank you. Though my sister's megrims are no concern of yours, I shall be most grateful if you can bring Sir Richard back. I will attend to Theo. You may tell him she will not attempt again to see the portrait. He threatened in the course of his diatribe to remove it to his own house, and to make her go there for her sittings. But though I know people do go to artists' homes to sit, my father would have a seizure if Theo ever did such a thing. She is his primary interest, you know, outside of his Vernis Martin vases, his coins, and his wine."

"Another collector's item, in fact," Crawley said.

"Why, no, that was not what I meant at all," Felicia said, but she was stricken by a sudden awareness that he was right. Her father did indeed look upon his younger daughter as a prize piece in an otherwise ordinary collection of children. He had some feeling for her brother, Jack, as his heir, and therefore for Jack's children, but he showed little interest in them, and none whatever in her. She saw that Crawley was watching her, and added quickly, "You are absurd, sir. I merely meant that because Papa has a concern for her, he would notice what she did—indeed, I should feel obliged to tell him—and he would never allow it. Nor would Theo go to Sir Richard's house," she added bluntly.

"Have you the housekeeper's key?" he asked.

"Sir Richard has taken it," she said.

"Then I doubt I will have any trouble convincing him to return." He turned to Lady Augusta. "But surely you, ma'am, did not come out at such an untimely hour merely to be an audience at what sounds like a rather tawdry brawl."

She chuckled. "No, I could not sleep for thinking about those dratted invitations, and that is why I am here. What are we going to do, Felicity? I cannot and will not allow my guest list to be printed in the newspaper like the doings of Parliament or, worse, the proceedings of a Magistrate's Court. It is one thing to have an account of one's social engagements printed after the fact, but aside from one's proper feelings of disgust at such a public display, Lady Thomond was quite right about the delicacy of it. Even if we wait until the day before and hope they get the list printed on the day, suppose we have not had all our responses by then? One cannot print names of persons who have not said they will come, for one would be accused of puffing off one's consequence in a most unseemly manner. And what if the *Times* were inadvertently to omit a name? Only think how offended that person would be!"

"He would merely think he had got a forged one, would he not?" Crawley asked in a tone clearly meant to be pacific.

But Lady Augusta was having none of that. "Merely? When he would still be offended to think he had been left off my list? Just suppose it were Langshire, for goodness' sake!"

"The *Times* would never omit the duke," Crawley said.

"Very likely they would not, but do not tell me that his grace will enjoy seeing his name listed with a host of other guests meaning to attend a ball."

"His name is printed every time he attends a Levee or a Drawing Room, is it not?" Crawley said.

Felicia shook her head. "That is not Aunt Augusta's point, sir. Such names are printed after the event. She is concerned lest it look as if we are puffing off the fact that a duke means to attend our ball."

"Langshire is small beer compared to the Prince of Wales," Crawley said with a grin.

Lady Augusta said tartly, "I wish you will keep to the point, my lord. I did not send the prince an invitation."

"But Prinny knows Vyne means to put his portrait of Miss Theo up against Lawrence's of the Princess of Wales, and I heard at Brooks's that he wants to see both portraits. Since he knows perfectly well that Dickon would not show his to the king himself before it is done, I should not be at all surprised if he decides to look in at your ball just to get an early look at it."

"It would be just like that officious fellow Townshend to bar the door, too," Lady Augusta said, "for I have already arranged with him to attend, you know. It is quite the thing to invite him. Everyone is doing so."

"Well, no one knows Prinny as well as Townshend does," Crawley said, glancing at Felicia. "I assure you, he would not suspect a forged invitation, nor would it occur to him to ask to see the prince's if he did. You are very quiet, Miss Adlam. I have promised you that Vyne will return. You may trust me."

Startled, Felicia said, "I cannot imagine how you manage to read one's thoughts as you do, sir. How did you know I was thinking about that just now?"

He smiled again. "Since your brow became all furrowed when I mentioned the prince's desire to see the portrait, it did not take a great deal of imagination to deduce that you were worried lest the portrait not be finished. Shall I put your mind at rest and go and wrestle with Dickon at once, or shall I first take that abominable young rascal Freddy out for his promised drive?"

"Oh, please, take Freddy. How very kind you are, sir! He has been in alt ever since you mentioned teaching him to drive. He was here when I came down this morning, demanding to know when you would take him. I sent him to Miss Ames, telling him he must wait there and do his lessons properly until you called for him, but I daresay he has accomplished little in the meantime."

Lady Augusta snorted. "There is a time and place for everything, Felicia, and that child don't deserve a reward."

Chuckling, Crawley said, "Now, Lady Augusta, you will agree that no act of kindness, no matter how small, is ever wasted. Send for the brat at once, Miss Adlam, and I will do what I can to keep him out of your hair for an hour or so."

She thanked him and rang for a footman to collect Freddy, who came running into the room a few short minutes later, demanding to know if Scraps could ride with them. When Crawley, responding with a flat negative, had taken him away, Felicia said to Lady Augusta, "His lordship is very kind, is he not, ma'am?"

"He is a rake and a fortune hunter, but women always love a rake, and I doubt you will fall victim to his charm, my dear."

"I own, I am not so sure of that," Felicia said. "It was much easier to deal with him when I thought he wanted only Theo."

"More fool he."

"He knew from the outset that she is an heiress, you see."

"And now he knows that you are, as well?"

Felicia nodded.

"I do see. Do you know, my dear, I had always heard that the Crawleys were very well to pass. I am certain there was never even the breath of a rumor that the old lord had run through his fortune, and the estates in Nottinghamshire are still very much in the family, I believe."

Felicia smiled. "His friends all say that Crawley would be much better off if he would merely attend to his business, but I collect that that is the last thing he wishes to do. He says life in the country bores him, and blames his ill fortune on wicked stewards and his father's ill-timed death."

"Then he has simply frittered away his fortune. Not a good prospect, Felicity, my dear, but I am not blind, you know. I saw how you looked at him."

Felicia flushed. "I find him charming, to be sure, ma'am, but I have no doubt that it is just as you say, and I have merely fallen for his charming ways. I will not do anything foolish."

"No, my dear," Lady Augusta said with a deep sigh, "I am very much afraid you never will."

"Oh, Aunt! As if it would be admirable if I did!"

Lady Augusta smiled at her. "I suppose I sound ridiculous. Forgive me. There is another thing you must forgive as well, I'm afraid. I have asked that Townshend fellow to attend me here. You will say I am foolish, but I cannot like a man of his cut coming to my house, where there is no gentleman to protect me."

Felicia smiled. "I am certain he is harmless, ma'am."

"To be sure, but one never wants to risk one's reputation, and you know how quickly some people will talk."

"At all events, there is no reason he should not attend you here. I find him most amusing."

Townshend arrived before Crawley and Freddy had returned, and was shown to the drawing room, where Lady Augusta and Felicia went to talk with him. In his inimitable fashion, he explained that he would hold himself responsible for the valuables in Lady Augusta's home, and see that no one entered who was not invited.

Felicia said, "We must tell you, Mr. Townshend, that my aunt cannot agree to let her guest list be published in the *Times*."

Lady Augusta said grandly, "Entirely too public the *Times* is, Mr. Townshend, as I am sure you will agree."

"I do, mum," Townshend agreed, folding his hands over his plump little paunch. "Very public. That be the point of it, don't you see? The more coves as know the list is published, the less likely you be to have folks coming in unwanted."

"Yes, I quite see that, but I still cannot allow it," Lady Augusta said firmly. "That is all there is to say."

"Very well, mum, but we must have a plan then."

"To be sure," she agreed, "and one good plan that works is better than a hundred doubtful ones."

Townshend blinked, and turned to Felicia. "Perhaps you might explain, mum. Have you a plan in mind already?"

She said, "My aunt will use her crested cards for the invitations, just as Lady Crofton did. That should make them quite easy to check, and I do not think she would object to a small notice in the papers, informing people that they will be admitted by invitation only, so everyone will bring them."

"Still there will be some as forgets," Townshend pointed out. "I'll want a list handy to cast my gazers over whenever some young blade comes up a-saying he forgot his invite. And I'll want to see your invitations before you send them out," he added. "Have you got one of them cards by you now, mum?"

"I do." Lady Augusta extracted a white card from her indispensable and handed it to him.

Townshend nodded. "Pretty engraving." He pulled a handful of similar cards from his coat pocket. "The ones as were the most difficult to detect were these, without personal crests or proper engraving. But look here, at Lady Westfall's card. Do you think that was a forgery?" He handed it to Felicia.

She looked at it, gave it to her aunt, and shook her head. "I do not know Lady Westfall's hand, but that looks like a proper invitation with a properly engraved crest," she said.

Townshend turned to Lady Augusta, who gave him back the card with a puzzled look on her face. "It does," she said.

"Every one of these"—Townshend waved the fistful of cards—"is a fake. The hand as writes them don't matter a whisker, for nearly everyone has a secretary, a friend, or family member what helps write the invitations; and, as you see by the Westfall card, an engraved crest ain't enough. I'll just leave these with you now, so that you can have a look-see. On the back of each one is the way we nipped out the fakes. Regarding the Westfall invite, it will say Lady Westfall's name ought to have been wrote first on each one. You do something like that. Choose words that'll be quick to notice, and that a forger mightn't think to write. Then hope the forger don't copy it all from a real one, and don't go blabbing to anyone what you did, see!"

Lady Augusta bristled, and Felicia said quickly, "We will be careful. Is there anything else, Mr. Townshend?"

He assured her that there was not, that he would look after everything just as he did for the Prince of Wales whenever that worthy demanded his services. At last Felicia was able to ring to have him shown out. Her aunt left shortly afterward, her feelings only slightly less ruffled than they had been, and with a sigh Felicia went upstairs to confer with her housekeeper.

When Freddy came to find her sometime later, he was aglow with his accomplishments. "He let me drive in the park, Aunt Felicia, and I did everything just as he told me. He said I was a bang-up driver, and that I had the lightest hands he'd ever seen in a lad my age. What do you think of that?"

She assured him that she was very proud of him, and he went on telling her in exact detail about every minute of the drive from Scraps's indignantly vocal protest at their departure without him, to his equally clamorous remarks upon their return. Only when Freddy chanced to mention that Crawley had sent him upstairs to finish his studies did she realize that he had left out one rather important detail.

"Is his lordship still in the house, Freddy?"

"Oh, yes, he is waiting in the drawing room. I told Peters I would fetch you so he needn't do so," he added casually.

"Well, then you ought to have done so straightaway, you unnatural boy. I must go down at once and hope his lordship does not think I have been snubbing him on purpose."

She entered the drawing room a few moments later to find Crawley standing just inside the doorway, looking down at the side table where Townshend had left the invitations.

"Oh, goodness," Felicia said, "I never meant to leave those there. I'll just put them in the drawer of my writing table." She collected them and put them away, turning back to him to ask, "Was there something in particular you wanted of me, sir?"

He had been watching her rather closely, she thought, but he smiled and said, "I was hoping for a reward for letting that dratted boy tool me all over Hyde Park. We saw Dickon driving his brutish chestnuts with Lawrence beside him, clinging to his seat for dear life whenever they shied at oncoming carriages or a sudden noise. Lord, but those horses are poorly trained! He's no business to have them in Town at all, but it will do no good to search him out just now, and I thought a change of company would be pleasant. May I take you for a drive, ma'am?"

Delighted, she told him she would just run upstairs to fetch her pelisse and be with him directly.

11

THE NEXT few days passed quickly, for Felicia's obligations included not only the usual family and household duties, but the laying-in of an unexpected shipment of wine from Oakley and Campion, a task that took several hours, since Lord Adlam, though extremely particular, saw no reason to exert himself when he could simply ask her to oversee its bestowal. And every spare minute between duties and engagements seemed to be spent in final fittings for new gowns. The Season was now in full swing, and both Adlam sisters required gowns for their aunt's ball and the opening of Almack's Assembly Rooms, as well as complete court dresses for the upcoming Drawing Room, where Lady Augusta was to present Theo to the queen.

The one thing Felicia did not have to worry about was the portrait, for true to his word, Crawley brought Sir Richard back to the house the very next day, and Theo, seeming chastened for the moment—or resigned—behaved, as far as her sister could tell, with all propriety and decorum.

The sisters did find time for an afternoon's shopping, and Felicia enjoyed two rides in the park with Crawley, although being forced to keep her mount to a walk or a trot made her wish it were possible to transport herself to Bradstoke just long enough for one wild gallop across the moors. She rather envied Freddy his daily lessons, too, for she thought learning to drive a curricle must be fun. She was kept entirely too busy to dwell for long on such thoughts, however.

At the queen's Drawing Room, Theo was in alt, and Felicia was pleased to see her in her finest looks. Both wore the requisite formal court dress with hoops, yards of lace, and white ostrich feathers in their headdresses. Theo's gown was white with gilded trimming and pale blue ribbons, and Felicia wore a pink satin half dress, its skirt opening in the front and descending in points over a white muslin underskirt.

"I never expected to see so many people," Theo said, gazing about in awe as they passed through one of the many state rooms of Queen's House leading into the famous State Drawing Room.

Lady Augusta fluttered her fan at the heat. "Since it is the first court day since his majesty's recovery from his illness, it is scarcely surprising that so many should attend."

"I had hoped to see the Princess of Wales," Theo said, smoothing a crease in one long, white silk glove.

Felicia smiled at her. "Concerned lest the Royal Academy select her portrait over yours, my dear?"

"Not at all," Theo said, laughing. "In point of fact, I heard that she is suffering from a mild indisposition and has been unable to sit for Mr. Lawrence for several days. I should not like my portrait to be chosen only because hers was not entered. I want everyone to know which is the best one."

Lady Augusta snorted. "Mighty sure of yourself, I must say, but self-conceit leads only to self-destruction, and it don't do to outshine royalty. You would be well served if her highness suddenly took it into her head to demand to see you, to determine if you were much to fret over. Then where would you be?"

Theo grinned saucily at her. "Why, I suppose I should be at Blackheath, ma'am. Is that not where she is living at present? I could not be so rude as to dismiss such a request, surely."

Lady Augusta shook her head in exasperation. "Let us move forward, so that we are not missed in the crush. There are to be several presentations, and you will not be the first, Theodosia. I believe that Viscountess Methuen is to have that honor."

"Who is she?" Theo demanded.

Lady Augusta shrugged. "Irish."

Felicia had been watching the gathering throng and paid no heed to the ensuing discussion of who was or was not present. From what she could see, nearly everyone who was anyone was there. She saw at least four dukes, including Langshire, and two marquesses whom she remembered from her previous

Season. But there were many other lords and ladies, most of
the political men, and all the new members of the administration, who had taken office a few days before, after Mr. Pitt's
resignation. She nodded and smiled to those she knew, and before long her party was joined by Lady Crawley and Belinda,
who had arrived shortly after them with Lady Dacres, Mrs.
Falworthy, and Miss Oakley.

Felicia had been presented during her first Season, so she
stayed with Lady Dacres while Belinda and Theo went on
with Lady Augusta and Lady Crawley. Mrs. Falworthy and
Miss Oakley remained with her, for Miss Oakley, though ac-
corded the privilege of attending the Drawing Room, did not
expect to be presented.

There were quite a number of presentations, as Lady Augusta had predicted, including six young ladies enjoying their
first Season, a captain of the navy on his appointment as a new
Lord of the Admiralty, and a stern-looking gentleman who
was announced to be the New Equerry to her majesty's son,
the Duke of Cumberland. By the time each member of the new
administration had been presented and allowed to kiss the
royal hand, the room was hot and stuffy, and by the time the
court officially closed at five o'clock, Felicia felt as though
she could scarcely breathe. But she soon learned that the
court's closing meant only that the queen and royal princesses
were departing. The rest of the company did not even begin to
leave the palace until after six.

Theo was displeased that neither Sir Richard nor Lord
Crawley had been among those attending the Drawing Room.
"I should have liked them both to see me in my finery," she
said, as they waited for her ladyship's carriage to draw up before the long red carpet laid along the walk leading from the
circular drive to the main entrance.

Belinda, close behind them, said, "I daresay we shall see
Dickon Saturday at Lady Castlereagh's ball, but Ned has gone
out of town. His friend Thorne was leaving today for Langshire, and Ned said something about riding to Watford with
him to watch a mill since he was not expected at Adlam House
this morning. Sir Richard can do no more work on your portrait, he said, until the background oils are completely dry."

Felicia smiled. "It was as well that Sir Richard did not want Theo to sit today. We have scarcely had a spare moment."

Theo tossed her head. "I told him a week ago that he needn't think I would sit today, or that I would be available the morning after the opening of Almack's, for I intend to stay until they put the orchestra to bed."

Felicia, assuring herself that she inquired only to prevent further such comments—unfortunately too easily overheard by others waiting for their carriages—said quickly to Belinda, "Did you say that your brother had left town?"

Belinda nodded. "He is free now, he said, to go about his own business for a few days. I think he and Thorne mean to go on to Newmarket for the races, and I think that Perry—that is, Lord Dawlish—must have gone with them today, though he never said he meant to do so. I had expected to see him here."

Felicia noted a look of self-consciousness on Belinda's face, and the younger girl avoided her gaze for a moment before she seemed to realize that she was doing so and made a visible effort to collect herself. Smiling at her, Felicia said, "No doubt there are matters of importance to occupy all three gentlemen. Sir Richard has frequently said he has any number of things he can do when Theo cannot sit for him."

"A comment clearly meant to depress my consequence," Theo said, tossing her head again, "but I happen to know that since the Princess of Wales has been unable to sit for Lawrence, Sir Richard thinks there will be no portrait to match mine. That, if you must know the truth, is why I was hoping to see her today. I want to see that man's crest lowered a bit, that's all."

They did see Sir Richard at Lady Castlereagh's ball two nights later, and by that time Felicia was able to provide Mr. Townshend with a copy of the invitation that had been sent out to their guests. The three ladies, and Lady Adlam, had argued and fretted over the exact wording for days, but when Felicia had recalled that all anyone need do was get hold of the invitation and copy it, they decided at last to seek some other method of foiling the forger.

"Such invitations are always written on cream-colored or

white cards, are they not?" Felicia said. "Aunt Augusta, would it be entirely unthinkable to use another color?"

Lady Augusta frowned. "It is simply not done, my dear."

Theo said, "Pink!"

Lady Adlam, reclining in comfort on a sofa with a blanket over her feet, sighed. "Oh, how pretty they would be, my love, but I do not think you ought to. So noticeable, you know."

Lady Augusta snapped, "That would not do at all."

"Oh, but it might do very well, ma'am," Felicia said. "Only think if we used gilt-edged pink cards and similar colors for our decorations. The ballroom in your house has pink and gold paper on the walls, does it not?" Seeing with relief that her aunt was at least willing to consider the notion, she pressed on, "Only think how your party will stand out from all the others if we tell all the ladies to wear at least a touch of pink, and provide pink nosegays for the gentlemen to pin on their lapels. You have already let it be known that Theo's portrait will be unveiled. We can use a pink satin drape for the easel, and tell the chef to use pink in the refreshments wherever he can. And with gilt-edged pink cards, surely the forger—whoever it is— would not dare try to copy them, for the stationers would know in an instant what must be the purpose. And everyone else would think we had been amazingly clever. Don't you agree?"

Lady Augusta did not agree at once, but in the end she had done so, and the cards had been ordered and laboriously inscribed in the elegant copperplate they all did so well.

Mr. Townshend was justifiably pleased with them, and Felicia was conscious of a wish that Crawley could be at hand to see that she had come up with an excellent notion without the least bit of advice from him. But the fact was that she missed him, and she wondered how long he meant to stay out of town. The Castlereagh ball was pleasant, and she danced frequently, as always, but it was not nearly so much fun as those parties to which Crawley and his friends had escorted them.

When Dawlish approached her midway through the evening, she greeted him with undisguised pleasure. "We had thought you must have gone out of town with Crawley," she told him, accepting his invitation to step outside for some fresh air.

The doors stood open, and there were others enjoying the coolness of the late evening on the broad brick terrace. The garden below had been lit by torches, and a silvery moon hovered overhead, casting its glow on the scene.

Dawlish drew Felicia a little to one side and said bluntly, "I say, Miss Adlam, is there aught awry with Miss Crawley? She has begun behaving in the most peculiar fashion. Her mama has noticed it. I've noticed it. Dashed well everyone has noticed."

Felicia could not pretend she did not understand him, for she, too, had been aware for some time that Belinda Crawley's behavior had altered, and not for the better. "I think, perhaps, she has merely become more confident of herself now that the Season has begun in earnest, sir. The first few weeks are always a bit unnerving for a young girl, you know."

"Dash it, ma'am, it ain't like it's her first season. I could understand it if it were Theo—Miss Theodosia—who were doing the changing. She *is* in her first, though, watching her hold court at every event she attends, no one would guess it. If it weren't for Vyne insisting she get her beauty sleep, and throwing fits, by what I hear, when she don't, Miss Theo would be the belle of the Season. But only look at Belinda." He seemed unaware that he had used her first name. "Why, there she is over there with that rascal Dacres, preening and flirting with her fan like a doxy. That won't do. Where the devil is Ned, that he don't stop her from making such a cake of herself. Dash it, I'm going to speak to her myself."

"Yes," Felicia said, beginning to enjoy herself, "you go and do that, my lord. I see Sir Richard, there by the window. I'll let him take me back inside, so you need not concern yourself."

It was just as well she did not easily take offense, since he had clearly forgotten her and already had taken several steps toward Belinda and Dacres. He was not deaf, however, and reminded, he turned quickly back, apologized, and motioned to Vyne to join them. No sooner had the artist done so, however, than Dawlish excused himself and hurried away.

"Enjoying yourself, Miss Adlam?"

She chuckled. "I think Dawlish has a stronger interest in Miss Crawley than he admits, don't you, sir?"

Vyne shrugged. "Won't do him any good. Belinda has decided to marry into great wealth. Dawlish wasn't born in a cottage, and his connections are excellent, but she thinks of him as a brother, you know, not as a suitor."

"That can change, sir, in the blink of an eye."

"Perhaps. Women are notoriously fickle."

"And men are not?"

He looked at her shrewdly. "Any particular man we might be discussing, or just men in general?"

Feeling warmth in her cheeks, she said with forced calm, "Certainly in general, sir. I merely made an observation. Men can be quite as fickle and rude, or as sensitive and frail as women can be. To separate feelings and emotions by sex has always seemed to me to be absurd. People are simply people."

"No doubt." His attention was clearly wandering. He collected himself with visible effort and said, "Your sister will stay up much too late, knowing she need not sit in the morning, but do not let her continue to fatigue herself unduly, or it will show in the painting. If it is to be finished in time for your aunt's ball, I cannot spend a great deal of time trying to recapture the look I want from sketches. It will be easier if she can pose, but she must look her best."

"How much is left to be done?"

"Only the final touches to the figure itself, and the glazing. Had to leave the gown till last, because it is white—I explained about that—and will take a deal of time to dry." He looked sharply at her. "I'd like your word, ma'am, that Miss Theodosia will have no new opportunity to get into that room."

"No, she has promised, sir, and Theo does not break her word when she gives it to me."

He studied her for a moment, seemed satisfied, and nodded. They went back into the ballroom, and Vyne left her with Lady Augusta, who also had comments to make about Theo, but Felicia was accustomed to her aunt's ways, and paid little heed to them. She had grown bored with the evening, and was quite willingly discussing the possibility of going on to Lady Hawthorne's drum when Dawlish approached, looking harassed, and said he must speak with her again at once.

"Devil of a thing, ma'am," he said, scarcely waiting until

they had moved a little distance from the others. "Can't understand it, but the fat is dashed well in the fire now, because Belinda thinks I have asked her to marry me!"

"Good gracious, sir, how came that about?"

"Dashed if I know," he said. "I was telling her that in my own opinion she ought not to be flirting so outrageously, or behaving as if she were a diamond of the first water, tossing her head and treating other folk like peasants, and when she demanded to know what business it was of mine, I said I dashed well wished her papa were still alive, because then I should know what to do about it, and dashed if she didn't say she couldn't think what I was about to be proposing marriage to her in such a slapdash way! Now, dash it, I ask you, ma'am, did that sound like a proposal?"

Felicia had all she could do to contain her amusement, but she managed it, and said, "Well, sir, you did say you wished you could speak with her father. Generally, when a young man wants to speak to a lady's father, it is to ask for her hand. And perhaps Belinda knows that you care for her."

"But I don't!"

"Don't you?"

He stared. "Well, not in that— Oh, good God, Miss Adlam, you don't know what you are saying. Ned will cut out my liver if I have led Bella to think I want to marry her."

"But don't you?"

He let out a long breath and nodded. "Made up my mind years ago that if I couldn't have Bella, I'd never marry. But Ned won't hear of it. Wants her to marry for money even more than she wants it, and he clearly don't think I've got enough. Stands to reason, don't it? As good as warned me off her, didn't he?"

"Did he?"

"Yes, by heaven, he did."

"I see. Well, perhaps you and Miss Crawley ought to have a real talk, sir, and find out what the pair of you want before this goes much further. It is possible that you are mistaken, and if you are not, there still may be a way out of the mire."

He sighed. "I suppose you are right. One hesitates, however, to annoy Ned, particularly just now when he has other things on his mind."

"More debts, I suppose," Felicia said with a sigh.

Dawlish looked at her as though he would deny the charge, but he seemed to have second thoughts and said merely, when Lady Augusta was seen to be approaching them in a purposeful manner, that Felicia might do well to take some of her own advice.

Lady Augusta had come to tell her they were ready to depart for Lady Hawthorne's house, and Felicia did not see Dawlish again that evening. In the days that followed, she had no time to consider anything beyond her own engagements and the preparations for their ball. Crawley did not return for Theo's next sitting, sending word from Newmarket that he would be delayed, and they did not hear from him again for some time.

Felicia, believing that he had got tired of playing nursemaid, decided he had more interesting things to do, but she expected daily to see him at one of their engagements or riding in the park. He did not return, however, even for the opening of Almack's, and she found the evening deadly dull, having no interest in flirting, which was the main pastime at the famous subscription balls. Indeed, London had begun to seem tiresome.

Much time in the days before the ball was spent at Lady Augusta's large house in Upper Brook Street, helping her make decisions regarding a myriad of last-minute details; and then, several days before the date, a new crisis occurred.

Theo came running to find Felicia. "Did we not send an invitation to Caroline Oakley?"

"Yes, of course, we did."

"Well, she never received it. I met Belinda in the park, and she told me Caro is afraid she has offended us."

The same afternoon, when Felicia received a demand from her aunt to know what had become of the invitations for the Ladies Crofton and Thomond, since they had not received them, she realized something was truly amiss, and remembering what had occurred with her letter from Bradstoke to Lady Augusta, sent an inquiry to the post office to ask if some similar incident had prevented the invitations from being delivered. Receiving a reply with her morning post and opening it to read a dignified disclaimer, she exclaimed, "The post office knows nothing about them. I cannot understand it, for the entire lot was set out in the hall and collected at once. What can have happened to them?"

Theo and Freddy were her only companions, the latter having come in but minutes before to suggest that since Lord Crawley had given up taking him driving, perhaps Miss Ames might escort him and Sara Ann to see the wild beasts at the Tower menagerie. Upon hearing Felicia's exclamation, he immediately assumed an expression of angelic innocence and said, "Happened to what, Aunt Felicia? Has something gone missing?"

Noting the look, Felicia watched him carefully and said, "A good number of the invitations to our ball have gone missing, Freddy. Can you think what might have happened to them?"

"How would I know about any old invitations?"

The innocent look was more intense than ever, but Felicia had begun to note that Master Freddy took care not to be caught in any outright lie, so she said quietly, "Do you know?"

His cheeks grew red, and he looked away from her.

"Freddy?"

He shrugged.

Theo said angrily, "You little beast, where are they?"

"Theo." Felicia quelled her with a look, then turned back to the little boy and said, "Freddy, I think you must tell us the truth, you know. This is a very serious matter."

He looked at her for a long moment, then said, "I'll get them." Turning on his heel, he ran out, and a moment later, they heard his footsteps clattering on the upper flight of stairs.

Theo said grimly, "I wish Jack and Nan would come to collect that little wretch. Really, Felicia, it is a wonder he has not burned us in our beds merely to see what it might be like. That is always the reason he gives for his mischief."

Felicia hoped Theo was wrong, but when Freddy handed her a stack of invitations minutes later, and she demanded that he explain himself, he shrugged and said, "I saw them sitting on the hall table waiting for the postman, and I just moved some of them to my bedchamber for a while to see what would happen."

Conscious of a wish that not Jack or Nan but Crawley were at hand to give this child his just deserts, Felicia struggled to remain calm and said through gritted teeth, "Freddy, you have been very naughty. You simply must not do such dreadful things."

"I didn't know it would make you angry. Are you going to send us back to India now?"

She stared at him. "Is that what you want? Is that why you do the dreadful things you do?"

"No. At home no one ever told me what was wanted. I had to find out for myself, and when we were in the way there, our papa and mama sent us to you. There is nowhere to send us from here but back to them, is there?"

"School," Theo told him. "The new term begins in a week, thank the good Lord, and I hope your masters beat you often."

"I should think they probably will," Freddy said with a sigh. Then, looking pensively at Felicia, he added, "I expect this is not a good time to mention that you still have not said if Miss Ames may take us to the Tower."

Felicia was conscious of an overwhelming desire to lose her temper. Really, she thought, repressing it with difficulty, civility was becoming a great deal more taxing than it ever had been before. She said carefully, "Not only is it not a good time, Freddy, but you must tell Miss Ames that although Sara Ann and Tom may go if they wish to do so, you are to have no treats at all until after the ball. Do you understand me?"

He nodded, looking serious but not, she thought, particularly chastened. Sending him to repeat her message to the governess and then to retire to his bedchamber to think about his sins, she sighed, and said to Theo, "I do not know what to make of that child. I cannot believe he truly means to be wicked, but it is as if he had no sense of right or wrong."

Theo nodded. "Tom told me once that Jack and Nan left the children entirely to the servants to raise, and the servants generally allowed them to do as they pleased. Tom, being the eldest, has always felt some responsibility to the younger children, and of course Sara Ann is just a baby by comparison, but Freddy feels no responsibility to anyone. School will be the making of him, I think," she added with a wise look.

Felicia frowned. "Crawley said the same thing, and I think his reasoning was much like yours, that he hoped they would beat proper behavior into him. But I cannot wish for that,

Theo. I want him to learn that his behavior makes a difference, both to himself and to those of us who love him."

Theo shrugged and turned the subject back to the invitations. Felicia decided to send footmen to deliver those addressed to persons most likely to be offended by the delay and to entrust the rest to the post. In the days that followed she had no time to miss Crawley, but she did note that Freddy's behavior was irreproachable. He tended to his lessons and was such a model of rectitude that Miss Ames expressed herself astonished and even Lady Adlam commented upon the change.

"He can be such a pleasant little fellow," she said to Felicia and Theo two afternoons before the ball, when they were counting replies to their invitations and inscribing a flattering number of acceptances on their guest list.

Felicia, knowing well that this encomium derived from nothing more than Freddy's having taken five minutes to hunt for his grandmother's vinaigrette, which Lady Adlam had managed to mislay in moving from the sofa in her sitting room to the one in the drawing room, felt no compelling urge to encourage this change of attitude, knowing it could easily alter again in the space of an hour. She agreed merely that Freddy had shown a good deal of kindness in searching for the vinaigrette.

Lord Adlam, who was perusing his afternoon post at the writing table, diverted her attention just then by saying in a tone of outrage, "Whatever can they be thinking of now?"

"What is it, Papa?"

He clicked his tongue angrily. "That rascal Bonaparte. If he forces the Portuguese to expel the English wine merchants from Oporto and Lisbon, the English trade there will fail altogether, since the Portuguese will be glad to get it into their own hands. His man in Lisbon wants to ship as soon as possible. They have thirty-six thousand pounds' worth of wine there—a good bit of it mine—and would be glad to remove it, but their man is afraid of being stopped if he attempts it."

"But I thought your wine had already been delivered, Papa."

"Pooh, nonsense, that was only what was left of a very fine cellar after the collector died. This is the best Portuguese wine I'm talking about, Felicity. We may never get any more!"

Fortunately, since she could think of nothing intelligent to say to soothe his outrage, Peters entered just then to announce the arrival of Mr. Townshend.

"I will come down to him, Peters," she said. But her father had paid attention for once and demanded to know who was this fellow Townshend to intrude at such a moment.

"A Bow Street man, Papa," she said calmly.

"Bow Street? Have nothing to do with him!"

"But I must. He is to provide security for Aunt Augusta's ball, and I collect that he has something to discuss with me."

"Not suitable," Adlam said testily. "Bring the fellow up here if we must see him at all, Peters. Not right my daughter should entertain a fellow of his stamp alone."

Felicia protested. "I am certain he would prefer a more private interview, sir. Perhaps if you and I were to see him downstairs. Mama will not wish to be disturbed."

"Nonsense, do her good to be disturbed. What are you waiting for, Peters? Show him up at once."

Peters fled, and Felicia, exchanging a speaking glance with Theo, accepted the inevitable.

Townshend was shown in a few moments later and displayed not the least discomfort at finding an audience awaiting him. Making a profound leg to Lady Adlam and another to his lordship, he turned with a businesslike air to Felicia and said, "It's done the business, Miss Adlam, just as we'd hoped it would. The culprit is known. The question is what to do now."

"What do you mean?" demanded Adlam. "Do you understand him, Theo, love? Felicity, what is the man nattering about?"

"I believe he has unmasked the person who has been forging invitations to *ton* parties, Papa. Is that it, Mr. Townshend?"

"That's it," the runner replied. "Nabbed her at the stationer's, just as I'd hoped, ordering cards. Had the nerve to inform the chap that Lady Augusta had misjudged the number of cards required, and had asked her to collect a few more. I'd had a word with the stationer beforehand, of course, and he kept her waiting whilst he sent for your humble servant."

Felicia, realizing that he was enjoying their suspense, said crisply, "A woman? Pray, who is it?"

He glanced at Theo. "Don't mind telling you, I suspected a few, but never this one."

Theo glared back at him. "I suppose you thought it was me."

"Don't say I didn't. Soon saw it was Lady Augusta got the invites, though, and wouldn't no one leave her off a guest list."

Felicia chuckled. "Oh, Theo, what a coup for you! You may tell all your friends you were a suspect. Won't they tease you!"

Theo's smile was crooked. "Sir Richard already said he wouldn't put such a thing past me, but that was because he was cross with me at the time. And, anyway, Crawley told him to stop talking nonsense. Said he had a good notion who the culprit was, and it was not Miss Theodosia Adlam. So there!"

Lord Adlam said curtly, "Suspected my Theo?" Nonsense. You must be mad, Townshend, if you ever thought my lovely daughter would do such a thing.

Theo said, "He just told us he knew it wasn't me, Papa. And Sir Richard isn't mad, either, not in the least, but I wonder if Crawley really knows who it is. Do you think he does, Felicia?"

Suddenly remembering the morning Townshend had left the fake invitations with her, that she had walked back into the room to find Crawley looking them over, Felicia said with a small gasp, "Good gracious, perhaps he thinks I'm the forger!" When everyone laughed, she explained, adding, "He gave me the oddest look, but I did not think much about it then. Now, I wonder."

"Well," Theo said soothingly, "he will soon know who the real forger is. Who is it, Mr. Townshend? Goodness, the person will be completely ruined."

"As to that, miss, it is no more than she deserves, but you could have knocked me over with a feather, for why the sister of someone as grand as Lady Dacres wants to go and do such a—"

"Mrs. Falworthy!" Theo and Felicia spoke at once.

"The very same. And mighty upset she was, too, to be confronted. But I'm at a loss for what to do with her now, I can tell you, for there is no law against what she has done. If a robbery had taken place as a result of them forgeries, well that would be a different matter altogether, but—"

"Good God," Theo said, looking in dismay at Felicia, "this is dreadful, Felicia. Poor Caroline!"

Lady Adlam, speaking for the first time since Townshend's arrival, reached for her salts and said in a wavering tone, "Who is Caroline? Really, Theo, darling, you make my head ache with all these names. Do I know this Mrs. Falworthy?"

"I don't know," Theo said. "She is Lady Dacres's sister."

"Oh, yes, a grasping sort, as I recall, and rather foolish. No doubt she deserves to be ruined."

"Perhaps she does, but Caroline does not," Theo said, "and she will be ruined by association, for it must look as though the whole had been done for her benefit, since Mrs. Falworthy has been sponsoring her. Caroline is Miss Oakley, Mama, and her—"

"Oakley? Oakley?" Lord Adlam gave them his full attention now. "Look here, is her father in the wine trade?"

Felicia stared at him. "Oakley and Campion. Of course, but I don't know, sir. Mr. Oakley is something in the city, to be sure, but I do not think we were ever told just what it is he does. He is very plump in the pocket. That I do know."

"Must be John Oakley of Golden Square. Dammit, send that fellow Townshend away directly, Felicity. You can't make trouble for Oakley's daughter. He's got to get me my wine!"

12

IN THE END it was decided that for Miss Oakley's sake, Townshend would simply inform Mrs. Falworthy that she must withdraw her sponsorship of the girl at once on the excuse of failing health, and then absent herself from Town for the rest of the Season. If she agreed to these conditions, then nothing more would be said and her identity would remain unknown to the rest of the *beau monde*. If, however, she did not agree, Mr. Townshend was to threaten to make it his business to make certain that everyone soon learned the exact identity of the forger.

Lady Adlam was confused. "I do not understand, Felicia," she said with a sigh. "Surely, if this Miss Oakley is a friend of yours, you did not omit her name or that of her patroness from your guest list."

Not wanting to demolish Freddy's recently earned credit with his grandmother, Felicia shot a warning look at Theo and said, "Through an oversight, Mama, some of the invitations were misplaced and not delivered when they ought to have been."

"And," Theo added, "we know Mrs. Falworthy's was amongst them, because Caroline's invitation was inscribed with hers and Caroline told Belinda she had not been invited. One supposes that Mrs. Falworthy was determined for them to come anyway, but she must know we'd recall not having sent them a card!"

Townshend, who had not departed yet, despite his host's rancor, said, "Didn't matter, miss. Meant to declare she'd got a fake one if anyone mentioned the fact. No cause to think her the forger, any more than any other victim, and she meant to see there were a good many of them. Asked for fifty cards, she did. Said she had waited and waited for an invitation and couldn't have her protégée miss the ball of the Season. Very important it was to her to show that she could get her young lady in anywhere. If you want my opinion, Mrs. Falworthy is a bit short of funds and looking to set herself up in the protégée business."

Felicia got rid of the runner shortly afterward, and to her father's repeated admonition that she was to say nothing that would put a rub in the way of Miss Oakley's pleasure, said she saw no reason for anyone to know the truth about Mrs. Falworthy. "You heard Mr. Townshend, Papa. No actual law was broken, so there is no reason to give out Mrs. Falworthy's name. I can easily promise you that neither Theo nor I will do so."

Theo protested, "But what is Caroline to do without a proper sponsor? She can scarcely go with her mother to such events as she has attended with Mrs. Falworthy, and she has no one else."

Felicia, surprised but pleased to see that Theo cared what became of Miss Oakley, said, "We will ask Aunt Augusta to take her under her wing. We might have to explain matters to her, Papa, but you will not mind that she knows, will you?"

He shook his head. "Augusta's not the sort of common gossip to open her budget over this sort of affair," he said. "Just see she knows she is not to speak." He got up, gathering his letters. "I am going to go and tend to my coins."

"I had better tell Aunt Augusta about this at once," Felicia said. "Do you want to come with me, Theo?"

Theo grimaced. "I do not know why it must be Aunt Augusta who looks after her, Felicia. I should think Lady Dacres would be a more appropriate person. After all, it is her sister who made such a mull of things, you know. Surely—"

Lady Adlam said shrilly, "Don't be nonsensical, Theodosia. Have you not said time and again that Dacres has been casting an eye in Miss Oakley's direction? Would you throw the two of them together in such a fashion and spoil your own chances?"

Theo flushed, but said steadily, "I think Dacres will marry where he chooses, in any event, and I would rather not have

Caroline Oakley following like my shadow wherever I go. I feel sorry for her, but I do not see why I must share Aunt Augusta with her. Lady Dacres is very conciliating. I am sure—"

"We cannot go to Lady Dacres," Felicia said quietly. "Papa is right about keeping the matter quiet, and it would not do, in any case, for us to betray to Lady Dacres that we know her sister did such a thing. To do so would be to make her uncomfortable in our presence. If she does recognize Miss Oakley's predicament, and chooses to help her, we will know it when Aunt Augusta invites Caroline to join us for dinner before your ball."

"I still do not think—"

Felicia raised a hand, silencing her. "I see I was wrong in thinking you had begun to put others before yourself, Theo. You may come with me to Upper Brook Street or not, as you choose."

Hunching a shoulder pettishly, Theo said, "I have things to do here, thank you, but I hope you will not be long, because the children will soon be clamoring to know where you have gone, and I do not wish to spend my whole afternoon entertaining them."

Knowing that such a likelihood was extremely remote, Felicia said merely that she would not be long. Then, smiling at Lady Adlam, she added apologetically, "I know you thought I would spend the afternoon with you today, ma'am, but you can see that this is a compelling matter that cannot be settled with a simple note to my aunt, and Theo will not desert you."

As diplomatically as possible, she cut short what promised to be a list of unhappy circumstances that had already befallen Lady Adlam that day, and bade her farewell. Stopping briefly in the schoolroom, she informed Freddy that if he continued to be a good boy, she would reward him with a special treat if not the day after the ball, when she would no doubt wish to rest, then certainly on Monday morning. "Perhaps the changing of the Horse Guard, dear. You will like that. Or Mr. Barker's panorama, or even the Tower menagerie. But you must be extra good these last two days." When he assured her that he would be "good as an angel," she hoped he meant at least that he would not annoy her mother or Theo in her absence, and hurried to Upper Brook Street.

Lady Augusta, when circumstances had been explained to her, clicked her tongue and exclaimed in distaste but agreed it was unfair to assume Miss Oakley had been aware of Mrs. Falworthy's machinations on her behalf. A note was composed to be sent off next day to the young lady, informing her that Lady Augusta had learned of Mrs. Falworthy's indisposition and desired Miss Oakley to be her guest at the forthcoming ball.

"I like the gel," Lady Augusta said. "No nonsense about her. She don't seem to have found your idiotish sister's airs and graces at all contagious, as certain others have done."

"Aunt!"

"I don't mince my words, Felicity, and if you can look me straight in the face and tell me Theodosia has not behaved as if she thinks herself Queen of the May, then I shall call myself a Dutchman. Fact is, my dear, your sister is greedy. Oh, she can be kind if it suits her, but far too often her kindness is mere condescension. She gathers flatterers, having never learned they are not to be trusted, though her own Papa flatters her and don't do much else. But the worst is that others try to emulate her. Only look at Belinda Crawley. I ask you, what on earth is that brother of hers about that he has not squelched her?"

Felicia had been waiting for an opening to defend her sister, but realized now she had nothing to say. Lady Augusta was right. Belinda's behavior, which everyone agreed was odd, was but a poor reflection of Theo's. What Theo did naturally and with a certain grace, Belinda did awkwardly because it did not suit her.

Lady Augusta said, "What *has* become of Crawley?"

"I don't know, ma'am. He went out of town some time ago, and though we expected him to return when Sir Richard was ready to finish Theo's portrait, he did not do so. His sister thinks he went to Newmarket for the races."

"That portrait is finished, is it not? I quite thought Vyne had assured you he would have it here tomorrow."

"Oh, yes, he took it away two days ago to finish the last glazing in his studio at home. Once it was dry enough to move, you know, there was no reason to leave it at Adlam House." And every reason, she thought, to take it away, Theo's curiosity having grown so great by then that Felicia had doubted that even having given her word would prove enough to keep her sister from breaking down the parlor door to see the portrait.

"Thought he said Theodosia could see the thing when it was done," Lady Augusta said.

"He did, but later he said she needed a lesson. After she tried to peek at it that one time, he told her she would have to wait to see it when everyone else did, at the ball. He has not yet even shown it to Papa."

"Serves Theodosia right. That man knows how to handle her. Pity he's a painter. Good enough family connections, of course, but an artist's in trade nonetheless, and your sister feels her worth too much to take a man only because he is good for her."

"Yes," Felicia agreed with a sigh, "she does."

Thinking of all the brangling that had gone on between the pair of them, she could not really agree that Vyne was good for Theo, but since she saw no good to be achieved by saying so, she changed the subject and soon took her leave, convinced that Lady Augusta would handle Miss Oakley with greater diplomacy than she had ever handled Theo.

Since she had walked from Park Lane to Upper Brook Street, she had no reason to wait for a carriage but set out at once on foot, walking briskly to the corner and turning into Park Lane, mentally listing the numerous small details that still required her attention before the ball. So absorbed in her thoughts was she that when a carriage drew up at the curbstone beside her, startling her, she shied back, nearly losing her balance.

"Good God, Miss Adlam, are you all right?"

"What the devil are you doing?"

"Aunt Felicia, look at me!"

All three voices assaulted her ears at once, and before she had recovered her senses to realize that the vehicle was Sir Richard's phaeton, carrying Crawley and her younger nephew as well as its owner, Crawley had jumped down and caught her by the arm almost, she thought, as if he feared she would run away.

"You nearly stepped in front of the horses," he snapped. "What the devil were you thinking, to be out walking without so much as a footman or maid to keep you awake to the traffic?"

Looking pointedly at his hand on her arm until he released her, Felicia took a small moment to twitch the sleeve of her pelisse into proper shape again before she said with a chill in her voice, "Had you drawn up in a civil manner, sir, I should not have been frightened out of my wits, but since you chose to bring your team to a plunging halt, of course I jumped. I was thinking of all I must do before my aunt's ball. I see you, Freddy," she added, smiling up at the little boy, who looked enormously pleased with himself. "Did these gentlemen find you roaming the streets, or did they pay a call to Adlam House?"

"Sir Richard called," Freddy said, "and when he said he was going to visit Lord Crawley, I asked if I could go, too, because I thought p'raps his lordship had forgotten my driving lessons, and Sir Richard said I might go with him, and what's more," he added happily, "when we got to Lord Crawley's house, there was no one to hold the horses, 'cause Sir Richard hadn't got his tiger, so he let me hold them, and he even told me I might walk them if he was gone for long. Only he wasn't." He sighed.

Crawley had her by the arm again. "Come along out of this chill," he said. "We will see you safely to your door." Bending nearer, he added, "That fool Dickon ought to have known better than to leave him alone in the carriage. I've told him he must not do it again, so you needn't trouble your head that he will."

She looked up gratefully. "Thank you, sir. That does relieve my mind. Freddy has been very good, but I am not fool enough to think he has become a pattern-card of virtue. Still, you needn't take me up beside you. The phaeton will be too crowded, and it is just a step now, not more than two blocks."

"Freddy can jump down and walk, to let you ride in comfort," Vyne said, ignoring the boy's indignant look.

Felicia chuckled. "He would not soon forgive you for that, sir, and truly, I prefer to walk."

"Let the boy drive you, Dickon," Crawley said recklessly. "I will give myself the pleasure of escorting Miss Adlam."

Knowing it was useless to object, and rather enjoying the

sensation of being looked after, Felicia watched silently as Freddy, with a look of intense concentration, took up the reins and gave Vyne's team the office to start.

"Dickon's blacks are entirely to be trusted, Miss Adlam," Crawley said calmly. "Had he brought his chestnuts, I'd have had his head for leaving that scamp in charge of them for so much as an instant. Dickon's got a natural ability to manage his horses, so he does not concern himself much with their faults, and as a result, his chestnuts are hard-mouthed brutes— a challenge even for me to drive, let alone a scrap of a lad like Freddy."

She smiled at him. "I did not think for a moment that you would have suggested letting him drive if you did not know it to be safe for him to do so."

"So you are learning to trust me, are you?"

His choice of words struck a nerve, and she realized she was still extremely vexed with him, but whether it was for jumping back into her life so casually after he had seemed to disappear, or for the disappearance itself, she was not certain. And oddly, despite her vexation, she did trust him. She hesitated to betray herself in any way by telling him so, however. And though she longed for the courage to ask if he trusted her, she could not bear to put him to such a test lest he fail it. She could recall too easily the measuring look on his face when she had surprised him looking at the forged invitations. At last she said simply, "I am glad you have returned. Do you mean to attend our ball?"

"Certainly. Why else do you think I came back?" This was said with a look of such warmth that she felt it to her toes, and her breath seemed to catch in her throat. Then, his expression changing to a look of comical chagrin, he added, "Of course, my sister would tell you that I came back on her account. What has the chit really been doing, to have put everyone in a bustle?"

"Why, nothing at all to speak about, sir."

"Don't play the half-wit with me, my dear girl. I have it on excellent authority that Bella has been making a complete fool of herself, affecting all the airs and graces of an imperial duchess. My sorely afflicted parent has commanded that I put a stop to it, but I confess, I do not know how."

She glanced up at him, wondering if for once he had come to seek advice rather than to give it, but he was looking at her in that warm way she had noticed earlier, and she could think of nothing sensible to say. She decided she would do well to speak to Dawlish at the earliest opportunity, however.

Crawley did not seem to expect a direct response from her, however, for all he said was, "I depend upon you to tell me all I have missed since I left Town." Willingly, she recited several amusing *crim con* stories, and was in the middle of one of them when they reached Adlam House, where Sir Richard, having sent Freddy on inside, was amusing himself while he waited to take Crawley up again by conversing with the mongrel, who was loudly objecting to the phaeton's presence at his curb. Crawley shooed him off, and told Vyne he would walk to Brooks's later to meet him if he still meant to go to the theater that evening. "Must discover this *New Way to Pay Old Debts*," he added, laughing.

"Oh," Felicia said, recognizing the title of the latest comedy to attract London theater-goers, "are you going to Covent Garden tonight? We are going, too, and then to dinner at Crofton House afterward. Shall . . . shall we see Lord Dawlish as well?"

Crawley looked at her sharply. "Don't tell me that in my absence you've gone over at the knees for Dawlish."

Feeling heat in her cheeks, she said, "No, no. We simply have not seen very much of him lately."

"Oh, you haven't!" His brows were knitted together, and she was grateful to Sir Richard for diverting him by shouting that he would join him for the theater but not to think he meant to spend the greater part of the evening doing the fancy. Then, with a flourish of his whip, he drove off, and Crawley, taking her by the arm again and urging her up the steps and through the door Freddy had left open, said curtly, "Tell me about Dawlish."

Startled, she said, "I don't remember what I was saying, and I don't believe you were paying very much attention in any case." She peered around the empty hall. "I do not know where Heath has got to. Do you want to come inside?"

His harsh expression relaxed, and shutting the door behind them, he said, "I must pay my respects to Lady Adlam, must I not? And to prove I was listening, I will repeat everything you said to me if you like. Before you got onto Dawlish, you were telling me about Lady Jersey's rout. Were there any more of the forged invitations in evidence there?"

"No! That is, I don't know." She turned quickly toward the stairway and moved ahead of him.

He followed, saying conversationally, "We must hope there will be none at your ball, must we not?"

"I do not believe there will be, sir," she said, striving to instill her voice with a calm she did not feel. Why it should be so difficult to dissemble, she could not think, but it was as if he were looking directly at her, and she wanted to tell him the whole tale. It would not do, however. She had given her word, and unless Mrs. Falworthy refused their conditions, she could not betray her to anyone, not even Crawley. Glancing back over her shoulder at him, and seeing him smile at her, she suddenly wanted very badly to tell him, if only to relieve herself of the worry that he might be thinking her the guilty one.

He was looking at her a little oddly now, she thought, and when she turned again, he said with his voice low in his throat, "You sound very sure of yourself, Felicia."

Rattled as much by his use of her name as by a comment that made her more certain than ever that he thought her guilty, she stammered, "You ought not . . . that is, I have not given you leave . . . Pray, sir, what are you doing?"

For he had caught her and turned her to face him. As she gaped at him in astonishment, he shot a quick glance around the still empty hall, put an arm around her shoulders, a hand gently to her chin, then tilted her head up, and kissed her open mouth.

She closed her mouth at once, but the warmth of his lips against hers was surprising, for it was not at all like the hasty kiss he had stolen from her at Devonshire House, and she had not thought anything could be so delightful. Her body swayed against his, and his arm tightened around her shoulders. The hand that held her chin moved to her waist, brushing against her breast in a way that sent fire through her body. He pulled her closer, as though he would make her a part of himself. Then his tongue touched her lips, moving gently as though he were tasting her.

Felicia felt dizzy. Somewhere deep inside she knew she ought to stop him, but she did not want to do so, for her body had come alive as it never had before and she did not want the glorious sensations to stop. She sighed, and her lips opened, welcoming him.

A stifled giggle from above startled them both and they sprang apart, looking up to see Freddy peering down at them.

"The beasts at the Tower *and* the changing of the Guard," he said, grinning at Felicia.

Crawley shook a fist at him. "One word out of you, my lad, and there will be no beasts, no guards, and no more driving for you. Do you hear me?"

Freddy winked at him. "I hear." And then when Crawley took a menacing step toward him, the boy laughed and said, "Oh, very well. I'm as mum as you like."

Felicia, watching him run off, sighed and said, "I confess, sir, I'll be relieved when he goes to school to know he is not at hand to play off more tricks. Of course once he learns how much his irresponsibility affects himself and those who love him, he will change, but until then . . ." She let her voice trail to silence when she realized that he was just smiling at her, waiting for her to stop talking. Turning and moving purposefully toward the drawing room, she firmly ignored an impulse to beg him to begin again where he had left off.

"When do they leave?" he asked, following her.

"We are to take them down on Wednesday," Felicia said. I would like to take all three children to the Royal Academy Exhibition when it opens Monday afternoon, to see Theo's portrait, for they have not seen it, either, of course, but I suppose that now I will also have to take Freddy to the Tower menagerie and to see the changing of the Guard that morning."

"He needn't go to both," Crawley said.

She flushed. "If you think I mean to take any chances with that rascal's mischievous tongue, you are much mistaken, sir."

"Why, Miss Adlam, I do not believe I have ever seen you put out of countenance before."

"Come and pay your respects to my mother, sir, before I have you thrown out. If I am the least discomposed, it is entirely your fault. Such a thing to do!"

He grinned at her. "I do not recall that you objected."

"And you are all the worse for pointing that out to me!"

He chuckled. "May I hope that you have saved at least two dances for me tomorrow night?"

"You may hope."

She had, but she saw no need to tell him so at once. It occurred to her some moments later, as she watched him use his charm to stir Lady Adlam to uncustomary animation, that she had been flirting with him, an activity that she generally considered foolish. And worse, that she was looking forward to doing a good deal more of it the following night. Not only that but she hoped she might experience another of his kisses as a result.

By the following night, she was in a state far from the serenity she usually enjoyed, worrying more about her hair and her gown than was customary. When Theo came into her bedchamber to ask what she thought of her ball gown, Felicia said, "Oh, Theo, how do I look? Is this flesh-colored muslin right for me?" Peering into the looking glass, she twitched the pink and black Vandyke trimming on her sleeves, then made a face at herself in the glass as she tried to adjust one of the pink ostrich feathers in her headdress.

Theo laughed. "Let me do that. You will pull that plume right out. We both look wonderful."

"Well, you do, certainly." She thought Theo's gown of pale pink muslin over an underbodice and petticoat of white sarcenet was extremely becoming. Blue and pink satin ribbons had been threaded through her golden curls and twisted into a rosette over her right ear, pink satin slippers peeped from beneath her flounced hem, and she carried a pair of long white silk gloves in her hand, but for once Theo seemed unaware of her beauty.

Felicia glanced back at her own reflection. "You do not think the flesh color too drab?"

"No, elegant. Felicia, what if my portrait is horrid?"

Felicia stared at her in the mirror. "How could it be? You are young and beautiful, and Sir Richard is the finest portrait artist of the day."

"But he paints what he sees," Theo reminded her, "and I think he doesn't see my beauty. I was horrid to him from the outset, and he is forever criticizing my behavior and telling me

I should be more conformable, though he certainly is not. He never likes what I wear. What if it all shows in the portrait?"

"Goose. I have seen how he looks at you, and I believe he corrects you because he cares rather more than he should. If you were not besieged by every fortune hunter in the *beau monde*, you would see what he really thinks of you."

To her surprise, Theo did not dismiss her words. Instead, she said solemnly, "I know he cares about me, Felicia, for he has told me so, but he cares more about painting, and about truth."

Felicia did her best to soothe these fears, and in the course of calming Theo did much to calm herself, so that by the time they reached Lady Augusta's house in Upper Brook Street, she was perfectly able to stand with her aunt and sister to greet their guests. Lord Adlam had been prevailed upon to lend his presence as host for the evening, and since he had learned that very day from Mr. Oakley that at least one shipment of his precious wine had been got safely out of Lisbon, he was in an excellent humor, delighted to present his younger daughter to an admiring world, and pleasant to his elder daughter whenever he chanced to recall her presence at his other side.

Felicia enjoyed the evening hugely. Lords Crawley and Dawlish, as well as Sir Richard Vyne, had accepted invitations to dinner, as had Lady Augusta's old friend Major Brinksby. But even the major's overloud and long-winded description of Lord Nelson's recent victory at Copenhagen could not depress the spirits of the other guests. At a quarter past seven the dinner party broke up, and with the exception of a few of Adlam's particular friends who adjourned with him to sample some of his champagne collection, everyone joined the many newly arriving guests in the ballroom at the rear of the big house.

Taking some pleasure in informing Crawley that her hand for the first set of country dances had long since been bespoken, Felicia took even more pleasure in agreeing to dance the first minuet with him. As they took their places in the set sometime later, she noted that Dawlish was with Belinda in the next set, and that Miss Crawley was looking rather mulish.

Turning her attention to her own partner, Felicia smiled at him and said, "The evening is going very well, I think."

"Excellently well," he agreed. "Your aunt had the foresight to provide a tea room, a card room, and four refreshment rooms. How could anything go amiss?"

She laughed. "The orchestra might be dismal, sir."

"No one would notice. I glanced into the nearest reception room ten minutes ago, and it was as if a swarm of locusts had discovered the table, all attired in knee breeches with pink nosegays on well-cut coats that as of this week they call Copenhagens. I fear all my coats have gone out of fashion since Nelson's victory." He stepped away from her as the pattern of the dance required, and she glanced toward the next set, seeing Belinda now staring at her feet and Dawlish looking very angry.

Intent upon diverting Crawley's attention so that he would not notice the byplay, she said as he came nearer again, "Where is Sir Richard? I have not seen him for some time now."

"He was watching your sister flirt with every person in breeches and got tired of it, I imagine, but they will be unveiling the portrait soon, will they not?"

"At midnight, just before they serve supper," she told him. "Aunt Augusta wanted Sir Richard to let her place the easel on a raised platform at the head of the ballroom, but he would not do it. He said Theo would perish with curiosity and would be like to snatch the veil away long before midnight. So a pair of his own servants are to carry the draped easel out at midnight and place it on the platform for the unveiling."

"And who is to do the honors?"

"Why, Theo, of course. Sir Richard suggested that Papa might, but of course, when Theo said she wanted the honor all to herself, Papa agreed at once. He does not like public spectacles of any kind. Sir Richard will be standing on one side and Theo on the other, and she will draw the cord to raise the drape."

She had forgotten that the orchestra was to play a fanfare to announce the ceremony, and became so wrapped up in her enjoyment that the drum roll and trumpets caught her by surprise. Crawley appeared at her side as if she had conjured him up by thinking about him, and she followed him through the crowd to the front, feeling rather disappointed that the Prince of Wales had not put in an appearance.

A space had opened between the crowd and the orchestra, and the platform was there with the draped easel upon it. Theo stood on one side, looking self-conscious and a little worried, with Vyne on the other side, looking stern but confident.

Crawley murmured, "This occasion calls for a pompous speech from someone. Where is your father?"

"Papa does not make speeches. Sir Richard told us Mr. West had offered to do a proper presentation, but he refused because he wanted everyone to see only Theo and her portrait, and not be diverted by the presence of the president of the Royal Academy."

The drum roll, which continued long after the trumpets fell silent, faded away at last, and Sir Richard with a brief glance around, as though to be certain the company was attentive, made a small gesture to Theo, who pulled the cord, raising the pink satin drape. The portrait, five feet high and three wide, was revealed at last to gasps of equal admiration and dismay.

Felicia saw at once that the artist had captured every ounce of Theo's beauty in a pose that showed her turned a little away and laughing back at him over one shoulder. Her skin glowed with youth; her eyes sparkled with laughter and mischief. The white of the gown bore a faint tinge of pink so pale as to be barely noticeable, with a satin sash of a much deeper rose. But with deep dismay, Felicia saw that Vyne had also captured every facet of Theo's personality as well. She could not tell how he had done it, but the portrait showed a vain young woman, laughing and happy but arrogantly sure of herself and her beauty. It was plain to anyone looking at her that she was for the most part unaware of and unconcerned with the rest of the world.

"Oh!" The brief silence that fell after the unveiling was shattered by the angry cry, and before anyone had any notion of what she meant to do, Theo snatched up the portrait and brought it crashing down upon Sir Richard's head. "You believe in truth, do you?" she cried. "Well, there's truth for you . . . you *painter*!" And with that, and without so much as a look at anyone else, Miss Theodosia Adlam swept out of the room.

For a long moment Sir Richard did not move. The canvas had broken and torn, and part of the top of his head could be seen poking through the opening. Slowly he reached up and lifted the portrait away. The hole was right in the middle.

"It's ruined," Felicia whispered, aghast. "It was magnificent, and now it's utterly ruined. Oh, I must go to—" She broke off, distracted when Crawley grabbed her arm.

"Not now," he said grimly.

"But I must. She will be so—"

"She deserves to be upset," he said. "And so does he. But you can't desert your aunt at a moment like this. Look at them."

She did, and knew he was right. The silence had ended. Everyone was talking, chattering about what had happened. Thinking about what Theo had done—in front of so many people—made Felicia shiver with horror. She was not at all sure she wanted to stay to support her aunt through what must follow, but she knew it would be worse if she too were to go rushing out of the room. Drawing a steadying breath, she said, "I cannot see Sir Richard. Where is he?"

"Gone," he said. "Took the damned portrait and walked out."

"It was a terrible thing to do to her," Felicia said. "He ought to have let her see it first, at least, but he ought never to have painted her looking like that."

"He couldn't help it," Crawley said. "It's the way he is. He paints what he sees. A man cannot change the way he is."

Overwhelmed by a surge of the anger that had once been so unfamiliar but was fast becoming habitual, Felicia could not stop the words that leapt to her tongue. "Even Freddy has learned that men can change if they want to. But first they have to grow up and learn to take responsibility for their own actions, to do the things they promise to do without making excuses or simply walking away when the duty they have accepted becomes tiresome."

He flushed, and she instantly wished the words unspoken, but it was too late. "Clearly, you have had a surfeit of my company for the evening, Miss Adlam. Perhaps before we meet again, you will learn that those who borrow responsibility for everyone else's problems and don't see their own, are as much in the wrong as we slackers." And before she could protest, he was gone.

13

FELICIA spent a sleepless night, for Crawley's words echoed over and over in her mind. She was certain he had meant that she assumed more responsibility than she had a right to assume, and marveled that he could think such a thing. Who else, she wondered, would look after things if she did not?

The next morning dawned dismally in a damp gray fog that blanketed the streets, doing little to lift her spirits. Theo kept to her own bedchamber until afternoon, insisting she wanted neither to speak to anyone nor to show her face abroad, but Lord Adlam had much to say over the breakfast table on the subject of persons who dared to offend his younger daughter.

"If he thinks I shall pay him for that piece of rubbish," he told Felicia angrily, "he has another think coming."

She did what she could to soothe his exacerbated feelings, but she did not succeed very well, and after he had gone, Mrs. Heath came to ask if she wanted the linen cabinets turned out, as was generally done in the spring, after which Miss Ames came to inform her that the children—Freddy in particular—rather hoped the promised expedition to the Tower might take place that day.

By exerting some tact, Felicia was able to deal adequately with Mrs. Heath and Miss Ames; however, there was little she could do to divert Lady Augusta, who, not content with numerous peppery comments she had made the previous night to anyone who would listen, turned up at Adlam House soon after the breakfast dishes had been cleared away, and was still having her say-so when Lady Adlam entered the morning room more than an hour later.

Felicia, seeing her mother pause on the threshold, and well aware that she had come down to arrange herself on the sofa in the drawing room as she did most days, got up and said, "As you see, Mama, Aunt Augusta has come to pay us an early call."

"Augusta," Lady Adlam said weakly, allowing Felicia to lend her an arm to the sofa, "oh, Augusta, what can have come over my wretched daughter that she could make such a spectacle of herself? Harroby has been telling me the most dreadful tales this morning. Did Theo truly screech at him and run away?"

"Worse than that," Lady Augusta replied acidly. "She tried to murder him with his own picture in front of four hundred witnesses."

With a wail of dismay, Lady Adlam clutched a hand to her bosom and said, "Murder! Oh, no! Tell me it is not so."

Annoyed, Felicia said, "It was not so bad as that, Mama, and only goes to show that you should not encourage Harroby to repeat gossip to you. To be sure, Theo hit him with the portrait—and how she managed to lift it and bring it down with enough energy to break the canvas, I am sure I do not know—but she never meant to hurt him, I assure you. Nor was he injured, except in his pride, I suppose, for now he will have nothing to compete against Lawrence's portrait of the Princess of Wales."

"Lawrence has no portrait," Lady Augusta said grimly. "I suppose no one has mentioned it to you, but Vyne sat next to me at dinner last night, and he said the Academy had refused in the end to grant Lawrence the extra time he required after the princess's illness to finish her portrait for the exhibition. At first, Vyne said, Lawrence threatened to withdraw his other pictures, and though that came to nothing, one supposes that now some lesser artist will win the portrait medal this year. The dinner to award the prizes is being held tonight, you know."

There was nothing much to say to that, and the conversation, in deference to Lady Adlam's wishes, became more desultory, but Felicia's mood did not improve. After Lady Augusta had gone home, Lady Adlam retired to her boudoir to nap, and Adlam took himself off to Oakley and Campion's to learn more about the wine being shipped from Lisbon.

Shortly afterward Tom came in to inform Felicia that if Freddy was to have even a small chance of continuing his improved behavior he must be taken outside to vent some energy, and she readily agreed to let him take the two younger children to sail boats on the Serpentine in Hyde Park. Glad to have one worry off her mind, she retired to the drawing room alone to attend to her correspondence, but managed to write only a few sentences before her mind drifted to other subjects, then fixed itself upon one tall, sadly irresponsible subject in particular.

She could no longer even attempt to deny her attraction to Crawley. He had dominated her thoughts from the moment of their first meeting, but although she had responded to his cheerful good humor—and to his moodier moments as well—she had not felt as if he encompassed her whole world until the second time he kissed her. Only then had she realized how much he affected her.

But it was useless to harbor such feelings. Not only was he an irresponsible fortune hunter but a fickle one as well. She repeated these sad warnings fiercely to herself, as she had done over and over during the long, sleepless, tearful night. Not easily given to tears, she had not wept long, and her sobs had been carefully muffled by her pillow so that no one else might hear her, but undeniably she had cried a little. Not for the first time, she wished there were someone in whom she might confide, someone who could explain her seemingly inescapable feelings for a man who was the antithesis of any she had ever thought she might love.

He was selfish and capricious, and thought he had only to tell other people to change in order to make them do so. Moreover, he had shown that he could be thoughtless and cruel, even to children. But he was kind, too, and warm, and when he looked at her or touched her, she felt protected and cared for in ways she had never felt before. He had said she was beautiful, and he had come to respect at least some of her opinions. Moreover, she had begun to turn to him more and more for the advice she had once scorned to accept. And although that was not enough, she feared that she had come to love him.

She realized that even if she had a confidante she would not know how to confide in one, for even as a child she had kept her private fears and troubles to herself, and she knew no other way. The only person to whom she had even partially revealed her inner thoughts was Crawley himself.

Not until she felt tears in her eyes did she realize she had succumbed to self-pity, and fight to collect herself. It was just as he had said the previous night. People did not really change, and it was foolish to sit, ignoring her tasks and wishing he might be different. It was useless too, however, to think she would succeed with her present correspondence, and having neither the heart nor the energy to leave the house to pay calls, she had nearly decided to go tell Mrs. Heath that they would, after all, turn out the linen cabinets, when Dawlish was announced.

Her mood improved at once, for not only could she now turn her thoughts to someone else's troubles, but she had had no opportunity yet to speak privately with him about his. He had not attended the play on Thursday, and the previous evening she had seen him only in company, most particularly with Belinda. When he was shown in, he looked harassed again, and it occurred to her that he had been looking so rather often of late.

He took a seat at once when she invited him to do so but refused refreshment, saying bluntly, "I need advice, ma'am, and I thought it best to come to you."

Gratified that someone truly believed her advice was sound, she smiled encouragingly and said, "It is Belinda, is it not? I saw you dancing with her last night."

"Obstinate chit," he growled. "Couldn't stand that preening nonsense anymore, so I took her aside and tried to put a flea in her ear. Her own brother won't attend to the problem, and she is used to talking things over with me, so I thought—particularly since she thinks I want to marry her—that I'd have a try, but it only made her angry. Danced with me once after that, before Miss Theo threw her temper tantrum, but only because I refused to let her beg off and she couldn't bear to be seen sitting out. She wouldn't speak a word to me. What am I to do, Miss Adlam?"

"You said you would talk with her," Felicia reminded him. "Not to scold, but to discover her true feelings toward you."

"I know, but I just can't bring myself to do it. First off, Ned would murder me, though I think I can bring him around in time—especially since his own affairs are in better trim—but I doubt that she will agree to any such thing now, and I'm not the man to put my head in a mangle for nothing."

"Does Lord Crawley have his affairs in better trim?" Felicia asked, forgetting Belinda instantly when her attention fastened on a more interesting point of Dawlish's speech. "I must suppose he won money at the Newmarket races, then. Did he, sir?"

He glanced at her as if he had not really been attending, then said, "Ned, you mean? Newmarket? Oh, yes, he did in fact. Dashed amazing thing. A mare named Tuneful, who has bolted every race she ever ran before, beat Popinjay, who's never been beat before. The odds were enormous, and Ned won about a thousand pounds."

"I see." Felicia sighed and forced her mind back to his problem. "I do not know what to tell you, sir, if you cannot bring yourself to declare your feelings to Belinda. If she thinks you took her to task out of brotherly affection—"

"I took her to task," he snapped, "because she has no business going about pretending to be as condescending and arrogant as your idiotish sister when she is nothing of—"

"Good afternoon, Lord Dawlish," Theo said from the doorway.

He spun around in his chair, dismay written all over his cherubic features, and gasped, "Miss Theo! I'd no notion you were anywhere about. Oh, look here, I'm dashed sorry. Never meant a word of it, I promise you."

Looking wan and red-eyed, she shook her head, stepping into the room and shutting the door behind her. "Don't apologize," she said bleakly. "I have been utterly scathing to Belinda. I must have told half a dozen people that she was behaving badly, but now that my eyes have been opened, I see with perfect clarity what you all saw before. She was imitating

me, was she not? What I disliked in her are the very things I
do myself."

"Now, I never meant that," Dawlish said desperately. Looking at Felicia, he said, "Tell her, ma'am. Tell her I'd never had
said a word if I'd thought she would hear— No, dash it, that
ain't what I mean either. Oh, what a muddle."

"I am glad you have come downstairs, Theo," Felicia said,
feeling sorry for Dawlish and striving for his sake to introduce
a note of normality into the conversation. "The house has been
very dull this afternoon. Dawlish has been our only caller."

He turned redder than ever, and Theo said, "There is no use
trying to wrap this in cotton wool, Felicia. You always try to
make things easier for everyone, but I am not a fool, and I
begin to see myself much more clearly than I like."

"No one said you were a fool, my dear."

"No, but you all allowed me to behave like one. It is very
lowering to think that Aunt Augusta was the only one who
tried to stop me before Richard made me see myself as others
do. He did, you know. He paints only truth, and his truth was
painfully plain to see in my portrait. It was a brilliant painting,
and I have written to him to apologize for spoiling it."

Felicia did not know what to say, but irrepressibly Dawlish
murmured, "Ought to apologize for calling him a painter.
Dashed if I don't think Dickon hated that even more than the
rest."

The comment got a wan smile from Theo. "I know that. I
apologized for the whole. I wrote that I had spoken out of
anger and that I know he is a great artist, better than anyone
else."

Felicia said, "You really ought not to have written to him at
all, dear. It was most improper, and if anyone else should learn
that you did so, it will only add to the scandal."

"I don't care about that. It was dreadfully difficult to write
to him, but I cannot bear for him to be angry with me, and so I
did it, and I sent Peters to take it to him straightaway so that I
could not change my mind."

"Good gracious, Theo, sending your footman to Vyne! People will think you were arranging a clandestine meeting, or
worse."

But Dawlish, in his continued attempt to make amends, instantly took Theo's side when she insisted that, since she rather than Vyne had been in the wrong, she had been obliged to write, and Felicia suddenly found herself wishing she could write a similar note to Crawley, apologizing for her own hasty words the night before. But she knew she could not. Not only would it be improper, but she did not think she could bring herself to apologize for speaking what was, after all, only the truth.

She realized the discussion between the other two had taken a sudden, more hazardous turn when Theo snapped, "It was not at all dreadful, was it, Felicia?"

Felicia said, "Don't speak to me so shrilly, Theo. I missed what was said, so I cannot answer your question."

Dawlish said, "You will have to agree with me, ma'am. I said that it was a dreadful picture to have painted of her."

Felicia, caught off her guard, glanced warily at Theo, but the younger girl still looked indignant. "Do you not think it was dreadful, my dear?"

"It told you, it was brilliant," Theo said. "I saw that at once. If it had been a portrait of someone we did not know, everyone would have exclaimed at how miraculous it was that any artist could get so much personality into a single picture. Richard would have won the gold medal, no matter what anyone else entered. And I spoiled that for him." Silent tears welled into her eyes and spilled down her cheeks.

Felicia got up at once and gave her a handkerchief, "Dry your tears, Theo. You must not distress Lord Dawlish."

"But I feel like crying," Theo wailed, sniffling loudly now, "and I warn you, I shall cry even harder Monday morning when the names of the medal winners are printed in the *Times*."

She refused to be consoled, particularly since there was no response whatever to her apology. There was no word from Crawley either, although Felicia tried not to think too much about him, and devoted her efforts—unsuccessfully, for the most part—to soothing her sister. However, Monday morning, when she entered the morning room to discover Lord Adlam reading his newspaper aloud to Theo, she saw no tears, only astonishment.

Adlam said, "Upon my word, Felicity, that fellow who

painted your sister's portrait has won a medal for it from the
Royal Academy. Thought it had been ruined, but the chap
must have been able to repair the damage, for only listen to
what I just read to Theo: 'The distinguished portrait artist, Sir
Richard Vyne, has been awarded a special gold medal by the
Royal Academy for a portrait described to us by the president
of the Academy as being so unique that one must see it to
enjoy it. Therefore the *Times* and other London newspapers
have agreed to forgo printing its description. The Exhibition
opens this very day at noon, so our readers may see this unusual work for themselves. Record crowds are expected to attend.' I should say they will," Adlam said, beaming at Theo,
"with such a portrait as yours to see, my dear, I shall go myself, I daresay. Haven't seen it yet, have I?"

"No, Papa," Theo said, looking perplexed, "but I do not believe it can be my portrait. The paper does not say so, after all,
and it may well be someone else's. To be sure, Richard has
not said anything about anyone else sitting for him, but he
must have other subjects. This picture must be one of them."

Adlam was clearly disappointed but cheered up again when
it occurred to him that he need not vie with the crowds expected at the exhibition opening merely to see someone else's
portrait. He bade them both a good day and retired to his
bookroom.

Theo bit her lip, turning urgently to Felicia. "I must go to
the exhibition, Felicia. I have got to see that portrait."

"Perhaps he did a second one of you," Felicia suggested.

"Perhaps. I don't know which would be worse," Theo confessed, "to see my true self displayed to all of London or to
see that he had won with someone else as his subject."

Remembering the paper's recommendation, Felicia said, "I
do not think we ought to go alone, Theo, not to the opening at
all events. There is a huge crowd expected."

"All the more reason to go early," Theo said grimly. "It is
nearly half past ten now. I cannot wait until I hear from someone else, Felicia. I must see the thing for myself, today. If you
do not go with me, I swear I will go alone."

"No, no, you must not do that. Perhaps we ought to tell
Papa it might be your portrait, after all, so that he will go with
us. Or perhaps Aunt Augusta would accompany us."

"No! I don't want Papa, and I simply cannot bear the thought of Aunt Augusta preaching maxims at me if Richard has painted more of my faults for everyone to see. Moreover, she would not go without Major Brinksby or some other gentleman."

This was unanswerable, and in fact another solution had occurred to Felicia, one that might solve her own problem as well. She said, "Would you object as much to Crawley's escort?"

"No, not at all," Theo said instantly, beaming, "but are you expecting him to call? He has not done so since the ball."

"No, but perhaps I could send a message, asking him if he would be so kind as to—"

Theo hugged her. "Do it."

"I feel odd even thinking of such a thing."

"Piffle, I am sure Aunt Augusta does that sort of thing all the time. She would not encourage Major Brinksby to call upon her often, so she must send him an occasional invitation, for he frequently escorts her to the theater or the opera. How else would she manage it?"

Felicia allowed herself to be talked into writing her note with what she felt must be truly suspicious ease, but Theo was too full of her own concerns to pay any heed to Felicia's. Excusing herself to change her dress, she left the room.

Felicia rang for a footman and sent him for writing materials, then spent the intervening moments trying to compose a proper but nonchalant request. She was interrupted in this endeavor by Freddy, who erupted into the morning room with a wide, expectant grin on his face.

"Today is the day," he announced happily.

"Day?" Felicia said. Seeing his happiness crumple, she remembered and said in dismay, "Oh, Freddy, darling, I'm dreadfully sorry, but we cannot go to the Tower today."

"You promised!"

"I know I did, but something of greater importance has come up and I must go with Aunt Theo to the Royal Academy Exhibition rather earlier than we had meant to go."

"Oh. Well, I'd rather see the beasts at the Tower, but I suppose the exhibition will be interesting."

"Oh, Freddy, I know I said I would take the three of you,

but now I do not think—" In the face of his dawning disappointment, she changed her mind and said, "Very well, but you will have to be a good boy, because there is to be a vast crowd, and so I am asking Lord Crawley to lend us his escort."

"I don't mind. Crawley's a great gun if only you don't put him in a pelter. Tom's gone out, but can Sara Ann go, too?"

"May she," Felicia said, correcting him automatically, but shrinking from the thought of having two children to deal with as well as Theo, whose behavior on this, even more than on most occasions, was certain to be unpredictable. "I do not like to say 'no' when I am allowing you to go," she began, only to be ruthlessly interrupted.

"She won't mind," Freddy said at once, then added with a mischievous look over his shoulder as he turned toward the door, "Only asked 'cause I thought I ought to, but it will be famous if only I get to go. Makes up for being left behind when Tom and Sara Ann got to go before."

"You deserved that," Felicia said, but she spoke to air, for he had gone.

The footman brought her writing materials, and she sat down to her task, wondering what on earth Crawley would think to get such a request after the way they had parted, but hoping fervently that he would not deny her his escort.

When Felicia's note was delivered, Crawley was not alone. Taking it from the footman's salver, he grinned at Dawlish, who reclined at his ease in a chair by the library hearth, with a glass of Madeira in hand, and said, "I recognize this handwriting, but I confess I never expected to see in on a billet addressed to me."

"Been meaning to speak to you about that," Dawlish said, sitting up straighter. "Only meant to help, you know, but—"

"Spare me your assistance, Mongrel." Crawley said, breaking the delicate seal and unfolding the single page. "You nearly always make matters worse when you attempt to help. Remember the excellent aid you rendered to Thorne? Nearly got him married to the wrong woman. Now, what is this she's written? Ah, I see, the exhibition. Theo must have seen the morning papers. I cannot imagine what ails Adlam that he must allow females to read what cannot be good for them."

"What is it?" Dawlish demanded.

"Miss Adlam, who spends her time trying to please everyone on this earth except those who deserve it, requires an escort for herself, her sister, and Master Freddy Adlam to the exhibition because she understands that rather too many persons are expected to attend it to make it safe for two unescorted females and a child. They should stay at home then. Sensible thing to do."

Dawlish shook his head and looked wise. "No use to expect Miss Theo to stay at home if she means to go out."

"I suppose not, but I can think of no good reason to let Miss Adlam drag me to what promises to be a ridiculously overcrowded event. We'd all do much better to wait until the second or third day."

"But Theo won't wait, and if she is determined to go, Miss Adlam will go with her."

"Serves Miss Adlam right," Crawley said. "Thinks she knows about everything and everybody, and can't stop for one moment to take someone else's excellent advice when it's offered."

"Talk of the pot calling the kettle black," Dawlish said, chuckling. "But I'll tell you something she don't know, though I'd have thought you'd have told her. I said something about your affairs being in a way to being settled—"

"Being helpful, I suppose. You talk too much, Perry."

"Fiddle, dashed well didn't talk enough. Realized when she asked if you'd won the money at Newmarket that she thought you'd been there the whole time you were gone. Not my business to tell her you'd gone on to Longworth, but you ought to tell her, Ned."

"Perhaps, in my own good time."

"No, dash it, that won't do. If you mean to tell her, you must tell her at once. And you mustn't refuse to take them to the exhibition, either. It's my belief that Miss Theo is in love with Dickon, for she said he had made her see herself as others see her—why, she actually understands that Belinda has been imitating her and that the behavior she criticized in Belinda was her own behavior, and that—" He broke off with a look of utter astonishment. "Good Lord, Ned, I've just done the same thing!"

Crawley, irritated, said, "Stop babbling, Mongrel. I must think what to do here."

Dawlish put down his wine glass and got up. "You think all you like, Ned. I've just realized that I can't go about giving folks advice that I refuse to take myself. I've some important things to discuss with your sister, and if I'm successful, I shall return to discuss them with you. In the meantime, my lad, harken well to what I tell you: People are too dashed inclined to condemn in others the very things they do themselves."

Staring at his retreating back, Crawley shook his head and muttered, "You, my friend, are suffering the consequences of an overlong acquaintance with Lady Augusta." But once Dawlish had gone, he got up and pulled the bell, telling the footman who responded to have Lady Crawley's town carriage brought around to the front door at once and to fetch a boy to him to take a message to Park Lane. Then, taking his pen knife from his waistcoat pocket, he moved purposefully toward his desk.

The footman cleared his throat.

His mind already on what he meant to write, Crawley said curtly, "Yes, why haven't you gone?"

"Begging your pardon, my lord, but her ladyship has driven out in her carriage. I believe she said she meant to call for Lady Dacres to go with her to the Royal Academy Exhibition."

"Damn. Very well, then, tell them to bring my curricle around. And never mind the lad." They would have to take the Adlam carriage, but he could tell them that much in person, and the sooner he got there, the better.

The footman had gone, and Crawley hurried upstairs to change his coat. When his valet pointed out that he had got something on his neckcloth, he ripped if off and decided to change his breeches and shirt as well. It took time and concentration to arrange his neckcloth again after he had dressed, and it was not until then that he wondered why no one had come to tell him that the curricle was at the door.

Checking to be sure he had money and a clean handkerchief, he took a final look in the glass, smoothed a crease in his neckcloth, picked up his gloves and hat, and hurried from the room. Encountering his sister on the stairs, he greeted her briskly and moved to pass her. She put out a hand to stop him.

"Ned, wait, someone said Perry had been here. Where is he?"

"Gone looking for you, he said."

"Oh, dear, I was walking in the park with Caroline Oakley, but when Dacres joined us, I could see that I was no longer wanted, so my maid and I came home. Will he come back again today, do you think?"

Her anxious expression gave him pause, recalling exactly what Dawlish had said, he frowned and said, "Look here, Bella, do you love Mongrel?"

"Don't call him by that horrid name! He stopped calling you Crawler ages and ages ago."

"Don't quibble. I am recalling any number of times that I have seen the two of you with your heads together, and I want—"

"Perry is a very good friend," she said indignantly. "I am sure he thinks of me only as a sister, but in some ways he has been a better brother to me than you have, Ned."

"I don't doubt that," he said with a grimace, "but I begin to think Mong—that is, Perry—don't think of you as a sister at all, Bella. He will be back, but I am not going to wait for him. You just tell him for me if he does anything to make you unhappy, I'll cut out his liver."

She stared, her mouth forming a small O, as she made a visible effort to comprehend precisely what he was telling her. He let her hold his stern gaze for a moment before he allowed his amusement to show. When it did, she flung her arms around him.

"Oh, Ned!"

"Unhand me, Bella. I've important matters of my own to attend. Perry will return soon. He won't have gone far."

He soon found, however, that he was mistaken, for when he reached the hall, the footman he had sent to call for his curricle hurried toward him. "My lord, I don't know what to say. I sent for the rig, right enough, and watched out the window so as I could tell you when it was brought round. But it didn't come, so I sent to the stables to hurry them along, and they said they had sent it off long ago. And one of the lads has just come running to tell me Lord Dawlish has taken it!"

"*What?*"

"Yes, my lord. He came downstairs all of a dither, demanding to know where Miss Belinda had gone, and someone said she had gone to call on Miss Oakley. Lord Dawlish rushed out of the house, and now the lad tells me he shouted out to your tiger that it was he who needed the curricle, then just swung up into it and snatched the reins. Last thing the lad heard was my lord telling the tiger they was bound for Golden Square. They'll be halfway there by now, my lord."

Rendered speechless for nearly thirty seconds, Crawley finally managed to say wrathfully, "Have my horse brought around at once, Jackson, unless his legs have chanced to fall off."

The young footman struggled with himself for a moment, but training stood him in good stead, and he managed a creditable bow, saying, "Very good, my lord. At once."

Crawley saw his shoulders shaking as he retreated toward the green baize door behind the stairs. The sight stirred his temper briefly, but a moment later he was smiling, and when his glossy black stallion was brought around in record time, he was a good deal cheered. Thunderbolt was a mettlesome creature he rarely rode outside the park, but the horse's energy suited his mood at the moment, and by the time they reached Adlam House, his cheerful demeanor was entirely restored.

Heath, answering his knock, said, "I shall ascertain if Lady Adlam is at home, my lord."

"I don't want her ladyship," Crawley said amiably. "Announce my arrival to Miss Adlam, if you please, and have Lady Adlam's carriage brought round at once. I daresay Miss Adlam was expecting me to bring my own, but I did not."

The butler looked momentarily confused. "There must be some mistake, my lord. The misses Adlam and Master Freddy departed more than half an hour ago in her ladyship's carriage."

Crawley looked at his watch and found that it was past noon. "Good God, I'd no idea so much time had passed. They must have thought I was not coming."

"Just so, sir, and Miss Theo, if I may take the liberty of saying so, had grown somewhat impatient."

Crawley looked up, suspecting an understatement. Encountering a speaking look in the butler's eyes, he winced. "I see. I will no doubt find them at Somerset House then." Hesitating only a moment, he decided he would make better time on horseback than if he tried to find a hack, but what on earth he would do with Thunderbolt at Somerset House he had no idea. He hoped he might find a lad clever enough to hold him.

The street in front of Somerset House was crowded, but when he neared the front entrance, he saw that people were moving inside in a steady stream. Finding a lad willing to hold his horse for a shilling, he rushed up the steps, only to encounter a brief delay when he discovered that there was an admission fee. He paid quickly, pushed his way past people, ignoring their indignant objections, and hurried through the first two halls to the room where the medal winners' works were displayed.

He did not see Felicia, Theo, or Vyne, but as he pushed his way toward the front, searching the faces of what seemed to be an increasingly mirthful crowd, he suddenly saw Lady Augusta, looking strangely bemused. Certain her nieces would be nearby, he made his way toward her, paying no heed whatever to the paintings on the wall.

"Lady Augusta, where are Felicia and Theo?"

She stood with Major Brinksby, and hearing her name, turned toward Crawley but looked at him as though she did not know him.

Major Brinksby squeezed past her and said, "Still in shock, don't you know. Never expected such a crazy thing."

Not having the least notion what the old bore was talking about this time and having only one purpose in mind, to reach Felicia as soon as possible and explain to her that it was not a lack of reliability that had kept him, Crawley said abruptly and rather loudly, "Where are Miss Adlam and her sister?"

"Gone," Brinksby said, spreading his hands. "Left in such haste they forgot the young fellow they brought with them. Oh, not to worry," he added, seeing Crawley look around. "Lad followed Vyne when he chased after the two young women."

"Vyne chased them?"

"Lord, yes. Funniest thing you ever saw. Younger chit—Theo, isn't it? She heard all the laughter, took one look at the Vyne entry and threw her hands over her face, then turned and pushed her way through the crowd like a madwoman. Older one took off after her, and Vyne and the lad followed as soon as they saw what was what. Crowd parted like the Red Sea in front of them. Wouldn't have missed it for a dinner with the king, I can tell you that."

"Where's the damned painting?" Crawley demanded.

"There." Major Brinksby, breaking into chuckles again, pointed a long bony finger, and Crawley saw it.

It was Theo's portrait—the damaged one—but Vyne had fashioned a cloth head painted to resemble himself and attached it to look as if it had been thrust through the opening in the canvas. The plaque beneath it gave the title of the piece:

Self-Portrait of the Artist, Meeting Truth

Crawley stared for a moment before his emotions overcame him. Then he threw back his head and laughed until the tears ran down his cheeks.

14

FELICIA, after enduring a carriage ride across London with a tearful Theo, no longer felt the least bit like apologizing to Crawley and, in fact, looked forward to murdering him, slowly and painfully, for ignoring her plea for an escort. First Theo wailed that she did not want to talk about Sir Richard, then she sobbed that she had ruined him, was ruined herself, and that in fact not one of her family would be able to show his face in public again. She succumbed finally to inconsolable weeping, deaf to anything Felicia tried to say to her.

Halfway home, Felicia remembered Freddy but solaced her dismay at forgetting him with a belief that he must have stayed with Lady Augusta and Major Brinksby, and would be perfectly safe with them. Until that moment, she had thought of nothing but catching up with and looking after the distraught Theo.

More than once in the carriage her thoughts veered back to Crawley, and her anger increased each time she remembered that she had made a simple request of a man who had taken it upon himself for sometime now to give her advice that was neither sought nor desired. But the one time she had asked for help, he had not so much as replied. She knew he must have received her request, for her footman had been told to make certain he was at home before giving up her message to anyone else, and she did not entertain for a moment the notion that a servant of Crawley's would neglect to pass on her message.

But Crawley had neither come nor written to say that he would not come, or that he would be delayed. And in light of Theo's impatience and repeated threats to go on alone, Felicia had felt obliged to go with her without waiting any longer. As it was, they had reached Somerset House to find themselves part of the huge crowd waiting to enter when the doors opened. A good many people passed into the medal winners' gallery before them, so that Theo had entered to the accompaniment of uproarious laughter and had no doubt believed herself the cause of all the merriment the instant she saw what Sir Richard had done.

Catching up with her after she had run away, Felicia had tried to soothe her overwrought feelings, but since her own thoughts were more firmly fixed upon Crawley's failure than upon Sir Richard's latest perfidy, she knew she was not giving her best efforts to Theo's needs and was not much surprised, therefore, that when they reached the house, Theo flung herself from the carriage and ran up the steps into the hall.

Their entrance coincided with Lord Adlam's emergence from his bookroom, so Felicia entered to see her sister running up the stairs and her father standing at the top of them, staring down at her in consternation.

When Theo brushed past him, he came partway down the steps and said sharply to Felicia, "What on earth have you done to distress poor Theodosia so?"

"Felicia," Lady Adlam called from the drawing-room side of the gallery, "what is wrong with Theo? She just ran past me without so much as a word, and I believe she was crying. You must do something at once. My poor nerves simply will not tolerate this sort of disturbance."

"Oh, Miss Adlam, there you are," Miss Ames said, appearing beside Lady Adlam and leaning over the rail. "Will you come up to Sara Ann, if you please? She is most distressed that both of her brothers will be leaving for school tomorrow, and I simply cannot seem to comfort her."

"Felicity," Lord Adlam said dangerously, "you've no time for any of the children's nonsense just now. I demand that you answer me. What have you done to—"

"I did nothing, Papa," Felicia said, striving with all her might to remain calm and think how to attend to each of these small crises. "Mama, I will come up to—"

Lord Adlam snapped, "You'll do nothing of the kind! Just

because you think you—" He broke off at the sound of a loud banging on the front door. "What the devil?"

Peters, emerging from the nether regions, ran across the marble floor and pulled open the door.

Sir Richard Vyne pushed past him into the hall. "Where is she?" he demanded. "I must talk to her at once."

A faint shriek and dull thud from above was followed by Miss Ames crying, "Merciful heavens, her ladyship has fainted!"

Lord Adlam glared at Vyne, then at Felicia before turning on his heel, striding back up the stairs, into his bookroom, and slamming the door behind him.

Felicia, distractedly gesturing dismissal at Peters, who still stood wide-eyed by the open door, changed her mind and said, "Peters, find Lady Adlam's woman and send her up to her ladyship at once. I will attend to Sir Richard."

"I don't need attending to! I want—"

"But, Miss, I think perhaps you should—"

"Do as I ask, please," Felicia said more tartly, wondering as she watched Peters obey her if next the maids would be daring to offer her advice. Turning back to Vyne, she said, "Pray, sir, will you not come into the parlor, where we may be private?"

"No! Look here, Miss Adlam, I am going to talk to Theo if I have to go upstairs and find her myself. And don't go thinking you can have your people throw me out of here, because I will only come back again and again until I do talk with her."

"I should think you have already said and done enough," Felicia said grimly. "You have made my sister a laughing-stock, sir, and I can promise you, she will not forgive you for that."

He glared. "Good God, they were not laughing at her! Wouldn't have even if they'd known her, which not more than a handful of them could have done. They were laughing, as I meant them to laugh, at an artist who had got too full of himself and his own inclinations to pay heed to anyone else's. 'Portrait of the Artist' was my reply to her damnfool apology, my way to tell her I was wrong to finish that portrait as I had begun it, that the truth was that if I had held by my own so-called principles, I should have painted my love of her for all the world to see. *That* was the real truth, only I was too blind to see it."

Felicia said weakly, "I thought you disliked her."

"Thought so myself until I realized that what I disliked in her most was simply that she didn't behave the way young ladies are supposed to behave. Once I realized that was it, I saw how hypocritical I was being. Can scarcely blame Theo for doing what I do myself at every opportunity. Flout the conventions whenever the mood strikes me, don't I? Once I saw that, I knew I loved her. I've got to tell her, Miss Adlam. Saw her run out and just dropped everything to follow her. Lucky thing I'd left my rig with a lad on the Embankment. If I'd had my tiger with me today, I'd have had to wait for him, and in that crowd, heaven alone knows where he'd have gone. As for finding a cab in that crush of people— Well, I'm glad I didn't have to, that's all. Will you take me up to her now?" The last question was asked in a more reasonable, even a pleading, tone.

Felicia wondered if he had found a lad to hold his carriage outside, too, or if he had simply left his horses tied to the area railing again. She sighed and said, "I will take you up to the drawing room, sir, and then I will see what I can do to persuade Theo to come down to talk to you. You must know, however, that I cannot permit you to go to her bedchamber. Nor can I force her to see you if she does not wish to do so."

He smiled ruefully. "I know that, and I make no such threat to you, but you need not tell her as much. Let her think me unreasonable and perhaps she will come down."

Casting a worried glance up at the bookroom door, Felicia decided she would do better to attend to Sir Richard and Theo before attempting to deal with her father, and said, "Come along then, sir. I will see what I can do."

Not until they were halfway up the stairway did she recall her mother's collapse. Seeing that Lady Adlam's woman and Miss Ames had taken her to her sitting room, she made a mental note to go to her as soon as she had settled Vyne and spoken to Theo.

Peters, approaching from the direction of the service stair, said, "Miss Adlam, please, if I might suggest that—"

"Not just yet, Peters," Felicia said, interrupting him ruthlessly for the simple reason that she did not think she could cope with any other crisis just yet. "Please take Sir Richard into the drawing room and fetch him whatever refreshment he requires. I am going up to Miss Theo."

"But, Miss Adlam, I do think you ought to—"

"Peters," Felicia said, controlling anger with difficulty, "please, do as I ask and see to Sir Richard. I will return directly, but I simply must attend to one matter at a time."

The footman bowed and turned away, and she hurried up to Theo, finding her still in a lachrymose state. Not until Felicia had exerted herself to the limits of both tact and patience did she realize that she had utterly misunderstood Theo's distress.

"You *don't* think he meant them to laugh at you?"

Theo wailed, "Oh, no, how could he? He is truthful, not cruel. But that he should have been put into such a position is all my fault. I hated him for daring to make me see the truth. How ridiculous! But oh, Felicia, how he must hate me now!"

"Nonsense, dear, you are shouldering the blame for something that was not your doing. And you must not be so foolish as to take all the guilt upon yourself, for he is equally guilty, and he knows it. He does not hate you. In point of fact, he is in the drawing room at this very moment and has threatened to take up residence there until you agree to speak with him."

"In the drawing room?"

"Yes, and I would have you know that it took skilled diplomacy to convince him that he could not simply rush up here to confront you where you stand."

Theo chuckled. "Do you advise me to speak with him then, Felicia, for I must warn you that you might not like what comes of it? I daresay, you know, that everyone will think he is more interested in my fortune than in my person."

"On the contrary. Do not be so quick to attribute motives to people without foundation, Theo. Why, I believe most people will think he is marrying you for your beauty in order to keep his best subject all to himself."

Theo's expression darkened. "A collector's piece? Will he think of me like Papa does, Felicia? I could not bear that."

"Stop assuming things, I tell you, without first talking to the man," Felicia said sharply. Then, astonished at herself, she added in a gentler tone, "You must discover for yourself what he thinks of you, my dear, but I believe you would be gravely mistaken to think he looks at you as Papa does. I will leave you now to tidy yourself, but I will tell him you are coming down."

Theo nodded and Felicia left her to attend to her appearance while she descended to inform Vyne of the success of her mission. Just outside the drawing-room door, however, she was intercepted by Miss Ames.

"Miss Felicia, her ladyship is resting comfortably now, so I must return to Sara Ann, but do you think you might come up with me to speak to her? You always have such a calming effect."

"Pray, go explain to Sara Ann that she must learn not to borrow trouble, and I will come up in a few minutes to add what I can to that," Felicia said, moving toward the drawing room. She reached for the door handle.

"Miss Felicia!"

Turning, she saw Peters hurrying up the stairway, and said wearily, "What is it now?"

"Begging your pardon, miss," he said, "but when Lord Crawley arrived, I noticed something mighty peculiar about—"

"Lord Crawley?" Anger warred with relief, and Vyne was temporarily forgotten. "Do not bring him up, Peters."

"Well, miss, I was going to put him in the parlor, but—"

"Excellent," Felicia said, thinking she could say all she wished to Crawley there, and not be interrupted. She realized that she had interrupted Peters, and that he was looking extremely frustrated. "Is there something more?"

With an unfootmanlike sigh, the young man said, "Indeed, there is, miss. I can't put him in the parlor because his lordship—the master, that is—came out of the bookroom just as I was about to do so and demanded that his lordship—Lord Crawley, that is—come straightaway up and talk to him. And he did. He's in there now. But that's not the worst," he added in a rush. "It's Master Freddy, Miss Felicia. I'm afraid he's . . ."

"He's what?" Felicia demanded. "Good God, Peters, don't stop. Tell me at once what he's done now."

"Well, I don't rightly know what to say it is he's done. I

tried to tell you before that you ought to send someone to look after Sir Richard's horses besides Master Freddy, but he did look as if he knew what he was about, so I held my tongue."

"Sir Richard's horses? Oh, good heavens, Peters, why did you not tell me?" At his look of silent reproach, she pushed a hand distractedly through her curls and said, "Oh, very well, I suppose you did try, but go and find someone to look after the team at once and tell Freddy I said he is to come inside." She glanced at the drawing-room door, inclined to tell Sir Richard to see to his own horses. However, matters were moving well there, and she did not want to put a rub in Theo's way. She decided to attend to the matter herself now and tell Sir Richard later what she thought of him. But Peters had not moved. "Well?"

"He's not there," the footman said bluntly. "Saw he wasn't when his lordship tied his horse to the railing and came inside."

"Not there? But of course he must be there!" Without another thought for Vyne or Crawley, or indeed for anyone else but Freddy, she pushed past the footman, snatched up her skirt, and hurried down the stairs to the front door, yanking it open and stepping out onto the step to see for herself.

A single black horse stood placidly, tied to the area railing at the foot of the steps, half on the flagway, half in the street. To the south, she saw only the little gray mongrel, sitting at the top of the area steps. But turning to the north, she beheld a yellow and green phaeton behind a team of bright chestnuts, moving rapidly toward her. She sighed in relief.

"Just wait till I get my hands on him," she muttered.

Freddy, seeing her, waved his whip and cried, "Look at me, Aunt Felicia! I've been all round the block without a single bit of difficulty. Aren't they a bang-up team?"

Finding it impossible to shout out to him in such a way in a public street, she merely waved and smiled, hiding her anger and distress. Showing off, he flicked the whip lightly, and then everything seemed to Felicia to happen at once.

The offside leader, feeling the whip, tossed its head and whinnied. The gray mongrel, barking excitedly, darted from the areaway to greet his favorite friend. Both leaders plunged in alarm, startling the wheelers, and one promptly nipped his leader's flank. The phaeton leapt forward. As it passed Felicia, standing frozen on the top step, she saw Freddy sawing madly at the reins in a futile attempt to halt the runaways.

Behind her, Peters cried, "I'll get his lordship!"

"Tell him to hurry," Felicia called, collecting herself in an instant. "I'm going after Freddy."

"Miss Felicia, you can't!"

Hurrying down the steps to the big black horse, she called back over her shoulder, "Nonsense, Peters, I must!"

With that, she untied the reins, pulled the horse nearer the steps, hitched up her muslin skirts, and flung herself onto its back, all quicker than thought. Realizing, even as she gathered the reins together that she could not maintain her balance in the saddle without sitting astride, she yanked her skirt up higher and threw her leg over. Ignoring the fact that she could not reach the stirrups properly, she kicked the horses's flanks hard. The huge black exploded in pursuit of the phaeton, impelled as much by the pummeling stirrups as by her kicks, and Felicia clung tight both to the reins and to his flying mane.

Inside the library Crawley was doing his best to disengage himself from Adlam without offending him, for the man had welcomed him in a much more friendly manner than was his normal custom to greet guests who did not bring wine, Vernis Martin, or other new oddities to add to his collection. Adlam had confided that he thought his entire family was going crazy and had welcomed the company of another sensible man.

Though Crawley wanted to encourage his host to like him, he wanted much more urgently to speak with Felicia, and when he thought he heard her voice on the gallery landing, he said pointedly that he had come to speak to Miss Adlam.

"Busy," Lord Adlam had said. "Whole place like Bedlam, and she's in the thick of it, like always. Very managing female, you know. Next thing you know we'll have my sister-in-law, Augusta, down upon us, demanding to know why I don't keep better order here. As if anyone could. Like pottery, do you?"

"My mother has some pretty pieces," Crawley said, glancing toward the door again. "I prefer wine to pottery, sir."

"So does that fellow Dacres, I'm told. Trying to winkle his way into Oakley's good graces. Can't say I like that."

Crawley smiled at him. "I think it's Oakley's daughter who draws Dacres, sir, not his wine."

"Prefers a woman to wine?" Adlam shook his head. "Always thought he was peculiar, but if that's the case, at least he won't be wanting to make up to my Theo. Let me pour you some of this Madeira. Special shipment Oakley got for me. Man's going to be knighted one day, mark my words." He turned toward a side table that bore a number of bottles and glasses.

Crawley was watching him and wondering how he would react to being told that men other than Dacres were interested in his younger daughter—and in his elder daughter, for that matter—when they were interrupted by Peters's precipitate entrance.

"Sir!"

"Good God," Adlam exclaimed. "What are you about, man?"

The footman said directly to Crawley. "You are needed, sir, immediately, if you please. It's Miss Adlam and young Freddy."

Crawley, about to demand a clearer explanation, saw a pleading look in the footman's face that caused him to say instead, "I will come at once. You will have to excuse me, sir. It appears that my presence is required elsewhere."

"Bedlam," said Adlam, picking up the glass he had already filled and turning with a dismissive shrug toward his desk.

"That was well done of you, sir," Peters said the minute they were safely alone in the hall.

"Never mind about that. What the devil is this all about? Where is Miss Adlam?"

"She jumped on that black horse of yours and rode off down the street after Master Freddy?"

Crawley stared at him blankly. "She what?"

"She jumped—"

"I heard you. I just don't believe you. Where the devil is Master Freddy that she must needs ride Thunderbolt after him."

"In Sir Richard's phaeton." Peters, spreading his hands defensively, said, "I ought to have made her listen to me. I know that, but the lad looked as if he could manage the team, and when everything else was in such a coil—"

"Which team?" Crawley's stomach had clenched.

"Why, chestnuts, sir. He was holding them for—"

But Crawley rushed out the door. "Which way?"

"South, sir, toward Hertford Street and Piccadilly."

"Good God! Get me a horse!"

Peters started to turn, then said in bewilderment, "A horse, sir, from the stables?"

"Damn you, of course not. Get— Never mind, I'll get it myself. Here you!" He shouted to a man riding a bay gelding out of the park gate across the way. "I need that nag of yours."

The man looked at him as if he were crazy. "Not my Cricket, you don't," he snapped.

But Crawley had run into the street by then and grabbed the horse's bridle. Looking up, he said with enough menace in his voice to quell a much larger and more determined man than the one he faced, "I need this horse. A child's life is in danger, and a woman's as well. Get down at once."

The man hesitated only a moment before sliding to the ground. "Then of course you may have my Cricket," he said, doffing his hat, "and I hope you find them safe and sound."

"So do I," Crawley retorted, leaping to the saddle, "because when I do, I'm going to strangle them both!"

Felicia kept her eyes riveted on the speeding phaeton and gave thanks that there was no more traffic than there was. A slower-moving carriage had been ahead of Freddy but the driver had turned into Stanhope Street, and the way was clear beyond Hertford Street to Piccadilly. By the time they passed Hertford Street, her heart was in her throat, for Piccadilly was a main thoroughfare. For a moment she hoped the cross street would stop them, and when the team scarcely paused before lurching left down the hill, she did not know whether to be glad or sorry that they had not turned toward the Hyde Park turnpike. With the echo of the huge black's hoofbeats pounding at her skull, she wondered if the keeper would have been able to stop them.

She paid no heed to pedestrians, certain there was nothing

they could do, and others on horseback seemed only to glare at the speeding phaeton, to notice only its pace and not that its single passenger was a small boy. There was, in fact, very little traffic along this broad stretch of Piccadilly, bordered as it was by the Green Park on the south and quiet residences on the north, but ahead, once they had passed Devonshire House and neared St. James's corner, it would be a different matter altogether. The street narrowed, and there would be more traffic. All her dependence was on the black, and on Freddy's ability to keep from being flung out into the road.

The black carried her at last to within arm's length of the phaeton but not before they had come perilously near to Devonshire House. Two blocks ahead lay St. James's Street.

Only when Felicia had pulled up alongside them did she realize that she might have trouble stopping such a team. But the sight of the blowing, wild-eyed chestnuts frightened her only until she saw Freddy's face. The little boy's visible terror instantly recalled her to her senses. Forcing her mind to focus itself on the nearest leader's bridle and nothing else, she urged the black nearer and nearer until she could reach out to the leader's cheek and grasp the straps where they crossed, just above the bit. To her dismay, the chestnut tossed its head free, nearly yanking her from her precarious perch on the saddle, and seemed to increase its pace. Kicking the black hard, Felicia leaned from the saddle again, praying for the strength she needed to stay mounted while she did what seemed to be the impossible.

St. James's Street was just ahead now, and the traffic on Piccadilly was accordingly much thicker. The phaeton took a path of its own down the center, between lanes of traffic. Frantically, hoping the black would not shy from oncoming traffic, Felicia grabbed the straps again and tugged, nearly heaving herself into the roadway in her effort. Again the chestnut tossed its head, but this time she managed to cling to the bridle strap. She was leaning into the black's neck now, her right hand, with the reins, clutching hard at its mane, her arm and elbow tight against its neck for leverage. She had little control over the horse this way, and had to trust it not to betray her, but she could not spare a thought for herself, or for anything but holding on to the chestnut.

She wanted to close her eyes. The traffic was terrifyingly near, all around her, and there was some sort of slowdown ahead with no opening to be seen. Shouting, "Whoa," at the top of her lungs and tugging with all her might, she realized that though the team was slowing a little, it would not be enough. She would never be able to stop them in time to avoid a terrible crash. Gritting her teeth, so absorbed in her task and the noise of the horses' hooves on the pavement and cries of alarm from helpless spectators that she did not hear anything else, she was nearly sobbing when the team began more noticeably to slow and finally to stop. Only when she sat upright and saw that they had stopped just sort of another carriage, was she able to relax, breathe a sigh of relief, and even to feel rather pleased with herself. It was then that she saw Crawley on the other side of the team.

She was glad to see him until he began shouting.

"What the devil were you about, woman?" he demanded with uncontrolled fury as he swung down from the gelding and went to the leaders' heads. "Have you no concern for your own safety, for the sanity of others, for your precious proprieties? Damn it all, you not only made a spectacle of yourself, riding down Piccadilly with that damned flimsy gown bunched around your hips and your bare legs waving for everyone to see, but you might very well have been killed! What on earth were you thinking?"

She opened her mouth to tell him of her terror for Freddy, but she had no time to speak before he went on, saying a good deal more than she had any wish to hear, his voice increasing in volume until he was bellowing at her as though she had been deaf.

Freddy sat perfectly still, but it was not long before Crawley's attention came to light on him. "And what the devil were you about, young man, to try such a damned fool thing as to drive Sir Richard's horses?"

Freddy blinked at him, glanced at Felicia, and then said, "I thought they needed walking. He was gone a long time."

"You took it upon yourself to make that decision when you had been given no permission to do so. Is that not right?"

Freddy paled. "Yes, sir, but Sir Richard said only the other day that I might walk them if he was away long, so I thought he would not mind. And, even though he did not say anything about walking them today, he did tell me to mind them while he was inside. I did just as you taught me till that dog ran under their feet and they bolted. I wasn't strong enough to hold them." Tears welled in his eyes. "I . . . I'm sorry."

"You'll be a deal sorrier before I've done with you, you young idiot. I mean to give you the thrashing of your l—"

Felicia interrupted furiously. "You will do no such cruel thing, my lord. The child did no more than he has been led to expect would be acceptable, and for that you have only yourself and Sir Richard to blame. He was perhaps a bit thoughtless—"

"He was a good deal thoughtless," Crawley snapped. "He was damned irresponsible to boot."

"He may have been irresponsible," Felicia said, her voice rising on the last word, "but children are expected to be irresponsible. One *expects* such behavior from a child."

"If I am meant to understand from that remark that I am too old to be irresponsible, you have missed your mark, my dear, and as usual do not know what you are talking about. But leave that. For the moment at hand, let me tell you what I think of your behavior, for a more irresponsible act than yours I should be hard-pressed to imagine. What the devil were you thinking?"

"Oh, stop asking me that!" Felicia shrieked. "I am sick and tired of being asked about my motives. Everyone says, 'oh, let Felicia do it. Ask Felicia! Tell Felicia your troubles, and Felicia will make them go away. Felicia knows what to do. Felicia is competent! Felicia is reliable! Felicia is always perfectly behaved and never puts a foot out of step.' Well, let me tell you, my lord, Felicia is none of those things. Felicia is a person like any other person, with faults and virtues all her own, and she neither wants nor needs to have the troubles of others thrust upon her, for she has plenty of her own and no one to tell them to, because no one cares. All anyone ever cares about, for better or for worse, is that Felicia always looks after others and does as she is told, never shaming her family with a public display of emotion, and never being a worry or a bother to anyone. And Felicia is bloody sick and tired of it all! So there!"

Applause broke out all around her, and when she snapped

her head around to stare in appalled dismay at the crowd that had gathered, Crawley said with a chuckle, "Never a public display, my dear? I think perhaps you have just blotted your perfect copybook." But Felicia barely heard him, for it was as if the earth had opened up beneath her at last. Without a word, she slumped where she sat and fainted dead away.

15

CRAWLEY leapt forward to catch Felicia before she fell off the black into the street. His first thought was that she had somehow been injured in her wild ride, and the terror that had haunted him as he chased her down Piccadilly rose again with a vengeance as he caught her and held her against his chest.

Freddy shouted, "What's wrong with Aunt Felicia?"

"Can I be of assistance," an elderly man demanded from a nearby carriage. "Bravest thing I ever saw, that young woman. Offer my assistance in any way. Put her in my coach, sir."

Crawley was tempted to accept the offer, but he did not know the man, and Felicia had begun to stir. He knew then that she had fainted upon becoming aware of what she had done and what a spectacle she had made of herself. She would not want a crowd of strangers, or even one stranger, hovering over her when she came to her senses. He must get her out of this before that happened. Turning quickly to the kind gentleman, he said, "If you would help with all these horses until I can get her settled in the phaeton, I will be most grateful, sir. That is all the aid I require, but I do require that much."

"Done," said the gentleman, opening the door of his coach and stepping down into the street.

The traffic had come to a complete halt, and the chestnuts, though still nervous, had settled down a bit. Freddy was able to hold them while the elderly gentleman tied the black and the bay gelding to the rear of the phaeton and Crawley lifted Felicia to the seat.

Crawley realized at once that she had not roused sufficiently to sit upright without support. Climbing up beside her, holding her, he looked speculatively at Freddy.

"Will she be all right, sir."

"She will. How are you?"

"I'll do," Freddy said gravely. "I never knew such a thing could happen. I deserve whatever you mean to do to me."

Crawley nodded. "You do, at that, but just now I want you to answer exactly the question I ask you. Don't say what you think I want to hear but only what you honestly believe."

Looking perplexed but willing, Freddy nodded.

"Very well. If I ask one of these gentlemen to guide the phaeton into Albemarle Street—that's the one just there to our left—do you think you can drive this team back to Park Lane? I will tell you how to go, and I'll be right here beside you, but if you are still too shaken to remember your lessons, I will have someone else do it. I don't think it wise to wait till your Aunt Felicia regains her senses, or to allow someone else to go with us back to the house if we can avoid that. But I will understand if you think the task a bit beyond your capabilities just now."

Instead of looking uncertain as Crawley had expected, Freddy glowed. "You would trust me? After what happened?"

"You kept your head when the horses bolted," Crawley told him. "You did nothing to make matters worse. You did not even cry out, which might well have frightened the team even more."

"I was too scared," Freddy confessed.

Smiling at him, Crawley said. "All the better that you can admit that. Can you do it, do you think?"

Freddy nodded, turning his attention back to the horses with that air of fixed concentration that Crawley had noted many times before in him.

The elderly gentleman, with the aid of several others, guided the phaeton, with the black and the bay tethered behind, into Albemarle Street, and from there Freddy drove through quiet Berkeley Square to Mount Street, and back to Park Lane. Long before they passed Charles Street, Crawley felt Felicia stiffen in his arms, but when he looked down at her, her eyes remained firmly closed. Since her cheeks were deeply flushed, and her breathing seemed to have quickened,

he decided it was better to say nothing, to let her pretend to be
still unconscious.

Felicia first became aware of the relative silence. The last
thing she recalled before fainting was a thunderous din and the
dreadful applause of the spectators. The thought that she, of all
people, could have provided such a public spectacle made her
wince with horror. Her only thought had been for Freddy, until
she had caught the runaway team.

The memory that she had not been solely responsible for
Freddy's rescue came back to her at nearly the same time that
she realized she was being held. She was not merely being
propped up against the seat of the moving carriage, either. She
was sitting on Crawley's lap, cushioned against his muscular
chest, with his strong arms around her, and her right cheek
resting comfortably against his shoulder. Through her lashes
she saw that Freddy was driving, and past him, she saw South
Audley Street, recognizable at once by the sight of Grosvenor
Square's west end a block away.

Realizing that they were close to Park Lane, she stirred,
meaning to take her place on the seat before she was seen by
anyone who might recognize her. Crawley's arms tightened.

"Be still," he murmured. "You are quite safe."

"I must get off you, sir," she said, opening her eyes at last
and looking at him.

"You will for once," he said firmly, "do as you are told.
Now be still or you will frighten the horses again."

Certain he exaggerated the danger, particularly since Freddy
relaxed his concentration long enough to shoot him a look of
indignation, Felicia nonetheless sighed and said, "You always
must know best, sir. It is what I like least about you."

"And I about you, my sweet Felicia. We must discuss the
problem in more detail, but not just at this present, if you do
not mind. Once we get you safely back to Adlam House, I
have a good many things to say to you. You have been a
goose, my dear, and deserve to be well scolded."

Remembering the dreadful things he had shouted at her and
the worse ones she had shrieked at him in the street, Felicia
was well aware of what she deserved. It was precisely the sort
of thing she had always dreaded, and now that the crisis was

over, she remembered with appalling clarity that she had simply rucked up her gown and flung her bare legs over the
black's broad back. What a sight she must have made! And
what she must have looked like when she fainted, she could
not bear to think about. Never again would she be able to hold
up her head among the members of the *beau monde*.

Crawley gave her a shake. "Bear up, sweetheart. I don't intend to eat you, merely to make a few matters quite clear."

Feeling sudden tears in her eyes, she muttered, "How do
you always know what I'm thinking?"

The sound of his chuckle was reassuring. "You speak as
much with your expressions as with your words, Miss Adlam.
Remember that in future, and always speak only the truth to
me."

"I do speak only the truth," she said indignantly.

"Bits of it," he retorted. "Sometimes, I fear, that bits are all
you can see, or all you think others can see."

Instantly she assumed he spoke of the forged invitations,
and she wanted nothing more than to tell him he had misunderstood that situation entirely. Since she could not tell him
the whole truth, however—he was certainly right about that
this time—she feared she could tell him nothing that would
convince him of her innocence. And since he would now add
her unspeakable conduct of this afternoon to his list of griev-
ances, she could not look forward with any confidence to a
tête à tête with him. But surely, he would not dare to demand
such a thing, not when they were not and probably never
would be more than just friends.

She tried again when they reached the house to disengage
herself from his embrace, but he would not allow it.

"Truly, sir," she said, "I am perfectly able to stand, even to
walk, by myself."

"Perhaps, but I have no intention of allowing you to do so.
Peters," he shouted to the footman who appeared in the open
doorway as the phaeton came to a halt, "come hold these
horses until I can rout out Vyne to look after them."

"Jack there will take them," Peters called back, gesturing to
a lad who was running up the areaway steps from the kitchen,
followed by the little gray dog. "I sent for him from the stables

after you rode off, sir, which is what I ought to have done when Sir Richard first arrived."

"And would have done," Felicia muttered, "had anyone listened when he tried to ask what ought to be done."

"Hush," Crawley told her, then added in a louder tone to Peters, "Good lad. Just come down then and help me get down without dropping Miss Felicia. She has been shaken up and must lie down to rest at once. Freddy, you go with Jack and take that mongrel with you. He mustn't be left out front again."

A window overhead was flung up, and Theo leaned out, calling, "What is wrong with Felicia, Crawley? Has she been injured?"

She was pulled back inside, and Sir Richard's head took her place. "Dreadful manners, that wench, to be shouting down to the street like that. What the devil are you doing with my rig, Ned? If those horses are blown—"

"They are," Crawley snapped, "and if you know what's good for you, you'll make yourself scarce before I explain to you in exact detail just why they are blown."

"Please," Felicia begged, "not here, my lord. May we not go inside? The neighbors will—"

"Hang the neighbors," he retorted, but he allowed Peters to help him get down so he would not have to relinquish his burden.

Sir Richard was shouting orders from the window now to the stable boy, telling him he meant to remain in Park Lane for dinner, so the rig might just as well be put up in the stable mews until he required it again.

Felicia was grateful when Crawley began moving toward the steps. Any moment now, she thought, and they would have gathered as great an audience as the horrid one in Piccadilly.

Her gratitude came too soon. Crawley stopped in his tracks when a familiar voice demanded, "What goes on here? Whatever is the matter with Felicity? I declare, this household is going to rack and ruin. First Selena faints dead away, then awakes insisting Sir Richard is going to murder us all in our beds. You must come up to her at once, Felicity. She has been distraught ever since my arrival, insisting that something dreadful must have occurred to keep you away from her just now."

Felicia struggled to get down, but Crawley held her. "Please, sir, I must go to her."

"No, she can wait. And so can anyone else who wants you. Forgive me, Lady Augusta, if I ask you to step aside and let me pass. I wish to get Felicia upstairs to the drawing room, where she may be made comfortable. She is a trifle shaken just now."

"Shaken? Good gracious, why should she be shaken? Peters related some unnatural tale or other to me, but it was so utterly ridiculous that I simply refused to listen. Would you believe he actually tried to convince me that dearest Felicity had ridden a horse in her afternoon frock? But I do not believe all I hear. Pure poppycock, that was, as I did not hesitate to tell him."

"Perfectly true poppycock, nonetheless," Crawley said, pushing past her into the hall with no further ado. He turned toward the stairs, and Felicia leaned her head against his shoulder.

Adlam stood at the top of the stairway, glaring at them. "May I inquire just what you think you are about, young man, to be carrying my daughter?"

"I am taking her upstairs to the drawing room, sir," Crawley replied, moving steadily toward him.

"Take her to her mother instead. Then, perhaps Augusta will let well enough alone, as she is always telling others to do, and stop deviling me, of all people, to look to Selena. Never paid a lick of heed to aught I tell her. Won't start now, I'm sure, but Felicity manages her well enough. And while you're about it, Felicity," he added, speaking just as though Felicia stood on her own two feet and no one else was within hearing, "speak to Theo. She has been telling me she means to marry that dratted painter, and I won't have it. Nonsense to think of throwing herself away on a man like that. A painter!" And turning on his heel, he disappeared into the bookroom. The door slammed behind him.

Crawley crossed the gallery toward the drawing room, but Felicia said, "Not in there, sir. Sir Richard and Theo are in there. Do put me down. I must go and talk to Papa and see what I can do to smooth things over for Theo. It will not do to have her plans go awry now when they are just in a way to being settled, and then I must go to Mama, for she must be thinking something dreadful has happened to me. Put me down, my lord!"

Clearly having gone deaf, he walked down the corridor and into the morning room, and kicked the door shut behind him. Over his shoulder, Felicia saw the outraged face of her aunt and realized that Lady Augusta had tried to follow them.

"My aunt! Oh, sir, you have shut the door in her face! She will be livid. Oh, you must—"

Her words broke off with a shriek when Crawley dumped her unceremoniously onto the sofa. There was an alarming crack from one of the slender mahogany legs, but it held. Indignantly, Felicia began to sit up but stopped midway when he said in a voice that froze her where she was, "Stay right there until I have finished talking to you."

"But I—"

"Silence," he roared.

Gasping, she fell back, wondering if he had gone mad.

"Now," he said in a more controlled tone, "you will listen to what I am going to tell you, and you will not speak until I have finished. Is that quite clear?"

She nodded, scarcely daring to breathe.

"You, Miss Adlam, spend entirely too much time trying to smooth the way for others, and all you get for your trouble is one headache after another. Your mother *enjoys* her ill health. Your father doesn't care a rap for anyone but himself, and the children—as Tom has proved very well—will do better for being allowed to cope with as many of their own difficulties as they can. I was never allowed to attend to such things, because I had a father who assumed he could do everything better than I could, and found it easier to do things himself. You are guilty of that, but you once compared me to Freddy, and in many ways you were right to do so. Now, however, I take the liberty to inform you that you are more like Sara Ann, in that you make up worries before you have cause. What is worse is that you ignore your own needs in favor of tending to the others.

"No, don't speak. I do not want to hear another word about

what you must do for the leeches in this house. I want to talk about you, and about me. You said something else a few moments ago that made me think, and I want you to think about it, too. You said the thing you liked least in me was that I always believe I know what is best to be done. Correct?"

"Well, to be quite—"

"Just answer yes or no, Felicia."

"Yes, then."

"Very good. Now, I said that was the same thing I liked least in you, did I not?"

"Yes." She wrinkled her brow. "I do behave that way from time to time, I suppose."

"So do I. I was not denying it. But something Dawlish said to me, and Belinda as well, I suppose, in her own way, has come back to haunt me, for I realized they were perfectly right. Dawlish said men are too apt to condemn in others the very things they do themselves. Think about that, Felicia."

Her eyes widened. "Why, only this afternoon, Sir Richard said he had come to realize that he condemned the same things in Theo's behavior that he does himself. I think Dawlish has been talking to others besides you, sir." She sat up straighter.

"No doubt, but look here, my dear girl," he said, sitting down beside her and taking her hand in his, "we are not much the same, aside from that one little factor. I know I have given you cause to think me irresponsible—"

"Great cause, sir."

"Yes, but that has changed."

"Only because you won a horse race?"

"No," he retorted, and she saw his lips tighten and knew he was restraining his temper. "Because I have reason now to care. I was not at Newmarket all the time I was gone from London. I was at Longworth. I had talked to my friend Thorne—"

"The marquess, you mean."

He nodded. "He recommended a fellow, Joe Penning, whom I hired as my new steward. I thought I could just leave matters in his hands until I had more time to deal with them, but Penning kept sending messages, asking me questions, until I realized I was really needed at home. To be truthful, I think Thorne put him up to it, but it doesn't matter, because I have learned that it does not do to leave my responsibilities in other men's hands. I went to Longworth to learn what I might from Penning and to let it be known that I mean to take the reins at last. I had come to hope, you see, that I might ask you to marry me."

She was conscious of a sinking feeling, and considering that she knew she loved him with all her heart, could not imagine why the notion that he wanted to marry her should suddenly be such a depressing one. Calmly, she said, "I am certain I could help you bring things into trim at Longworth, sir, but I am not certain that we would be a good match for one another."

"Good God," he snapped, "I don't want your help!"

Flushing with embarrassment, she turned her face away, fighting back tears. "I beg your pardon. I must have misunderstood you. I thought you were asking me to marry you, but I quite understand that you meant only that the thought had crossed your mind again. No doubt my behavior today, coupled with what you thought before—erroneously, I promise you, but I cannot tell you more than that . . . that is—" She broke off, tangled in her thoughts and at a loss for what else to say.

There was a long silence, and when she dared to look at him again, she saw that he was regarding her with astonishment. At last, he said, "What did I think before now? I swear, woman, you are borrowing trouble again. Sometimes you would try the patience of a saint, the way you assume the worst!"

In the face of his displeasure, she wanted to drop the whole subject, to smooth the angry look away and make him smile again. But she could see that nothing but truth would avail her now, and so she said, striving to sound matter-of-fact, "But I do know you thought I was responsible for those forged invitations, and—"

"Why would I think any such thing?"

"Didn't you?"

"Never! Good Lord, Felicia, I have shown you over and over that your thoughts are utterly transparent to me. Don't you think I would have known if you had been deceiving me in such a great way as that?"

"But when you saw the samples Mr. Townshend had left me—"

"Is that where you got them? I did wonder, but one look at you convinced me that wherever they had come from their presence in your drawing room was entirely innocent. When I learned of Mrs. Falworthy's sudden indisposition and subsequent absence from town, I assumed I was correct in believing she had devised the scheme to puff off her consequence as a sponsor."

He paused, and when she could find nothing to say, he smiled at her. "I'll tell you what it is, my love. You are too accustomed for your own good to trying to anticipate the needs of all your family, and trying to please everyone. Since you are not nearly as good at reading their minds, or mine, as I am at reading yours, let me draw from Lady Augusta's vast supply of maxims to tell you that you cannot please everyone, and if you continue to yield to the caprices of all, you will soon have nothing to yield. There is a time and a place for everything, and if you try to please all, you end by pleasing none. You must therefore learn to let well enough—"

"Oh, stop!" Felicia cried, shaking her head and laughing. "You are much worse than Aunt Augusta, and I can just imagine you at her age, spouting the same sort of fustian. It is, I might add, a truly appalling thought, sir."

"My given name is Edward," he told her, reaching down and pulling her to her feet. "Members of my family call me Ned."

Feeling suddenly extremely relieved and, oddly, a bit shy, Felicia looked at his chest and said, "Do they?"

"They do. Look up at me, Felicity, my love."

She did. "I wish you will decide what to call me, sir—that is, N-Ned." Feeling more heat in her cheeks, she swallowed, then added, "You just called me Felicity, you know, and only Aunt Augusta does that. Everyone else calls me Felicia."

"I like Felicity," he said, gently drawing her closer. "When I read your first letter, I imagined a soft and gentle girl, all womanly curves and laughter, a girl with far too much responsibility for her young shoulders to bear. Then, when I learned that you were generally called Felicia, I saw an entirely different person in my mind's eye, somehow older, more mature, more capable and less yielding."

"That is the true Felicia, sir," she said, looking straight at him now.

"Is it?" he asked, bending to kiss her.

His lips, warm against hers, recalled her instantly to the last time he had kissed her, and it seemed that her body recalled it as well, for it molded itself against his as though it belonged there, as though they were one person. Felicia felt as if she were melting. She felt warm and protected, and safe, and for a few blissful moments, she thought about what it would be like to cast all her burdens aside and run away with this man. Then she remembered that he did not really want to marry her, and her bliss turned to ashes. She stiffened in his arms.

"What?" he murmured, kissing her cheek, then her hair, and stroking her back, his arm hard against the side of her breast.

"I suppose you have proved what you wanted to prove," she muttered to his chest, fighting the tears again and wondering why it was that this man could so easily make her want to cry.

"That you are soft and desirable? Does that displease you so much? I promise you, it does not displease me."

"You are very charming, sir, so charming, in fact, that you made me forget for a time that you are a fortune hunter. You slipped up only once just now, but that was enough. You don't want me or my help, only my money."

He held her away and looked down at her, his consternation giving way almost instantly to amusement. "You really are not very good at reading the truth in people, are you, my love?"

"I am not your love. You said so."

"I said no such thing. I said, if you will but bend your stubborn little mind to recalling our exact exchange of words, that I did not want you only for the help you could give me in bringing Longworth into trim again. I mean that. I did not intend to imply that I will not value your assistance, merely that that was not at all the primary reason I wish to marry you."

She savored the words. "You do wish it, then, truly?"

"I intend to ask your father for your hand just as soon as I can persuade him to listen to me. He seems disinclined to discuss anything sensibly at this exact moment, but I daresay I will be able to bring him around before the day is done."

"Not easily, sir, if he realizes you mean to take me away from here. And what will they do without me?"

"I don't much care what they do," he retorted, bending to kiss her again.

"Well, I do," she said, eluding him. "You may be quite right in saying that I have allowed myself to become too much enmeshed in trying to please everyone, but I have done it for years, and they will not accept a change easily. Perhaps if we could have them all to stay at Longworth—" She broke off, biting her lip at the look on his face. When he did not explode but only shook his head, she said, "Very well then, but the children will want to stay with us, and I do not think I could bear to make them live with Papa and Mama."

"Nor would I allow it, even if your brother would," Crawley said. "I am not such an ogre as that, love. Sara Ann will make her home with us for as long as need be, and the boys will both come to us for their holidays. As for your parents, you will certainly invite them to visit two or three times a year. For that matter, Longworth is not so far from Bradstoke that you cannot visit them as frequently as you choose. Now, do you think you can manage to accept me as a husband?"

"With all my h—"

"I cannot stand it a minute longer," Lady Augusta announced, bursting into the room, then coming to an abrupt halt, her eyebrows soaring upward. "What on earth are you about, Felicity, to be allowing Crawley to paw you about like that? A proper lady does not behave so, and I have always had good cause, until today at all events, to be proud of your behavior. But a lady is known by the company she keeps and by the way she comports herself, and this will not do. Bad enough that Theodosia seems bent upon encouraging the attentions of that dreadful artist after he made such a mockery of her lovely portrait, but I cannot and will not stand for one of my nieces allowing a gentleman to make free with her person. Unhand her, sir, at once."

Instead of obeying, Crawley put his arm around Felicia's shoulders and drew her closer. "I must disappoint you, Lady Augusta," he said. "Your niece has agreed to marry me, and I mean to see that she does so just as soon as I can procure a special license."

Lady Augusta said haughtily, "One must suppose you covet her fortune, sir. She is far too good for you."

"I cannot deny that I shall welcome her fortune, ma'am," he said, looking down at Felicia with a smile, "but any of it that I use for Longworth will be replaced as soon as the estate is in trim again. I mean that money to go to our daughters, and since we may have a good many, every penny will be needed. As to the other, you are entirely right. She is far too good. I mean to teach her to be less well behaved in future."

Lady Augusta said, "You are most peculiar, Crawley, but I confess, such words make me think the better of you, rather than the worse. You will not believe me, I daresay, but—"

"Here you are, Felicia!" Theo pushed open the door that Lady Augusta had left ajar and burst into the room, her face wreathed in smiles. "Only wait till you hear what I have to tell you. Richard has just—"

"Aunt Felicia, Aunt Felicia," Sara Ann called, pushing past Sir Richard, who had entered on Theo's heels, "I have been looking and looking for you. Tom says both he and Freddy must go away, and I cannot bear them to. Oh, please, Aunt Felicia—"

Tom, coming in behind the little girl, caught her up in his arms, saying, "I have been telling her she need not worry, Aunt Felicia, but she insists she must discuss the matter with you, and I've just heard what Freddy did with Sir Richard's rig. I hope you mean to give that young rascal—"

Freddy, running in behind him, shouted, "Don't you say it, Thomas! I have already told Crawley he may do what he thinks right, and I don't need you to—"

"Out!" Crawley roared. "Every last one of you!"

There was instant silence.

"Dear me," Lady Crawley said, hovering on the threshold, her hands clasped at her bosom, her lower lip trembling ominously.

Felicia, conscious of a strong wish that she had never recovered from her faint, looked up at her beloved, to see how he would handle this.

Crawley drew a long breath, looked around the room, and said quietly, "Felicia cannot attend to your wants just now.

She has agreed to become my wife, and we are going to go for a walk in the park, alone. Is that not true, my love?"

"Oh, yes," Felicia agreed fervently, ignoring the stupefied silence that seemed to fill the room around them.

Crawley put out his arm, and obediently she placed her hand upon it and walked with him from the room. The last thing she heard as they hurried down the stairs was Lady Augusta declaring from the gallery above, "To do the right thing at the right season is a great art, my dears. My blessings on you both!"

Crawley shut the door behind them and took her into his arms.

"Not on a public street," she protested.

"Hush, sweetheart, we have Lady Augusta's blessing."

Looking up at him to see his eyes lit with warmth and laughter, she tossed caution to the winds. "Very well, my love, since you insist, I shall begin as I hope to go on." And welcoming his kisses, exhilarating in the way her body responded instantly to his, Felicia relaxed in his arms and counted the rest of the world well lost.

TALES OF THE HEART

LOVE IN THE HIGHEST CIRCLES